The HEART Only KNOWS

OTHER BOOKS AND BOOKS ON CASSETTE
BY KERRY BLAIR:

The Heart Has Its Reasons

The Heart Has Forever

The HEART Only KNOWS

a novel

KERRY BLAIR

Covenant Communications, Inc.

Printed in the United States of America
First Printing: August 2001

08 07 06 05 04 03 02 01   10 9 8 7 6 5 4 3 2 1

ISBN 1-57734-861-3

SPECIAL THANKS TO:

*Hilary for research, refreshments,
and for helping me to avoid a major baseball blunder.*

*Jennifer, Andrea, Kaylie, Amy, Suzzie, Christy, Sheree, Shannon,
Jennika, Megan, Lindsey, and the many other Young Women who write
to me to share their lives and their loves and their talents. I cherish each
of you and stand all amazed as I watch you Stand for Truth and
Righteousness. You are a joy and an inspiration in my life.*

Valerie Holladay, editor auerum, editor egregia et fidelis *(Latin for
"awesome lady who is outstanding at her craft and very much appreciated").*

*My family. Especially to Greg, who is my brother and best friend—
not to mention my hero.*

Only the heart knows how to find what is precious.

FYODOR DOSTOYEVSKY

CHAPTER 1

Andi Reynolds didn't believe in harbingers, omens, or foreboding. It was difficult, then, for her to explain the flutter of her heart and sudden clamminess of her palms as she gazed up at the solitary crow perched in the rotted pine.

One crow for sorrow, two crows for joy . . .

Despite herself, Andi gripped her book as she glanced around. These woods were full of crows; there must be another one somewhere in sight. She knew from working at a zoo that crows are sociable creatures. It was only reasonable to suppose that this one was part of a flock.

Murder, she reminded herself. *A company of crows is called a murder.*

Her emerald eyes scanned the wide Arizona sky above the Mogollion Rim, but there was only the one crow to be seen. *One crow for sorrow.* Andi's heart went from a flutter to a steady thump, and her breath came a little faster. At the bird's sudden, raucous cry, she pressed the book to her chest, then closed her eyes and drew a deliberate, calming breath. This was ridiculous. She wasn't afraid of a *crow*, for heaven sakes.

Let my heart be still a moment and this mystery explore.

A dimple winked into Andi's cheek as she opened her eyes and smiled, remembering. Last night her brother had held a flashlight under his chin and recited "The Raven" for his part in the family reunion talent show. Apparently, pieces of Poe's classic were still caught in her subconscious, but that was just silly. It was almost noon on a bright and beautiful day in early September, not "once upon a midnight dreary," and she had to stop all this "wondering, fearing, doubting, dreaming."

Well, she thought as her dimples deepened, *perhaps not the dreaming.* All the dreaming she had done of late was of her fiancé, Greg Howland, and their still-too-distant wedding day. She pulled a cell phone from the pocket of her jeans to consult the time. Greg should be calling any minute now, which was why she had left the campground—to have a measure of privacy when he called to tell her about his visit to the District Attorney's office in Mesa.

A sudden realization came tapping at the door of Andi's conscious mind. While all the lovely wondering and dreaming she had done lately was of Greg, all the odd doubting and fearing of the last few days was for him as well. It wasn't foreboding she felt now as much as it was certainty of things unseen: Greg was in trouble. She knew it. She had known it for some time in fact—despite his denials—but she hadn't known the cure for his cares and could only guess at the cause.

But in an hour or so, she thought, as she continued to scan the sky for the black birds, she would finally see him again and hold him close and know that he was safe—if only for the moment—in her arms. But the sky was empty and the nagging fear returned. Shouldn't he have finished with the District Attorney by now? Greg had said he would call to tell her when he was on the way. Where was he?

One crow for sorrow, she recited, looking up at the majestic, ebony bird, *but only because one is such a lonely number.* Checking her phone to make certain it was on and that she was still within the cell area, Andi slipped it back into her pocket. The crow cawed out mournfully.

"Keep calling," she counseled it softly. "Your love will come."

Nevermore.

Andi frowned, then tried to shake off this final flight of her fancy by reminding herself that Poe had placed his raven on a bust of Pallas, the Greek goddess of wisdom, to show the folly of allowing superstition to overcome reason.

Thank goodness I've always been a reasonable sort of person, she thought as she turned away from the withered pine toward a more verdant part of the forest. *And thank goodness I'm studying Shakespeare this semester instead of Poe.*

She dropped the thin volume of *Romeo and Juliet* onto the soft carpet of pine needles and removed the phone from her pocket before sitting down. *If Romeo and Juliet had each had a cell phone,* she thought, *their romance would have turned out better.* She opened the book and turned to the part of the play where she'd left off earlier. *True, Romeo might still have been exiled to Mantua, and Juliet might have had to stay behind on that balcony in Verona, but at least they could have talked about it.*

Certainly Andi couldn't imagine asking, "Wherefore art thou?" of Greg and receiving no response. And there was no telling on any given day wherefore art he *was,* although it was never, unfortunately, in the bushes below her window. Being engaged to a professional athlete was not without its drawbacks. For one, it meant that she saw Greg more often on television and in newspapers than she did in person. But she was fortunate, she knew, to live in a time when she could at least talk to him. Without a doubt, hearing her love's voice every day helped stave off the fatal combination of melancholy and miscommunication which had sent Juliet to the apothecary in the first place.

Andi opened her book and tried to concentrate on Juliet's concerns rather than her own but found her attention wandering back to Greg. What was taking him so long? She fingered her phone and watched a squirrel gathering piñon nuts. When the rodent paused with full cheeks and seemed to regard her quizzically, she held up the phone. "I'm expecting a call," she told it. "Cell phones are the greatest invention of the twentieth century."

"Absolutely," a voice agreed.

As a part-time keeper at the Phoenix Zoo, Andi was used to talking to animals—but not to hearing them respond.

"If it's a choice between antibiotics and cellular communication," the voice continued, "give me a telephone any day." Andi's cousin leaned around the wide trunk of a nearby tree, where she had apparently been sitting—no doubt communing with nature, Andi thought.

"Oh, hi, Zona," she said, doing her best to muster a weak smile. If she had made a list of people she hoped to avoid by leaving the campground, Zona May Reynolds would have been at the very top. Andi tried not to stare at her cousin's boysenberry-hued hair and quadruple-pierced ears, but the only alternative was to gape at her outlandish outfit. Who but Zona wore a Speedo tank top with Bermuda shorts and combat boots? She looked like she had tumbled out of one of Andi's little sister's books—the one where you turned the tri-cut pages tomake a picture of something comic—in this case, a mermaid/ tourist/fireman. Andi regretted the involuntary note of dismay in her voice as she asked, "What are you doing all the way out here?"

Zona lifted her own wonder of modern technology—a 35mm camera. "Photographing the wildlife," she said, "before somebody captures it all to put in zoos." Her crazily plucked brows rose in challenge.

If Andi had learned anything in the last day and a half of the reunion, it was that Zona May was not only anti-zoo, she was anti-Church and anti-everything-else right now. Unless you were prepared for a debate you couldn't win, it was prudent to defer to her on relatively minor issues like animal rights, and to avoid major issues like women and the priesthood at all costs. "Well, I came out to talk to—"

"The squirrels?" Zona interrupted.

"No," Andi said. "To Greg."

"Oh, right," Zona said. "The Jock. AKA Poster Boy for the Decline of Western Civilization." She got to her feet, making no effort to brush the forest floor from her baggy shorts before reaching for her camera bag. "I predict you'll get more intelligent responses from the squirrels."

Andi's eyes flashed, but Zona's departure and the digital melody of the phone saved her the necessity of a retort. She tossed her mane of auburn curls over her shoulder and pressed the button to turn on the phone. "Greg!" she said without waiting for a confirmation. "Where are you?"

"Just leaving town," he responded. His voice was deep and quiet and unbelievably dear. Andi's fingers curled around the phone as he added, "The deposition took a little longer than I expected."

"What did they say?" she asked. "Do they have enough on Zeke to convict him?" Greg's former publicist, Zeke Martoni, had attempted to blackmail the ballplayer, using his relationship with Greg's older brother to gain information for gambling on the World Series. Jim Howland had been ill, and Zeke had not only taken advantage of him, he soon had Jim addicted to drugs that dulled both his senses and his pain. Now Jim was dead, and Zeke had been indicted for extortion. Knowing this, Andi was even more concerned by Greg's reticence. She gripped the phone tighter. "Greg?"

He cleared his throat. "The DA said my testimony ought to guarantee Zeke fifty years behind bars."

Andi listened for elation—or at least satisfaction—in his voice, but it wasn't there. Instead, he sounded weary, and she prayed for words of encouragement. "Martoni will be almost a hundred years old if he gets out," she said finally. "At least we can be pleased about that."

"I guess fifty years in prison is going to have to do," Greg said. "At least until a better punishment can be arranged for eternity."

"Eternity?" Andi repeated as she looked up at the tips of the gently swaying trees. "Isn't that how long it's been since I've seen you?" As top pitcher for the Arizona Diamondbacks, Greg had been on the road with them for more than a week, but to Andi it had seemed more like a lifetime. "I've missed you," she whispered, surprised and pleased to find that her worries about Martoni were quickly overshadowed by the dappled sunshine on her face and the joy of knowing she and Greg would be together soon. "When will you be here?"

"About an hour and a half," he guessed. "Better tell the Board of Inquiry to assemble."

She smiled up into the sky—a sky as deep and blue as Greg's incredible eyes. "My family will love you as much as I do," she promised.

"Uh, huh," he said. "Tell me that one again. It's my favorite fairy tale."

He wasn't as serious now, Andi thought in relief. *Probably*. She could almost see his lopsided grin when he added, "I'll tell it to you then. Once upon a time there was a beautiful princess who lived in a tall ivory tower. Everybody in her kingdom was a scholar or an attorney or a physicist." He paused when she giggled then concluded ruefully, "And they all prayed each and every day for a hick ballplayer to come along to dumb down their bloodlines and—"

"You're the smartest man I know," Andi interrupted.

"Smart enough to marry you." His voice was rich and low and full of longing.

Andi was about to remind him that fairy tales always ended in "happily ever after" when the crow above her spread its blue-black wings and sailed from its perch on the pine to a fallen log not eight feet from Andi's knees. There it sat perfectly still, seeming to read her mind with its knowing yellow eyes. The blissful words she might have said died on her lips, and goosebumps rose on her bare arms.

'Tis the wind and nothing more.

"Hurry, Greg," she whispered.

"Andi? Is something wrong?"

"No," she said and the crow cocked its feathered head.

One crow for sorrow.

"Hurry and finish the story, Greg," she urged.

"Huh?"

"The fairy tale." Her voice sounded strained even to her ears, and she tried to lighten it by teasing. "Don't you know how to end a fairy tale?"

"You mean 'and they lived happily ever after'?"

"Yes," she said. Andi turned her back to the bird. "Promise me that we'll live happily ever after." She longed to be held in Greg's strong arms, but for now she would settle for just a note of reassurance in his voice. "Greg?" But there was only silence.

Slowly she removed the now quiet phone from her ear. He must have entered the first of the many canyons between Phoenix and the Rim. Their connection had been lost.

HAPTER 2

Driving as fast as he dared and mostly lost in his thoughts, Greg saw the rough-hewn mile marker a moment too late and had to turn sharply onto the unpaved Forest Service road. A die-cast toy car that had been on the dash rolled to the floor near his right foot. He frowned as he nudged the tiny red Jeep out from beneath the gas pedal and over to the passenger side.

Why did you keep the thing, anyway? he asked himself. *You should have thrown it away when you first opened the box instead of thinking you might give it to Enos.*

From the corner of his eye, Greg watched the perfect replica of the vehicle he drove bounce across the floorboard. The short hairs prickled along the back of his neck, and he knew at once that he couldn't give the toy to Andi's little brother. Despite the fact that there had been no note enclosed, Greg had a good idea who had sent him the "gift." He only wished he knew why.

He hit a rough spot on the road a little too hard and was pleased when the bump caused the miniature Jeep to roll under the seat.

Out of sight, out of mind.

If only it were that easy.

Hoping to distract himself from thinking any more about the deposition he had given this morning and the rotten year with Zeke Martoni which had preceded it, Greg reached for his cell phone. When it showed that he was once again within an area where the reception would be clear, he pressed an auto-call button at the top. It was past time to check in with his mother.

"Greg! I was hoping it would be you," Sadie Howland greeted him, then paused to listen to the sound of the engine before adding, "You're not calling from your car again, are you? Talking on the phone while you're driving isn't safe, son. You know it isn't."

"It's a Forest Service road, Ma," Greg said. "There's nothing on it to hit." Except for that squirrel. And he'd missed it. Barely.

"Are you wearing a seatbelt?"

"Yes, ma'am," he grinned, "and clean underwear." He could almost hear her nod approvingly two thousand miles away in Iowa, where she'd recently moved to care for his two nephews when their mother had abandoned them a year after Jim Howland's death from cancer. "How are the boys?"

"They're still wound up from your visit," she said. "Wish't you could have stayed longer."

"I know, Ma," Greg said. "Baseball season's almost over. I'll get out there more. Or you can always bring Justin and Jason out here and live with me."

"They've got school, Greg."

"I'll bet there're one or two elementary schools in Arizona."

They'd had this debate and Greg knew that if he were ever going to win it he'd have already done so. At least he wasn't as worried about his family. When he'd seen them during the Diamondbacks' recent series with the Cubs, his mother had looked ten years younger and his nephews seemed happier than they'd been since before Jim's death.

"They've gotta keep their roots in," Sadie said. "Roots is all those little boys have left."

"No," Greg said. "They have you."

"I talked to your father this morning," she added. "That was real nice of you, Greg, to invite him to your game in Chicago and all."

"It was no big deal."

They both knew better. Roy Howland had completed a detox program for alcoholism and was now living in an AA halfway house in Chicago, but his abusive nature had made Greg's childhood too horrific for him to embrace his father without reservation now. Sadie knew better than anyone what it took to forgive the past beatings, to acknowledge that Roy was trying to change, and to be sincerely, if cautiously, supportive.

"It was Christian," she repeated firmly, "real Christian of you, Greg."

And that was the watchword, Greg thought. If he'd learned nothing else in the past few months, it was that a Christlike path was the only walk worth taking. Look what it had done for his mother.

"Did you see that lawyer fella this morning?" she asked after a moment.

"Yeah," Greg said, not bothering to tell her—again—that the fella was actually a lady.

"Good," Sadie said. "I can't tell you how glad I am to know that Zeke is finally out of our lives for good."

For good?

Greg hung up a few minutes later and drove down the rutted road with his mother's words lingering in his mind. He'd love to believe that she was right. Certainly the DA this morning had seemed to confirm that Zeke was on his way out of their lives. Why, then, did his gut reaction tell him that the battle had only begun and that while Zeke might finally be going, Greg had better not count on him going quietly.

Well, the phone calls for one thing.

Over the last ten days, Greg's cell phone had rung every night at bedtime but the calling number was always as "unavailable" as the caller was. The first night it happened, Greg was in New York, where he'd pitched a grueling ten-inning game and then fallen asleep almost before he hit the bed in the hotel. When the phone rang he didn't waste precious darkness worrying about a lousy wrong number. When there was no response, he tossed the phone back on the bedside table and pulled the pillow over his head.

The next night, after the second call, Greg thought about the "wrong number" for less than a minute then dismissed it as a coincidence. But the next night he had wondered if the calls really *were* a coincidence. By the fourth night it was pretty apparent they weren't, so the next morning he had his number changed. That night the phone rang right on schedule. Greg had the number changed again the next day but still lay awake waiting for the phone to ring. It did.

The phantom calls that were merely annoying at first had become uncanny and, although Greg wouldn't admit it, almost unnerving. He changed his number twice more, telling Andi and his mother only that he was having trouble with his service. Still the phone rang every night—later and later—as if the mysterious caller knew that Greg would be awake and waiting for the call. The caller was right.

Then, when he'd come home from the road trip last night, the box containing the toy Jeep was waiting. Greg knew it was a playing piece in Martoni's latest game, but he wished he knew the rules.

Not that it would do any good to have a whole game book, he admitted to himself now. *Zeke Martoni doesn't play by any rules.*

When he got back into town tonight, if the hour wasn't too late, Greg thought, he would call Dan Ferris. Ferris was his bishop and a detective in the Mesa Police Department. Greg had planned to call him every day since he'd first begun to suspect that the midnight calls were coming from Zeke, but he'd always found a convenient excuse to put it off. The root of his procrastination was the fear that he would sound paranoid and, worse, needy.

Needy was the last thing Greg Howland intended to be ever again. He had grown up needy, always the poorest boy in school in almost every way. When he was ten years old, he had determined to change that—someday, somehow—and it took all his resolve, every iota of his strength, and each thin strand of his hope and faith do it. At twenty-four he was physically strong, financially secure, and spiritually more attuned. But looking back at where he had been was still appallingly painful and going back was simply unthinkable. That's why it was so hard for Greg to ask for help. Even when he needed it. Which he probably didn't.

Probably.

But if he ever did, he kept telling himself, he'd call Dan Ferris.

In the meantime he was almost to the campground. Anticipation and apprehension vied for chief emotion. As much as he couldn't wait to see Andi, he didn't relish the assignment he'd set for himself: to tell her that he wouldn't see her again until after Martoni's trial. If Zeke *was* playing some kind of game, Greg knew that he wouldn't hesitate to use Andi as a pawn. Since she meant everything to him, he must convince Zeke that she meant nothing. If it took dating every female in the United States to lead Martoni to believe he was still playing the field, then that's what he would do. (And when the Diamondbacks played the Expos, he'd date some Canadian women for good measure.)

It's the best plan you have, he told himself again, *and the least you can do.*

Just then an angel appeared from around the bend. She wore a striped T-shirt tucked into faded jeans, and tennis shoes instead of silver sandals, but the way her long, spiraled tresses reflected back the bronze and gold of the late summer sun left no doubt in Greg's mind that Andi Reynolds was a heavenly apparition—and the only angel he'd ever pray to see. He swallowed hard and slowed the Jeep. Obviously, "the least he could do" was going to be the hardest thing he'd ever done.

CHAPTER 3

By the time he climbed from the car and Andi rushed into his arms, Greg had begun to think he could wait an hour or two—or eight—to tell her his plans. Gratified to see that tall trees obscured the view from the campground for the most part, he held her close, breathing in the heady, spicy scent of her and wishing that they could stand here, just like this, for the rest of their lives. When Andi at last raised her flushed, happy face to him, Greg lowered his head and covered her lips with his own in a tender kiss. Needing at last to breathe, he drew marginally away. "Hi there."

"Hello," Andi murmured, her eyes still closed and her lips achingly alluring.

Greg forced his eyes away from those lips to trace the outline of her porcelain features and recommit each tiny freckle across her nose to memory. When her eyes finally opened, soft and wide and deeper than the forest green, Greg smiled into them with quiet devotion. "So," he said to prove to himself that he could gaze at Andi *and* speak, "how's the reunion?"

"Now that you're here," she replied, nestling her cheek against his chest, "it's simply wonderful, thanks."

"You don't know how much I've missed you." Greg's lips brushed Andi's forehead and the tip of her nose on their way back to her mouth. He had just found it when he heard a rustling in the bushes followed by a "Thwang!"

Startled, he turned to look down at the source of the peculiar sound. A little boy of three or four stood carefully beyond arm's reach with a plastic bow drawn and aimed at Greg's kneecap. Though the drawstring was arrow-less, the child pulled it taut, squinted one eye to focus, then released his imaginary dart.

"Thwang! I got you again!" he declared, his voice triumphant.

With one arm still around Andi's shoulder, Greg grinned down at the child. "Sorry Cupid, but you're too late. I'm already smitten."

The little boy's face screwed up into a look of disgust. "I'm Robin Hood!" he announced as though it were a fact that should be obvious to anyone who had ventured this far into Sherwood Forest.

"This is Rufus," Andi said quickly. "He belongs to my cousin Ida June." Her voice lowered so only Greg could hear. "No Dr. Seuss for him. Ida June believes in classical education for preschoolers."

"Yeah?" Greg said with only the slightest raise of one sandy blond eyebrow. "Well, it's nice to meet you, Rufus Hood." He glanced back toward the campground then down at the little boy. "Should he be out here all by himself? Where are the rest of the Merry Men?"

"I followed Andi," the little boy volunteered. "I'm too . . . too . . ." Rufus paused, unsure of the big word his mother always used to describe him. In a moment he remembered and brightened. "Too *precocious* to play with other children." He lifted his round little chin in a defiant gesture that reminded Greg of Andi. "Precocious means smart."

Andi stood on tiptoe to whisper in Greg's ear. "It really means that Rufus bites."

"Ah."

Rufus' eyes narrowed as he stepped back to consider Greg's imposing stature. "Are you the Sheriff of Nottingham?"

"Not a chance," Greg said.

"Rufus, this is Greg," Andi said.

Rufus evaluated him with the appraising eye mastered only by four-year-olds. "Are you part of my forever family?"

"Well, not yet."

"Then who are you?"

Greg filled his lungs with cool mountain air and decided that he was going to love Andi's family reunion, Board of Inquiry not withstanding. After two years of everybody with a newspaper, television set or cereal box knowing who he was, for the next few hours he would be the only thing he wanted to be: Andi Reynolds' fiancé.

"Do you want to know what I am, Rufus?" he asked, closing the gap between himself and the child in a single long stride. "I'm a horse!"

Rufus squealed in glee as Greg swung him up and onto his broad shoulders. He laughed so hard he almost fell off when the young pitcher gave a pretty fair whinny and began to paw the forest loam with one of the shoes a major corporation not only provided, but paid him a small fortune to wear.

"To Nottingham, horse!" the little boy cried, pointing his bow toward the Reynolds' camp and swinging his pudgy legs to spur Greg on.

"What about Maid Marian?" the horse asked, winking at Andi. "Shouldn't I carry her, too?"

"I'll walk, thanks," Andi said with a smile. "Or should I drive your Jeep over and park it with the other cars?"

"No," Greg said. "Leave it right there."

"You don't trust me?"

"I trust you all right." Greg grinned. "I trust you to walk me back out here when I have to leave tonight—hopefully without an armed escort this time." He bounced Rufus enough to set off another gale of squeals.

Andi's dimples deepened with the color in her cheeks. "You're right. This is the perfect spot for your Jeep."

For just a moment, Greg's grin disappeared as he realized that that one or two or eight hours would be here before he knew it and then he'd have to tell Andi that he couldn't see her for a month or more. Even worse, he would have to spend the next month or so following through with his decision.

Impatient, the little boy squirmed atop Greg's shoulders. "Are you a horse or not?"

"Sure I am, Rufus Hood," Greg said. He reached up with strong arms to hold the child in place. "And you'd better hold on tight 'cause I'm the fastest, strongest, wildest horse in Sherwood Forest." When he looked again at Andi and saw the love so clearly evident on her face, something caught in his throat and took his breath away. "Come on, Marian," he said when he could speak. "We'll race you to Nottingham!"

CHAPTER 4

Zeke Martoni didn't know what he would do with Greg Howland at the conclusion of their little game. He leaned back in the leather chair and lit a long cigar with a monogrammed silver lighter. He could think better with a good smoke.

Sure, some of the boys in the Syndicate—the ones who helped fund the lifestyle to which Zeke intended to ever be accustomed—would feel safer with Howland dead. Men like Greg Howland were a bad risk. Not only had the kid refused to try a few drugs and rig a few games, he'd gone to the police, like the idiot he was. That was when he'd made it personal. Now, while the other boys only wanted Howland to disappear, Martoni wanted something more. He wanted something that the kid feared more than death, something that would finally even the score.

Stretching his long legs languidly, he raised a manicured hand to smooth the raven-black hair above his ears. Then he exhaled thoughtfully and watched the smoke ring rise toward the ceiling and drift away in a hazy, ever-expanding circle.

He had once believed that every man had his price, believed that most men could be bought for gold, but that sometimes the price came higher: fame or, more often, power. When he had first met Howland, baseball had already given the young upstart more money than he'd ever expected to see in a lifetime. Still, Zeke had seen the potential for more. He'd expertly assessed Howland's All-American good looks and quiet, unassuming nature, and he alone had known how to exploit them to their full potential. In a single year he had not only tripled Howland's fortune through endorsements, he'd given him enough status and fame to ensure the satiation of any appetite. But Howland, the fool, apparently had none. So, instead of gratitude and loyalty to his maker, the kid had shown Martoni nothing but disdain and disrespect.

Zeke had turned then to Howland's brother—a simpleminded pawn—but lost him to brain cancer before he could be of any real use. At last, having only power left with which to bargain, Zeke had offered this last gift to the young ballplayer—only to have it brushed scornfully away.

But Zeke had learned. He had grown stronger and more cunning while he watched Howland grow weaker still by turning to "God." Let the kid cite the "law and the prophets" to his heart's content, Martoni thought; he had commandments of his own to keep. Certainly, "thou shalt not kill" was not among them, but "to every thing there is a season" was.

He held the thin cigar between his fingers and thumb and considered the glowing tip. Tomorrow afternoon Howland would be back at Bank One Ballpark, and Zeke was ready to up the ante.

Let the games begin.

HAPTER 5

Flanna Martyn Reynolds was in fine form. Within three minutes of Greg's arrival at the reunion, the wheelchair-bound matriarch not only had his attention, she clearly had his heart. And he had hers. She had already declared that if she were thirty years younger, she'd marry him herself. (That she had been sixty-five years old in 1970 and Greg had not yet been born never entered her mind—and there was certainly nobody in this family of scholars and physicists foolish enough to mention it.)

"Yea, a fanciful tale it is," Granny Reynolds said, her gnarled, spotted hand gripping Greg's, "but, oh lad, 'tis grand!" Though Flanna's thick red hair had long ago faded to brass, then eventually turned as soft and white as the late summer clouds, her eyes were shamrock green and as lovely as her lilting Irish brogue. She raised them now to Greg as she had the day she'd used them to captivate Andi's great-grandfather— an American missionary in Galway. "And remember the story, you will," she implored, "and tell your own wee ones?"

As if, Andi thought, *any of the rest of us will ever forget it.* As long as she could recall, Granny Reynolds had lapsed into the legend of Katie O'Grady Reynolds as easily as she slipped into a nap in the middle of a sentence. But it had been only this year that Andi had understood Kathleen. That a nineteen-year-old daughter of an Irish-gentry family would sacrifice her sheltered future to marry a poor, America-bound blacksmith she'd known less than a fortnight had always been an enigma to her sensible descendant. So what if Aidan

Reynolds was dashing? Dashing doesn't put food on the table. So what if he was handsome? Even handsome children need a roof over their head—preferably one they can inherit. And so what if a future in America seemed romantic? Romance is a poor substitute for reason when security is at stake.

Since romance and reason marked the diametric points on Andi's life-compass, and since she was determined to plot her course by the latter, Katie O'Grady Reynolds had remained an enigma. Until the day Andi had met a certain sweet, shy pitcher and finally understood one of her father's favorite sayings: *Mutato nomine de te fabula narratur.* (In English, "With the name changed, the story applies to you.")

Andi caught Greg's eye over Granny's head and, when he smiled, felt as warm and gooey inside as marshmallows left too long by the campfire. Follow him to another country? Andi would follow him to another world.

A few minutes into Granny's story—at about the point where newlyweds Katie and Aidan crossed the gangplank on their way to the steerage deck of the *Wingate*, the old woman began to snore softly. Andi took quick advantage of this opportunity to introduce Greg to her aunts and uncles and then finally to walk with him toward the lake where he could see her brothers and sisters and meet the younger Reynolds kin.

"Who is that?" Greg asked, motioning with his chin toward a distant tree. "And another question, what is she doing?"

It took some effort for Andi to shift her eyes away from Greg long enough to look toward where her cousin hung upside down from the tree, her short, spiked hair almost touching the ground. It was Zona of course. In her tattered attire and unorthodox position, she looked to Andi like some kind of freaky, homeless bat.

Of course, she'd never say so. She said, "That's my cousin, Zona May. And I think that perhaps she's meditating . . . or something."

Greg's eyebrow rose, but before he could reply, Andi's younger sister Clytie came over the rise from the lake. Andi watched his face break into an affectionate smile. As the girl approached, Greg knelt to retie his shoe. He didn't rise, Andi noted with a smile of her own, when the ostensible task was complete. Clytie Reynolds was an achondroplastic dwarf, and because she was only three and a half feet tall, the top of her blond head scarcely reached Greg's waist.

"Greg!" Clytie cried, shooting forward to wrap her short, pudgy arms around his neck. "I missed you!"

"Hi, Clytie," he said, holding her tight for a moment before rolling back on his heels to look carefully into her pretty face. "How are you?"

"Great!" she chirped, too quickly and too loudly. Noting the deepening look of concern on his face, she said more softly, "I mean, I'm good, Greg. Really."

"I'm glad," he said, but Andi knew he wasn't any more convinced than Clytie was convincing. It had been only four weeks since they had lost Thaddeus Bisher, a mutual friend, to a brain tumor. *Or rather*, Andi amended, *Greg lost a friend and Clytie lost a love.*

"So," Greg said, forcing a grin, "how's school now that you're a mighty senior?"

Andi thought that she could see his heart fall with Clytie's expression. He hadn't realized high school meant more to her little sister than classes and graduation. It meant homecomings, parties, and proms—all without Thaddeus or, likely, any date at all. Andi knew that if biting off his tongue could have brought the question back, Greg would have done so gladly. "Look, Clytie—" he began.

"I know," she interrupted, reaching for his hand. "I'm okay, Greg. Honest."

He squeezed the little hand.

"Have you met my cousins?" she asked.

"Well, I'm pretty well acquainted with Rufus." That's all he said, but Andi giggled, remembering that it had taken the combined efforts of the child's mother and grandfather to pry him from Greg's shoulders so the ballplayer could talk with Granny Reynolds. "But the person I think I really want to meet is Zona May," he said, motioning with a thumb toward the tree he and Andi had just passed.

Clytie looked at her cousin and wrinkled her nose. "What is she doing?"

"Andi says she's meditating," Greg said with a grin, "or something."

Clytie shrugged. "At least she makes Darlene look normal." Realizing immediately that her offhand remark might be unkind twice over, Clytie bit her lip.

Greg couldn't help but chuckle. Their sister Darlene was famous in the Reynolds' family circle for eccentricities exceeding even the broad range of most thirteen-year-old girls. "Darlene's great," Greg said sincerely. "And I really do want to meet Zona."

"She just got out of the Peace Corps," Clytie offered with obvious admiration. "Wasn't she in the South Pacific, Andi?"

"Yes," Andi said, "but I don't remember the name of the island."

"Ida June says she must be crazy to have spent three years sleeping in huts and eating bugs," Clytie continued, "but Mother says that Zona was teaching and trying to find homes for babies nobody wanted."

This obviously put Batgirl in a different category as far as Greg was concerned. They watched Zona swing agilely down from the tree and assume a Lotus position.

"What is she doing now that she's back?" Greg asked. "Teaching yoga?"

"I heard somebody say she's moving to Mesa," Clytie volunteered, "but I don't know what she'll do there."

"She's a professional photographer," Andi said, biting back an involuntary smile when Greg flinched. It wasn't that he disliked photographers individually, she knew; it was more that he detested them collectively. And certainly with good reason. Recently named "The Most Eligible Man in America," Greg had been on the cover of every tabloid in the country at least a dozen times. "She won't take pictures of you," Andi promised.

"I wouldn't think so," he said as he pulled his eyes away from Andi's cousin. "It's pretty obvious that if Zona May's interested in anything on this plane of existence, it isn't me."

"Maybe *she's* not interested in you," Andi smiled, "but here comes your biggest fan." The whooping and hollering from the top of the hill could only mean one thing: Enos had seen Greg.

* * *

"You can be our pitcher," nine-year-old Enos declared generously, extending a bright yellow whiffle ball to Greg, but not letting go of it until they'd reviewed the league rules. "Can you throw underhand?"

"Sure," Greg said. He wouldn't want to do it in the World Series probably, but he ought to be able to lob this Swiss-cheese of a ball somewhere in the vicinity of the rock that marked home plate for Enos' own Reynolds Reunion Classic.

"Don't throw it *too* hard," Enos cautioned, using the end of his glove to push his glasses back up the bridge of his freckled nose. "You'll be pitching to some *girls*, you know."

Greg nodded solemnly. "I'll lay off the bean balls."

From the opposing team's "bench"—a ragged line of lawn chairs, camp stools, and boulders—Zona May hollered, "Hit me with your best shot, Ace!"

A tempting offer if ever Greg had heard one. He allowed himself the luxury of considering the idea before dismissing it, as he had all the other comments she had made about him throughout the afternoon.

About his career:

In her dictionary, "pitcher" came right after "mercenary" and right before "rodent."

About his education:

She hoped that when he got that math degree from Northwestern, they taught him to count high enough to balance his checkbook.

And even about his hair color:

Did he want to split a bottle of peroxide with her sometime? (Though she might have realized he was a natural blond by the way his fair skin colored so quickly at the suggestion.)

"And there aren't any walks," Enos concluded. "The other guys just stand there until they hit the ball or strike out."

"I like that rule," Greg said. "Maybe I oughta suggest it to the commissioner of baseball."

Finally convinced that the reigning Cy Young Award winner could hold down the mound—if there had been one—Enos handed him the ball. Greg watched him trot back behind the plate, crouch down, and begin to flash the hand signs he had seen actual catchers use on TV. Greg tried not to laugh.

"Ready?" he asked his team, glancing toward third base where Andi's stocky Aunt Minerva (the physicist) was already in a crouch, swinging her pudgy arms and chanting, "Hey, batta, batta, batta!" Andi's father (the college professor) stood ramrod stiff at second. Between them was little Rufus. *Talk about giving the term "shortstop" a whole new meaning.* Clytie, Andi, and Darlene played outfield. Clytie admired the wildflowers in left while Darlene rebraided her hair in right. Only Andi saw Greg look back, and she waved happily at him. He smiled—at least he hoped it was a grin and not a grimace—before turning to nod at her eighteen-year-old brother, Brad, on first base. *Every single person who gets past Brad is gonna make it home,* he told himself.

"Play ball!" Granny called from the sidelines. As they did whenever Granny Reynolds spoke, the family obeyed.

Whiffle balls, Greg soon discovered, have both good points and bad. On the one hand, they don't have much weight to them, making a curve ball more along the line of a looper, and a sinker more like an impossibility. On the plus side, they don't have much weight to them, so when you get it right back at you (as Greg did the first time he pitched to Zona May), there's less chance of it killing you. Greg grabbed the screaming yellow missile just before it reached his forehead and fired it off to Brad. Unfortunately, there were just two things in the world quicker than Zona May's tongue, and they were her legs. She beat his throw by a mile. Maybe a mile and a half.

"You okay, Ace?" she asked from atop the paper plate base. "They're not gonna take all your shiny little trophies back for that, are they?"

There are worse things than having Zona May humiliate you in front of Andi's family, Greg reminded himself grimly. *She could play for the Mets, for instance, and humiliate you coast to coast.*

"That's okay, babe!" Aunt Minerva shouted encouragingly from third. "You'll get the next one!" The next one had big blue eyes, long strawberry-blond pigtails, and a batting zone of approximately three inches. Greg's heart melted as it always did for Andi's littlest sister Francie.

"Watch out, Ace!" Zona taunted. "She looks like a real killer."

Greg ignored Zona. Or tried to. "Hold the bat up, Francie," he said. Then he took a couple of steps forward to make sure he didn't miss it. Anything was possible with Andi's family looking on.

"Can I hit the ball, Greg?" Francie asked hopefully.

"Sure you can, sweetheart," he said. "Hold the bat up a little higher." When she did, he tossed the ball and hit the bat right in the center. "Run, Francie!" he urged.

"Hey!" Enos protested from behind the plate. He lunged forward as Francie headed toward first. Grabbing the ball, Enos threw it for all he was worth—six feet to Brad's right and directly into the outfield.

Darlene didn't notice. She was busy examining the chipped polish on her left thumbnail.

Greg watched Zona dance on home plate and Francie close in on third before he finally turned around. "Andi!" he called. "Could you, uh . . . Would you please go get the ball?"

"Oh!" Andi said, seeing that it had rolled to a stop at the base of a log. "Of course."

"Thanks," he said, pulling the brim of his cap down over his eyes before turning back to face Uncle "Slugger" Willard.

Charlie Brown had seen better days on the mound.

CHAPTER 6

The sun had set leaving the pines a soft pink sky above and deep purple shadows beneath as Greg and Andi stood beside his Jeep. He'd been "going" for twenty minutes now but couldn't seem to say goodbye—or any of the other words he'd planned so carefully on the way to the reunion. Knowing it might be weeks before he would again touch Andi's cheek or gaze into her eyes, Greg frankly didn't want to go.

Nor did Andi want him to. Despite having to share him with her family—or perhaps because of it—she couldn't remember a happier day than this. Except, perhaps, for the day last spring when Greg had asked her to marry him. Or the day she slipped the beautiful diamond and emerald engagement ring on her finger, certain at last that "eternity" and "Greg" would always be synonymous in her heart. She smiled up at him, her joy illuminating her features. The best days of her life had one thing in common, and he stood before her now, as reluctant to leave as she was to see him go. Even knowing that all the best days to come would be with Greg, Andi wanted to savor every remaining moment of this one. "I want to say—"

"I have to tell you—"

They spoke at once and stopped as if on cue. "Go ahead," Andi said.

"No, you," Greg said, then shook his head. He'd put this off too long already. "No, me."

Andi smiled and leaned into him, nestling her head against his wide chest. She could feel the strength of the muscles there and hear the pulse of blood into his gentle heart. "Then you," she sighed happily.

He raised a hand to stroke her silky curls but dropped it back to his side at the first touch. This was too hard already. "Andi, I'm not going to be able to see you again for a few weeks."

The pressure against his chest increased as Andi nodded in resignation. "I hate baseball," she said.

Greg let out a breath, tempted to allow her to believe it was his career that would come between them again. But he knew she wouldn't believe it for long. The Diamondbacks would play at least some games in Phoenix over the next few weeks. How many excuses could he possibly devise not to see her for even a few hours between them? Besides, he'd always been a lousy liar. "It isn't baseball, Andi," he said. "It's Zeke."

Andi felt cold. She'd forgotten the "one crow for sorrow" the moment her love had arrived, but she remembered it now at the mention of Martoni's name. Suddenly she needed Greg's warmth and strength and tightened her hold on him.

"I thought about it on the way up here," Greg continued, "and I'm worried about him, Andi. I'm worried about *you*. I think the best thing to do until Martoni goes to prison is to make him believe there's nothing between us anymore."

Andi looked up into his candid face. "Nothing he could use against you, you mean?"

Her eyes were wide with concern and Greg lowered his own, berating himself for worrying her—and for drawing her into this mess in the first place. "Something like that," he mumbled.

"Greg, what's happening?" Andi asked with growing alarm. That his expressions were so easily read was not always a blessing. Was he truly frightened? "You've talked to Zeke Martoni," she guessed. In the next breath she asked, "What does Bishop Ferris say about it?"

"I haven't talked to Zeke," Greg assured her. "And I'll call the bishop when I need to." He suspected that he had already said too much without even telling her about the mysterious phone calls and anonymously mailed Jeep. He'd tell her about them when he knew what they meant himself. "It's . . . I don't know what it is, Andi. Just a bad feeling, I guess."

Suddenly, Andi Reynolds believed in "bad feelings." She almost believed in premonitions and omens as well—but only good ones— and she had the best. Before she could reach in her pocket for it, Greg moved her gently to arm's reach and continued, "So I'm not going to see you again until after Zeke's court date. In the meantime, I'm going to find somebody to date in public—maybe lots of some-bodies." When her green eyes narrowed, he added quickly, "I have to, Andi. I want Zeke to see, if he's watching, that there's nothing between you and me."

"But there is."

"Of course there is," he said in frustration. "I love you Andi, you know that, but . . . "

No buts. They needed a good omen now and she had just the one. Andi fished a wide, silver CTR ring from the front pocket of her jeans and held it up to him. She'd been planning this for a week. "It's your engagement ring," she said.

His face softened. "It is?"

"Yes." She reached for his hand and tried to put it on his finger, but it wouldn't go. Andi bit her lip in frustration and felt tears rise in the back of her throat. It wasn't a bad sign—it wasn't. The ring just didn't fit. She should have bought a larger size. She knew Greg was left-handed and used that hand every day to grip a baseball. She should have—

What little was left of coherent thought disappeared when Greg lifted her face and kissed her tenderly.

"Thank you," he whispered.

"It doesn't fit." In another moment she was going to cry.

"It will," he said. "I'll have it fitted tomorrow—or tonight if I can find someplace that will open."

Andi nodded and tried to pull herself together. "The letters stand for . . . for . . . "

He smiled. "Choose The Right?"

"No," she said. She'd planned to tell him that they stood for "Certifying for Temple Readiness," but actually she'd had another acronym in mind: *Claimed. Taken. Restricted.* Despite the fact that Greg's current press agent, Dawson Geitler, worked fourteen-hour days to keep their relationship out of the headlines—or maybe because of it—she really intended the ring as a not-so-subtle signal to every female he encountered that Greg Howland was no longer "The Most Eligible Man in America." Now he was hers.

He kept looking at her with that boyish, lopsided grin, and she was lost. All she could think was: *Stop smiling and kiss me again!* Let him assume the letters stood for "Choose the Right." Nothing could be righter than this.

Greg agreed. Below the cuff on his shirtsleeves, the muscles bunched in ropy lines as he encircled her waist and kissed her like he meant this kiss to last until November. When his lips finally drew away, his arms stayed tight around her waist.

Which was good, Andi thought, or she would have likely collapsed at his feet.

"I'll miss you," he said.

Abruptly, Andi's head began to clear. "The letters stand for *Claimed, Taken, and Restricted,*" she said. This time when she lifted her face to his, there was a distinctly stubborn tilt to her chin that said if Greg thought he was dating any "somebodies" while promised to her, he'd better think again. "Are we engaged or not?"

Greg loosened his grip. "Of course we are, Andi, but you need to be reasonable—"

"No!" she practically shouted the word, and to her surprise she was neither sorry nor embarrassed. In fact, she felt pretty darn good. But how did she explain what she felt to Greg?

"All my life," she began again, in an even tone of voice, "people have told me *not* to be so reasonable. I've done everything right, Greg, and I've played everything absolutely safe—until I met you. Now I don't care about being safe. I only care about being with you."

He wasn't going to be easy to convince. Andi could tell by the set of his jaw and the appearance of the fine lines at the corners of his eyes. She paused a moment to consider—and seek inspiration—then smiled. "Well, if you insist I be reasonable," she said, the amber flecks dancing in her eyes, "I guess I'll just have to go home and marry Sterling Channing."

Andi had dated the practically perfect Sterling almost exclusively in high school then waited faithfully for 728 days for him to return home from his mission. She had planned to wait the full two years, of course, but the last two days had proved her undoing: she had met Greg.

Greg grimaced at the thought of "Elder Charming." "You don't have to be quite *that* reasonable."

"Oh?" she asked innocently. "Then you want me to play the field like you? Shall I date every man in the Valley, or will all the men in Mesa do?"

Greg hadn't meant that she should date anyone at all. After a second or two, he saw that she knew it. "This is serious, Andi."

"I know it is." Greg's arm had slipped from around her waist, so Andi reached forward to press her small hands into his large ones as she looked into his face. "I know it's serious, Greg," she repeated. "That's why I want to be with you. When we're together, I'm not afraid."

Clearly she was not and Greg wished he could say the same. But he knew Zeke Martoni and Andi didn't. Zeke's world was far enough from her realm of experience to qualify as another universe. Looking down into Andi's angelic face, Greg knew that he would move the earth and quite possibly the sun, moon, and stars, if that's what it took to keep her and Martoni a galaxy apart. Holding tight to both of her hands with one of his own, he raised the other to cradle her cheek in his palm. "Andi, you have to trust me on this one."

His eyes were hopeful and tender and a nameless blue that was deeper than the darkening sky. But there was also a careworn aspect to them that brought sudden tears to Andi's own. Hadn't Greg already carried his share of the weight of the world? Must he now also give up their love for a time to protect her? Surely he knew that she had already entrusted him with her heart and soul—what was her life after that? Still, Andi couldn't bear to add to Greg's burden by letting this perfect day end in disagreement, so she nodded and settled back into his arms for a farewell kiss.

Let him think it was settled and she was safe. Certainly, she wasn't afraid anymore. Fear cannot coexist with faith—or fury—and Andi was growing angrier than she knew she could be. She might not know, really, who Zeke Martoni was or what he had up his sleeve, but she knew that he hadn't reckoned on dealing with her. If Katie O'Grady could leave a life of ease to cross an ocean in steerage and then traverse almost a thousand miles on foot to be with

Aidan Reynolds, then there was little way to tell what her great-great-great-great-granddaughter Ariadne Reynolds could do to be with the man she loved.

HAPTER 7

"I have the world's greatest idea!" Darlene announced as she entered her older sisters' room uninvited and plopped herself down on Clytie's frilly bed.

Instinctively, Andi slapped her textbook closed, pushed it to the end of her own bed, and sat up in alarm. Darlene's "great" ideas could always be filed under D all right—for Disaster.

"What is it?" Andi asked, reluctant to hear the answer. It was too bad, she thought, that Clytie was out in the yard with their mother. Clytie was much better at diffusing their mostly misguided younger sister than Andi was.

"Well," Darlene began, "you know how I did such a good job of fixing up you and Greg?"

All of Darlene's contributions to her romance with Greg had come directly from the D-Files, but Andi nodded anyway.

"And you know how Zona lives right down the street from my school?"

This time, Andi was slower to nod. She knew of course that Zona had rented a studio apartment a few miles from the Reynolds' house and had taken the word "studio" a bit too seriously to Andi's way of thinking. Even so, she'd helped Zona hang thick blackout curtains over the only small window in the room to turn the cramped quarters into a photographer's darkroom. When she'd returned a week later, Zona's place was littered not only with negatives and prints, but also with clothes and books and half-full tofu containers. The latter had sprouted microcosmic rain forests—presumably because there was room in the mini-fridge for food or photographer's chemicals and Zona had chosen the latter. Heaven only knew where she slept in all the mess. Possibly she hung upside down from the shower rod in the tiny bathroom. Andi also knew where Darlene's junior high was. She just didn't know, quite, how the two were related.

Darlene was happy to tell her. "Well," she said, "Zona rides her bike—that weird three-wheeled thing with the big basket of cameras—past the school every day when we're out on the field for P.E."

And you're going to slash the bike's tires, Andi thought, *before anybody finds out that you and Zona are related*. Not that she could blame Darlene, exactly. With her mango-orange (or some other fruity color-of-the-week) spiked hair, safari-style shorts, and striped knee socks, Zona usually looked more like a traveling sideshow than a free-lance photographer.

"And every day," Darlene continued before Andi could say a word, "the boys' football coach stares at her."

I imagine, Andi sighed to herself. "And your great idea is . . . ?"

"To fix them up, of course!"

Andi was nonplussed. Had Clytie given Darlene meddling lessons? Clearly she'd picked up the matchmaking bug somewhere. Andi's first impulse was to squelch the idea, but she paused at her sister's shy, hopeful smile and the way the freckles on her pixie face crinkled into the creases around her nose. A few months ago, Andi realized, she would have called her sister silly and sent her on her way. Now she slowly returned the smile. This idea of Darlene's *was* silly, certainly, but what could it hurt to giggle with her little sister for a few minutes? She hadn't engaged in nearly enough "girl talk" in her reasonable life. Besides, Darlene would surely forget this idea and be on to another potential disaster before suppertime.

Andi wrapped her arms around her knees. "What do you have in mind?"

"Well . . ." When it came right down to it, Darlene was only a romance wannabe. But she leaned forward eagerly, thrilled to have her big sister's attention. "Do you have any ideas?"

"Um . . ." Romance wasn't exactly Andi's forte either. She searched her mind for a love story she might have read. The only thing that came to mind was *Romeo and Juliet,* and without the cell phones *that* hadn't worked out well enough to be worth mentioning. Then she remembered a romantic comedy she'd seen based on the story of Cyrano d'Bergerac.

"Well," Andi said, "there's a famous story of a man who wanted to court a beautiful woman, and he did it by getting his friend to write love letters to her in his behalf."

"Did that work?" Darlene asked.

"I'm not sure," Andi said honestly. "Steve Martin got the girl, but I don't remember which character he was."

"Why don't we do that?" Darlene suggested eagerly.

The eager "we" gave Andi pause. Here she was practically suggesting that Darlene pass herself off as the football coach to court Zona May. This wasn't merely silly; this was a Darlene-Disaster waiting to happen. And she would be an accessory. "We *don't* do it," Andi said quickly. "We were just talking about it for fun."

"It sounds like a good idea—" Darlene began.

"It isn't!" Andi interrupted. She scooted forward. "Darlene, listen. You can't pick two people at random and try to put them together romantically. It isn't, um, it isn't nice."

"But I told you that Coach already looks at Zona," Darlene said.

"A lot of people look at Zona," Andi said, choosing her words carefully. "But that doesn't mean that they want to marry her."

"I don't know if Coach should *marry* Zona," Darlene agreed. "At least, not right off. I think that people should date first. Don't you?"

"Yes," Andi said. "I mean, no. I mean that Zona and that coach should date only if they want to and even then it should be their idea, not yours."

"But how do they know if they want to date?" Darlene asked.

Suddenly, Andi's temples throbbed. If this was girl talk, she hadn't missed anything after all. She was simply not good at it. "They . . . I don't know, Darlene. They just know they want to. So they do. Do date, I mean."

"You wanted to date Greg when you first met him," Darlene pointed out, "but you didn't date him. You decided to marry him instead."

"Well, it wasn't exactly like that," Andi replied, although she knew that from a certain point of view it pretty much was. "I *couldn't* date him because he wasn't a member of the Church then—"

"And his family weren't members either," Darlene added helpfully. "And he didn't go on a mission and—"

"I know, Darlene," Andi interrupted. How had this discussion shifted from Zona to her anyway? And how did she ever explain herself to a girl whose brain worked more like a blender than a word processor? "I was right to set the standards that I did," she began again, "and I hope you do, too, as long as you remember then to judge people the way God does, by the intent of their hearts. Understand?"

"No," Darlene said. "And I still don't understand why you and Greg don't date now. Isn't that what people are supposed to do before they get married?"

"You'd think so," Andi said, mostly to herself. She'd talked to Greg every day on the phone and she'd seen his press agent, Dawson, almost as often, but she hadn't seen Greg once since the reunion.

Darlene leaned forward on the bed. "So Greg was *supposed* to go out to dinner with that other lady?"

"No," Andi said. "He was *not* supposed to do that."

But he had. The very next night after telling her about Zeke—the night before she had returned from the reunion—Greg had had Dawson arrange a late, after-game dinner with a popular TV personality. Of course it had made the local papers the next day. The day after that, it made the national papers and *Entertainment Tonight.* Greg, who usually hated publicity of any kind, was thrilled with this. Andi was less thrilled, but more determined to convince him that Zeke Martoni wasn't half the threat *she* would be if he tried that "dating" thing again anytime soon. Anytime ever.

She looked up to see that Darlene's hazel eyes were wide. "You know that Greg's famous," she tried to explain, "and he thinks it would be . . . difficult . . . if people find out we're engaged. See?"

"I guess so."

Obviously, Darlene didn't see. Just as obviously, Andi couldn't explain it, so she said, "Good."

"Now can we talk about what we're going to do about Zona and Coach?"

Andi sighed. She should never have started this conversation thinking her sister would soon forget it. Pit bulls dropped knuckle bones more easily than Darlene was dropping this. "We aren't going to do anything," Andi said firmly. "If the coach is looking at Zona . . . that way . . . then he'll do something himself."

"I think she needs to think somebody likes her," Darlene insisted. "It might make her happy. And nice. Like it did . . ."

Andi smiled at the pink rising on her sister's freckled cheeks. "Like it did me? You're right, Darlene. I probably *have* been nicer since I fell in love with Greg. But Zona has to find that out for herself."

"You're sure?"

"I'm certain," Andi said. She reached for her textbook as Darlene rose from Clytie's bed, but she didn't open it. Instead she watched her sister leave the room. "I hope you're half as sure as I am," she said softly, "or I may have just helped instigate a major Darlene-Disaster."

HAPTER 8

Darlene *was* sure. Sure that she was right about her cousin Zona May. And she was sure that Andi's idea was a good one, too. The problem was that Darlene didn't think she could write the letter herself. In the first place, she didn't know what grownup people in love said to each other. In the second place, English wasn't her best subject. What would Zona think about a letter from a teacher— even a P.E. teacher—who couldn't spell and was likely to put the apostrophes in the wrong places? No, Darlene knew she needed help. But who?

She crossed her arms on the sill and gazed out the living room window as she thought it out. Her big brother, Brad, had just graduated from high school, so he was an adult, if not a great grammarian. But should somebody who was filling out his mission papers also be writing the kind of letter Darlene had in mind? She doubted it.

Clytie was in the front yard with their mother planting gazanias along the top of the driveway. Darlene watched her sister and wondered if Clytie might want to conspire on Project Love Letter. She was a great speller and had read just about every romance novel ever written. Darlene started to rise, then slumped back into the chair. In the first place, Margaret Reynolds was out there, too. Darlene knew that her mother wouldn't approve of this project any more than Andi had. Besides, Clytie's boyfriend had died and talking about love letters might make her sad. She decided not to mention the project to Clytie at all.

While she moped, she watched a beat-up Volkswagen beetle move up the street in fits and starts. It was Ian, the paperboy. Ian lived in a trailer down by the Salt River and delivered newspapers to help his single mother make a living. Until a month or two ago, he'd done his job from the seat of a bike, even in July when it was 110 degrees and too miserably hot for most people to venture out long enough to pick up a paper from the driveway. Now Ian had a car, but it didn't look to Darlene like much of an upgrade. Clearly it wasn't air-conditioned since Ian's dark, curly hair was damp and his face was flushed. Darlene had heard that he was near the top of his class at the high school, but near the bottom of everybody's social list but Clytie's. Of course, Darlene reflected, that was Clytie for you. *She* firmly believed that the only excuse to look down on anybody was if you were going to pick them up.

When Ian stopped at the corner for an oncoming silver Volvo, Darlene perked up a little. It was Dawson Geitler's car. Maybe Greg had sent him over again with something for Andi. Why Greg didn't come himself anymore still puzzled her, but Andi had just said it was "complicated" and her mother had said it was "none of her concern," and Darlene knew better than to even ask her father. But, maybe she could ask Dawson. He worked for Greg as a press agent and . . . The sheer inspiration of the next thought brought Darlene to her feet. A press agent wrote stories for newspapers and magazines, right? Here she had been worried when all along she'd known a real, live writer. This was great!

"Thank you!" Darlene told God on her way out the front door— even though she hadn't thought to enlist His help in the first place.

"A love letter?" Dawson asked a few minutes later. He had rolled down the car window since it was impossible to open the door with Darlene leaning on it, and he certainly didn't want her fingerprints smudging up his freshly polished glass. "What could you possibly want with a love letter?"

For just a moment Darlene doubted her inspiration. Dawson Geitler *was* kinda old (he was probably at least thirty), and he *was* kinda bald (just a little spot on the very top of his head, but it was shiny when the sun hit it, like it did right now), and he *was* kinda boring. Still, he *was* the only writer she knew in the world, and she was sure he could spell all kinds of great words and be counted on to keep his apostrophes right where he wanted them, too.

"I have this friend," Darlene began breathlessly. "And she, I mean he, I mean . . . well, I have these two friends actually and—"

"Could we discuss this indoors?" Dawson asked. Margaret Reynolds and Clytie were troweling away, and he could almost see the mold particles fill the air around his sinuses. He pulled a fresh handkerchief from his starched and pressed shirt pocket and held it to his nose. "Please?"

"Oh, okay," Darlene agreed, reaching for the door handle to hurry him along.

Wonderful, Dawson thought, *grimy fingerprints on the chrome*. If Greg didn't pay him so well, chances were he'd—well, he'd be here anyway. Greg Howland was not only his employer, he was probably the most genuinely nice guy Dawson had ever met. Geitler hadn't met very many nice guys in the course of his work, nor did he form friendships easily, but when he did he was fiercely loyal. Now Greg was his friend, and he was in trouble. That was why Dawson had come to see Andi. He followed Darlene up the steps into the Reynolds' spacious home.

Darlene pulled him to a sofa and planted her sneakered feet squarely in front of him. "So, I have this friend which—"

"*Who*."

Darlene stamped her foot. "Listen! I'm trying to tell you who!"

"People are *who*," Dawson said, "and things are *that*, and *which* is another part of speech altogether. So you have friends who."

"Who what?"

"I'm attempting to help you with your grammar, Darlene," Dawson said tiredly.

"Grammar?" Her face brightened. "Oh, grammar! Great! That's why I want to talk to you—about this friend which—I mean that—I mean who—needs your help."

"My help?"

Darlene put her hands on her narrow hips impatiently. "You're a writer, aren't you?"

Dawson's master's degree was from the Columbia School of Journalism, and his internship had been with the *Washington Post*, though how, he thought now, his rather impressive credentials could possibly assist a friend of Darlene's was rather unclear. He inclined his head in assent and asked, "What, specifically, does your friend need?"

"She needs a letter."

"Of reference?"

"Of what?" Darlene asked, the picture of puzzlement.

He might as well be talking to the Reynolds' pet duck, Dawson thought, for all the sense this made. His eyes wandered to the window, and he watched the mallard watching Clytie struggle with a long hose. Her impossibly short arms were ill equipped for the task of untangling it, and Icarus the duck looked as though he wished he could help.

"My friend doesn't need something out of an encyclopedia," Darlene said impatiently, applying the only definition of "reference" she knew. "She needs to think that somebody likes her. I want you to write her a love letter."

Dawson raised a finger and used it to push his Franklin-style glasses back up the bridge of his narrow nose. "I think you have me confused with Cyrano d'Bergerac."

"Yes!" Darlene cried. "That's just the guy! See, this . . . friend . . . of mine doesn't ever smile."

Dawson continued to look out the window at little Clytie. In her own obtuse way, Darlene must be talking about her sister. Greg was worried about Clytie, too, Dawson knew. He had been since their friend Thaddeus died.

"And I thought that if she got a letter," Darlene continued, "like from a secret admirer, it would make her feel happy. Every girl likes to feel like somebody likes her," she added without a pause for air, "even if she never finds out who it is."

"And if she did find out?" Dawson asked slowly. He couldn't believe that he was even considering the idea of writing to Clytie. But he could see Darlene's point. What could it hurt to write a little something to lift the girl's spirits and help her see that there could be another young man in the world who found her appealing? Greg would do it if Darlene asked him, Dawson was sure of it.

"She wouldn't find out!" Darlene insisted. Maybe Andi was right. Maybe she should leave the coach's name off the letter. "Maybe she wouldn't *ever* find out," she repeated, refining the idea in her mind as she went along. "Don't you think it would be more exciting to have the letter come from a mystery man?"

Dawson ignored the question. "What would the mystery man write?"

For a split second, Darlene was at a loss for words. She screwed up her face. What *would* somebody write to Zona? "Well," she said finally, "he could write that he sees her almost every day and . . . and . . . "

"Couldn't help but admire her individualism, courage, and determination," Dawson mused, noting with pleasure Clytie's success in taming the garden hose.

"Well . . . okay," Darlene said reluctantly. It wasn't surprising to her that Dawson was still single if that was the best he could come up with. Still, it was a start. Even though it didn't sound all that lovey-dovey, the big words were impressive and Zona was about as "individual" as a person could be. And didn't it take determination to dress so weird and courage to ride her bike through the traffic the way she did? "He could say that for a start, I guess," Darlene agreed. "Will he? I mean, will you?"

Dawson hesitated only a moment more. "I will," he said. He pulled a small leather notebook from his laptop computer case and a fountain pen from the pocket of his suit. "I'll do it while you go tell Andi that I'm here to see her."

Dear Clytie, Dawson wrote. *I have the privilege of seeing you almost every day.* Pausing, he began again, changing "privilege" to "joy" in the hope of making it sound less formal, then he added, *I find you a remarkable young woman. I am often struck by your individualism, sweetness of nature, and determination*—and what? he wondered. At a loss, he added a period and signed it, *A Secret Admirer.*

Skimming the brief lines, Dawson knew he would never be mistaken for Cyrano on the basis of this note. Still, he had tried to do a good turn. The effort was to his credit, if not the product. He folded it carefully and passed it discreetly to Darlene when she followed Andi into the room.

Andi scarcely noticed. She was justifiably upset at Greg, and if the messenger was the only person around on whom to vent her frustrations, then so be it. "I don't know why he sent you this time, Dawson, but . . ."

"Actually, Greg didn't send me."

" . . . if he thinks he's going to—" Andi caught herself in mid-sentence. "He didn't?"

"No. I wanted to talk to you myself," Dawson said, "about Greg."

Alarmed in spite of herself, Andi dropped down next to him on the sofa. She frowned at an odd twitch that had developed around his eyes and wished he would control it somehow and get to the point about Greg. Suddenly, Andi realized he was trying to signal her to get rid of Darlene. She turned to her sister. "Darlene, don't you have something to do?"

Darlene fingered the corner of Dawson's note. "Yes!"

When she had gone, Andi turned back to Geitler. "What about Greg?"

"I don't know," Dawson said. "I had hoped maybe you could tell me something. He's been acting rather odd of late. First, he asked me to arrange a date for him with somebody high profile—he didn't care who—and then he told me to go through with the contest."

"What contest?" Andi asked.

"I wondered if you knew," Dawson said. "You see, I had suggested it—as Greg's publicist—last spring. It was before I knew you were engaged," he added hastily.

"What contest, Dawson?" Andi repeated.

"Well . . ." Dawson hesitated at the look on her face. He suspected that she had never particularly liked him and knew this wasn't going to do anything to change it. "It's an essay contest to win a front-row seat at a ball game, followed by a dinner date with Greg Howland and a teammate."

Andi's frown deepened. "And he wants you to do it now?"

"We've already advertised it." Dawson fidgeted with his fountain pen. "This isn't like him, Andi. Is everything, er, on track between the two of you? Perhaps you've had an, er, a disagreement?"

Andi shook her head slowly. "The last time I saw Greg was at the reunion, and it was wonderful." She considered. "He did tell me then, and again on the phone since, that he's worried about Zeke Martoni being out on bail. He doesn't want him to know we're engaged."

This was more than Greg had told Dawson. "Hence the date with the anchorwoman," he mused. "And the contest."

"Well," Andi said, "that's the reason he gave me for that 'date' of his. He conveniently forgot to mention the contest."

"But Martoni's been out a couple of months now," Dawson reasoned. "Why the sudden concern? Has Greg been threatened?"

Andi shook her head. "Not that he's told me about, at least."

"Something must have happened." Dawson stuck the pen in his pocket. Obviously he wasn't the only one Greg was keeping in the dark. "Perhaps he's concerned because the trial is coming up."

Andi nodded then leaned forward, her eyes wide. "Have you ever met him?"

"Martoni?" The revulsion on Dawson's face would have saved him the trouble of answering. "Yes, I met him once. I went to interview him when he was still in jail." He winced at Andi's start of surprise then the corner of his mouth turned down. "That was when I was still writing the, you know . . . thing . . . about Greg."

"I don't know," Andi said. "What thing?"

Dawson adjusted his glasses, surprised that Howland hadn't told her about the exposé he'd been writing when he first came to work for the famous young ballplayer. Either Greg was exceptionally loyal to his friends or particularly tight-lipped about his trials. Perhaps he was both. "I once entertained the notion of publishing an unauthorized biography about Greg," he admitted.

So, Andi thought, there *had* been a good reason for her not to trust Dawson Geitler.

"But I didn't," he added. "And I never will."

And that, Andi supposed, was all Greg would remember about it. If he could forgive and forget so completely, surely she could. "Tell me about Martoni," she said.

Dawson rarely responded to even simple requests for information without careful consideration, so it was almost a minute before he responded. "He hates Greg," he said without preamble. "The man could lie convincingly about anything and everything except that. Maybe that's what made him so anxious to talk to me in the first place. He hoped to use me to get to Greg." When Dawson finally looked up, his eyes reflected his concern. "I don't know very much of what's gone on between them, Andi, but I know that Martoni believes he has a score to settle."

Andi's hands felt cold as she clasped them together in her lap. "Then you think that Martoni's dangerous?"

"My impression," Dawson responded, this time without hesitation, "is that Zeke Martoni would go to any length to ruin Greg. And I think he's the kind of man who's capable of doing whatever it takes to get what he wants."

CHAPTER 9

Greg sat on the curb in the players' parking garage at Bank One Ballpark and wondered just what Zeke Martoni might be capable of.

He hadn't consulted Dan Ferris, although he wanted to. Or intended to. Or at least knew that he should. He told himself that he'd call just as soon as he'd figured out what to say.

Should he start with: *Sergeant Ferris, I've been getting these phone calls but nobody is ever on the line. I think it's Zeke Martoni—I'm sure of it—but I can't prove it. I also think he mailed me a toy car. And now he's done something really criminal—he's washed my Jeep.*

Or should he say, *Bishop Ferris, I haven't been sleeping much at night and now I think I'm seeing things. I could have sworn my Jeep was dirty when I drove it in here today, and now it looks like new. But the parking attendant insists that the only person who's been near that car is me.*

Or should he continue to sit here on the curb at 11:15 at night and stare at a Jeep that had obviously been washed, waxed, and probably spit-polished in the twelve-odd hours Greg had been at the ballpark?

What else has Zeke done to it? he wondered. *Cut the brake line? Put an explosive device on the starter?*

Probably not the latter, Greg decided. Zeke might be criminal, but he wasn't insane enough to blow up part of Bank One Ballpark. In all likelihood Martoni had done nothing more sinister than steal it long enough to wash it. This game was a psychological one—for now—calculated to keep Greg off balance and on edge.

And the thing that really bothered the young pitcher was how well it worked.

"Hey, man! Whatcha doin'?"

Greg jumped half a foot at the deep, heavily accented voice. Then he ran a palm across his face and tried to muster a weak smile for Jorge Andres, the D-Backs' new Dominican catcher.

"You okay, man?" the stocky catcher asked.

"Yeah, Jorge," Greg managed. "Sure. I'm great."

Jorge looked from Greg and the duffel at his feet to his shiny car and back. "Why you sittin' there, man? You lose your keys? Your car broke?"

"No," Greg said, tossing his keys into the air and catching them in his fist as he rose to his feet. "I've got my keys and there's nothing wrong with my car."

But by the time he was standing, he had changed his mind again about driving it. Why take a chance—to prove to Zeke Martoni that he was a man? Forget it. He'd save all he had to prove for when and where it counted: in a court of law. In the meantime, he'd take a cab home tonight and have a mechanic come in tomorrow to find out what, if anything, Zeke was up to.

He said, "I mean, yeah, I think there might be something wrong with the Jeep."

"So, you want a ride?"

Greg hesitated. He'd heard the locker room rumors that Jorge acted behind the wheel the way he did behind the plate, taking out any and everything that got in his way. That the man was already driving his third truck this season made Greg think he was likely better off taking his chances with Zeke after all. "Well, I don't want to put you out any, Jorge," he said. "You probably go another way and—"

"No problem, man!" Jorge said. He reached for Greg's duffel before Greg could and slung it over his shoulder with his own.

Jorge Andres was built like a bulldog and had roughly the same genetic imprint. Greg knew that he wouldn't get that bag back until Jorge decided to give it to him. Resigned finally to his fate, he followed Andres to his truck.

Andres' driving was as bad as everybody had said, and probably worse than they had imagined. *This guy doesn't need a truck*, Greg thought, *he needs a tank. At the very least, he ought to keep his catcher's armor strapped on until he gets home.*

Without armor of his own, Greg held out little hope for his seatbelt, his airbag, or his chance for survival. He could only hold on and hope that a scripture he had read that morning—the one about "thy years are known and thy days shall not be numbered less"—applied to him as well as Joseph Smith.

Jorge took the freeway exit ramp at roughly the speed the space shuttle reenters the atmosphere. Still, he turned his head to look at Greg. "You wanna stop for a beer?"

Greg considered saying yes, if only because it involved a stop, but then shook his head. "No," he said. "I don't drink."

"You don't drink nothing?" Jorge asked.

"Well, no alcohol."

"That's what the guys say," Jorge confirmed, "but I wondered."

Greg didn't respond. He couldn't blame Jorge for fishing for more information. The "guys," he knew, said that and much more about him but rarely *to* him. The laughter was mostly behind his back. Depending on how you looked at it, it was either a perk or a drawback to being a so-called superstar. The only man on the team with enough courage to deride Greg to his face was fading legend Wes Westen, and Greg had a hard time holding it against him. After all, Greg's trade to the team as the new ace had moved the other pitchers down a slot, with the result that Westen was bumped off the bench altogether and had landed in the bullpen. Then, as if to add insult to injury, the press gave the former five-time all-star a heck of a hard time about it.

"Your momma?"

"Huh?" Greg startled from his thoughts. He must have missed something in the moment he'd been imagining their truck wrapped three times around that palm tree Jorge had just managed to miss by a frond's length.

"Your momma?" Jorge repeated amiably. "She tol' you not to drink?"

With his drunk, abusive father's example so painfully obvious, she hadn't had to. "Well, no," Greg said, "I—"

"My momma, that's what she tol' me," Jorge continued. "'Play baseball,' she say. 'Don' play aroun'. Make money,' she say. 'Then you gets yourself right down home.'"

Home for Jorge was in one of the poorest spots on earth. Like a number of well-known players, he had grown up in the Dominican Republic using a stick for a bat and a rock for a ball and a piece of cardboard for a glove. Not, when Greg thought about it, all that different from his own start in the dirt fields of Iowa.

Under the glow of a much-too-near light pole, Greg saw Jorge's white teeth gleam in his open, honest face and warmly returned the smile. "What your mother said, that's good advice, Jorge."

"And I'm takin' it."

"Good for you."

Jorge looked up at the lighted street sign he had approached at over 50 mph. Then he glanced at Greg. "This your street?"

"Yeah," Greg said as they sped through the intersection. "It . . . uh . . . it *was*."

"We there, man!"

Greg's eyes closed involuntarily as Jorge spun the wheel, jumped the narrow brick median, and headed back toward Greg's expensive gated community.

"Can your little Jeep do that, man?" Jorge asked gleefully.

"Not legally."

"It's midnight, man!"

"Jorge," Greg said with more patience than he felt, "the great state of Arizona doesn't suspend its traffic laws just because the streets are nearly empty."

"No?"

"No. And you have to stop for that—" Too late. The formerly high-tech security gate was so much scrap metal now, ripped from its hinges and deposited on the street in front of a truly astonished guard.

"Gate?" Jorge asked sheepishly.

"Yeah, gate." Greg swung open his door before the gatekeeper could find his cell phone and dial 911. At other times it wasn't so bad being who he was, he thought. Fame (and a checkbook) had a way of turning major mistakes (like riding with Jorge) into minor (if costly) inconveniences. "I'll take care of it, Jorge," he said. "Thanks for the ride."

"You sure?"

"Yeah." Greg turned back when he heard Jorge put the truck into reverse. "Hey!" he called "Be careful, will you? We've still got a World Series to win."

Jorge raised both thumbs high—with the result that neither hand was on the steering wheel.

Greg shuddered. Jorge Andres: best catcher in the league, worst driver on the planet.

CHAPTER 10

Mid-September and *still* eighty-five degrees in the middle of the night. Greg slowed from a jog to a walk as he rounded the corner, then stopped short at the sight of the car parked in front of his townhouse. Next he broke into a run.

Andi opened the car door just as he reached it.

"Andi!" Greg said. He was happy to see her, but he was unhappy to see her out so late alone. He was relieved that she was okay but dismayed that she didn't share his perception of risk. And he was mostly out of breath from the long sprint from the front gate in the heat. He wished there was a tree in the yard to lean against. A saguaro cactus doesn't replace a willow tree for some things, no matter how beautiful and practical a desert landscape is in the Valley of the Sun.

"Greg!" Andi said, scooting out from her car to wrap her arms blissfully around his neck.

It was all Greg could do to force himself to untangle those arms and move her gently out to an arm's length. "What are you doing here, Andi?"

Clearly, that wasn't the welcome she wanted. Her chin lifted and her eyes flashed. "If the mountain won't come to Mohammed . . . "

Greg frowned. "I told you—"

"You haven't told me anything," Andi interrupted. "Just like you haven't told Dawson Geitler anything that makes sense. And Bishop Ferris said he hasn't talked to you at all for a least a week. You don't even return his calls, Greg." Andi's eyes were wide and faintly accusing. "Why?"

"There isn't anything to tell anyone," he said, averting his eyes even though he knew he was telling a version of the truth—the very one, in fact, that he spent most of his time convincing himself to believe.

"Where is your Jeep?" she asked suddenly.

Obviously, it would have been too much to hope that she wouldn't notice he was on foot. "I left it in the garage downtown."

"Why?"

"Because . . ." What truth should he tell her now? What would a girl most like to hear about her fiancé: that he was being stalked by an amoral criminal or that he was suffering from a particularly acute case of paranoia?

"Because . . . ?" she prompted.

Would the digital whine of his cell phone save him by distracting Andi? Greg wondered as he pulled it from his pocket, or only dig him a deeper pit? He looked away from her frown. "Hello?"

It was definitely a deeper pit. Zeke Martoni's voice was just as Greg remembered it—throaty and low and as smooth as frosted glass. "So, Grego," the man said. "I'm hurt you didn't appreciate the little favor I did you."

"Don't do me any favors, Zeke."

At the look on Andi's face, Greg mentally kicked himself to Chicago and back for saying the name out loud. "It's okay," he whispered to her above the mouthpiece. "Just give me a minute."

"Sorry, kid," Zeke said, apparently not missing a word. "I thought you'd be in bed by now, and from everything I know about you, I didn't dream you'd have company."

Greg felt the blood pound in his ears as he struggled to frame his reply in front of Andi. Before he could, however, Zeke spoke again.

"You oughta take better care of that car of yours, kid," he said. "Looks to me like you got in some deeper dirt than ya meant to. It's hard to get the muck off when you've been in too deep, Grego. Ya know what I mean?"

Greg was afraid that he did.

"And I didn't just clean up after ya this time, kid," Martoni continued smoothly. "I had 'em check the points while I was at it.

And you know what? Your timing was off. That can be dangerous, Grego. Nothing can louse a guy up faster than bad timing."

The blood that had felt so hot a few minutes ago now seemed to have drained away, or perhaps it had merely been replaced with water chilled by Zeke's words.

"Remember what I said, kid," Zeke said. "I'll keep in touch."

Greg held the phone to his ear seconds after the connection had been cut. Finally he lowered it slowly, his fingers so numb it was a wonder it didn't slip to the ground.

"That was Martoni?" Andi asked immediately. "What did he say?"

Greg shook his head. "I don't know." He needed a few minutes to think, but he apparently wasn't going to get them.

"Call Bishop Ferris right now," she said.

"No." But he caught the flash in Andi's eye and added, "It's too late. I'll call him tomorrow morning."

Finally, Andi edged closer, but whether it was to comfort him or be comforted, Greg couldn't say. He held out his arms and when she moved quickly into them, he embraced her gratefully.

"Did he threaten you?" she asked softly into his chest.

Did he? Greg wondered, replaying the brief conversation in his head. Certainly Zeke's tone had been menacing, but the words themselves—if put down on paper and read in the context of a dirty jeep as Zeke would insist he had meant them—were certainly harmless.

"No," Greg said finally, stroking her curls. "He was playing word games, Andi. That's all. It didn't mean anything."

She stood there for a moment, content to be with him, then forced herself to pull back a little to look searchingly up into his face. "Is it so very hard for you to trust people, Greg? To trust me?"

Greg started and his hands fell to his sides. Recovering, he raised them to clasp Andi's. "I don't know what you mean," he said. "Of course I trust you."

"But you don't," she said softly. "Not really. Maybe you can't . . . yet."

Since Greg apparently would never call Bishop Ferris, Andi had called him herself this afternoon and her bishop, as always, had been calm and perceptive and wise. He'd helped Andi to understand how deeply Greg's father had hurt him and caused him to withdraw at an early age into a self-sufficient, emotionally insulated world of his own creation. Then, when his only ally—his brother, Jim—had died, it only confirmed to that frightened, wary part of Greg that there was truly nothing, and no one, in the world to trust. Certainly the gospel had made a tremendous difference in his life, and without a doubt Greg had come a long way in a little time. But it would take patience, understanding, and commitment on their part, Bishop Ferris said, to help him to come further.

It was help that Andi feared Greg would be unwilling or unable to accept. "I know you want to protect me, Greg," she ventured, "but can't you see that I want to protect you, too?"

He held her close and pressed his lips to the crown of her head. "I'm fine, Andi," he said. "There's nothing for you to worry about."

She wanted to shake him. To slap him. To do whatever it would take to make him understand that she loved him and wanted to share everything—good, bad, and undecided. "I want to worry about whatever it is *you're* worried about," she persisted.

"Then all you have to worry about is yourself." He forced a smile just before his lips brushed her forehead. "Okay?"

No, Andi thought. But she raised her lips to his instead of opening them to protest. She wasn't going to win this battle with words—at least not tonight and probably never with words alone. But she was going to win it just the same. She would prove to Greg somehow that he wasn't alone anymore—and that he would never, in fact, be alone again. As her arms locked around his neck, she prayed that the Lord would show her the way.

CHAPTER 11

Martoni tossed the phone onto the brocade couch across from his chair and followed it with two expensive Italian loafers. Then he reached for the decanter on the polished table at his side and poured precisely two inches of amber liquor into the crystal glass.

A man deserved to relax after such a satisfying day's work.

It was too bad the kid hadn't taken the car home, he thought, appreciating the burn that slid across his tongue and down his throat to warm his vitals. Howland's cowardice would set him back a little, and there wasn't much time for setbacks before the trial.

In some ways, Zeke would have liked to cut to the chase. But it would be a shame to waste what he had planned. This way would be more subtle. And shrewd. And conscienceless. Three virtues Zeke most deeply appreciated in himself.

Besides, this way was more fun.

He imagined the stew Howland must have been in to leave his precious Jeep in the parking garage. He allowed himself the luxury of reveling in this side benefit of his patience. What was the petty inconvenience of a single day's delay compared to Howland spending another sleepless night?

And the fun had just begun. By the time he was finished, Zeke intended to have the DA's star witness doubting his own credibility. Although he was quite sure that the baseball altar boy could be counted on to tell the truth, he was equally sure that the truth was malleable and that a jury—like the rest *of the half-witted world—could be counted on to embrace the version of truth that best suited its appetite for the sensational.*

A tiny fly, attracted to the light on the table, landed atop the almost empty decanter. Zeke observed it with quiet interest. He would play with Howland a little longer, the same way he would play with a fly: he would calmly, and with great detachment, pull off the wings and watch it stagger and try to flee.

He could always kill it later.

CHAPTER 12

Andi woke with a start. As she had for the past six months, she'd been dreaming about Greg. But this dream wasn't one of quiet kisses and pleasant plans. In fact, this dream hadn't been a dream at all. It had been a nightmare.

She lay still for a moment staring at the cream-colored wall as she tried to call back images from just beyond this side of consciousness. But the dream was gone. Only the shiver of apprehension it sent down her spine remained. Greg was in trouble, and she didn't know what to do about it—asleep or awake.

She pulled the soft blanket up to her chin and rolled away from the wall toward the window across the room. It was still dark outside but close enough to dawn that she might as well get up. She had a busy day. She had to be at work at the zoo by six and then she had class after. Besides, sleep—after that dream—was an impossibility.

Andi sat and drew up her knees and thought of Greg. With him working nights and her working days, it was easy for him to claim he wasn't avoiding her, but Andi knew better. She might not know exactly what Greg faced in Zeke Martoni, but she knew it couldn't possibly be easier for him to face it alone. She wanted to be Greg's helpmeet forever. *And how appropriate*, she thought unhappily, *since that's approximately the length of time it's going to take him to turn to me for help.*

She squared her shoulders and shook back her thick curls. *Then I won't wait for Greg to turn to me.* Last night Mohammed had gone to the mountain, but today she would try it the other way around. Mountains *could* be moved, after all—even mountains as stubborn as Greg. It only took determination, faith in the cause, and some well-placed connections.

In an hour or two she would call a couple of those connections, she decided—Bishop Ferris and Dawson Geitler—but she would start with the best-placed connection of all. Andi knew the source of strength and inspiration to which mountain-movers had been turning for all time. She threw off the blanket, and with scarcely a glance at Clytie still asleep in the next bed, she knelt beside her own and began to pray.

* * *

It was going to be a long day.

Dawson Geitler stuck a bottle of pain relievers into his coat pocket then reconsidered, removed two from the bottle before replacing it in his pocket, and chewed them thoughtfully on the way over to his computer. The scrupulously neat desk took up almost all of his tiny, immaculate apartment. Dawson had never noticed that his quarters were cramped—possibly because work took up almost all of his narrow, well-organized life.

He pulled out his chair and glanced at the clock, gratified to see that it was not yet 6 A.M. He still had two hours before he needed to pick up Greg to shoot the public service announcements they had agreed to back in June. After that session, there was a segment to wrap for the Diamondbacks' weekly TV special and a World Series promotion to film. Baseball franchises, Dawson mused, were nothing if not optimistic.

He checked his other pocket for antacids and found he had only two rolls. That meant that he'd have to stop at a drugstore on his way into Mesa. And he'd better pick up more Excedrin while he was at it. Since his job was to keep camera-shy Greg Howland smiling into lenses all day, he'd better be prepared for both indigestion and one heck of a headache.

In the meantime he decided to use his spare hour to look over the latest batch of "Win a Date with Greg Howland" contest essays. He opened the manila envelope and pulled out a thick stack, waving away the overpowering scent of conflicting perfumes. There had been no mention of awarding extra points for drenching the submissions in Chanel or planting lipstick kisses on the envelopes, but you'd never know it to look at this lot.

The first entry, Dawson was pleased to note, had neither cologne nor lipstick. It was from a man. He lay it hastily aside. The next one began, *You want to choose me because you're hot and I'm*—Dawson stuck it beneath the first. The next one said *I regret to inform you that I am dying of . . .* Dawson adjusted his glasses, but could still not decipher the disease, though he could see right through the transparent ploy. He set it on the "no" stack. Whatever she was dying of, he hoped she learned to spell it before she "expired."

He categorized ten more "definitely not" essays, six "probably nots," and only one "maybe if I'm desperate" when the phone rang.

Yes, Dawson thought, rehearsing what he would say if it was Greg. *It's too late to tell them you don't want to do the promotions.*

"I'm sorry to call so early," the feminine voice said in response to his greeting, "but I have to feed the alligators in a few minutes, and I was afraid that I'd miss you if I waited until I finished."

Dawson knew only one alligator feeder. "Good morning, Andi," he said.

"I'll get right to the point."

She always did and Dawson always admired her for it.

"Have you chosen a winner for that contest you told me about?"

He looked down at the papers on his desk. If Andi Reynolds wanted to judge this sorry lot, it was fine with him. "No," he said. "In fact—"

"I want to enter," she said. After a brief pause, she added, "I want to win."

Instinctively, Dawson reached for the roll of antacids. "I see."

"I don't want you to cheat," Andi explained quickly. "At least, not really."

Dawson waited for her to continue.

She did. Rapidly. "You're supposed to choose the most convincing essay, right? The one that states most plainly why the writer should win the date with Greg?"

"Yes," Dawson said carefully.

"I've written an essay," she said. "May I read it to you over the phone? I want to win a date for *tomorrow* night." Before he could object on the grounds of such short notice, she hurried on, "I *have* to see Greg before he leaves town again on Saturday."

"But—"

"You never said when the date would take place," Andi pointed out.

A calculated oversight on Dawson's part to give Greg time to sort out what he was doing.

"So I could win today and go on the date tomorrow, couldn't I?"

"I—"

"Good," she said as though he had acquiesced. "Here's my essay. Do you have a pen?"

"Yes," Dawson said, but he didn't reach for it.

"I believe that I should win the date with Greg Howland," Andi said slowly enough for him to transcribe every word, "because *as his fiancée*, I am in a unique position to make his life—and yours, Dawson—*truly miserable* if he dates anyone else." After a moment she asked sweetly, "Did you get all that?"

Dawson stuck the phone under his chin as he gathered his "probably nots" and "definitely nots" and "desperate" stacks and returned them neatly to the top of the pile of essays.

"Well?" Andi asked impatiently when he didn't respond. "What do you say?"

"I think the appropriate response is 'Congratulations, Miss Reynolds,'" Dawson replied. "You just won a date with Greg Howland."

"Thank you, Dawson," she said. "But could we, um, keep this a secret? I don't want Greg to know what we've planned before tomorrow night. There are a couple of other things I need to do first."

Dawson thought of the mood his young employer would be in today given his schedule and agreed wholeheartedly. "There are arrangements I need to make, too," he said, wondering if seeking other employment should be among them. "I'll check with

Mr. Andres, for instance, and make sure this change will fit his schedule. It is, as you'll recall, a double date."

* * *

Double date, Andi thought, climbing from the zoo cart at the edge of the Tropics Trail to see to the egrets. She'd forgotten that part of the deal. *Who can I take with me?*

Her best friend, Justine, was the first person who came to mind. She'd go in a split second, but she'd probably have to break a date with Sterling Channing to do it. They'd been dating pretty steadily since Andi's engagement to Greg. And though Andi didn't feel guilty about breaking up with her former boyfriend, she still didn't want to risk "Greg" and "broken commitment" entering Sterling's mind in the same sentence.

As she removed a water-filled bucket from the back of the cart, Andi reviewed a mental checklist of her closest friends: *Mission. Engaged. BYU. Missionary. Rotten cold. BYU/Ricks*. It was hopeless.

No it isn't, she told herself firmly. *It's just another mountain*. And a small one. She'd think of someone.

Andi unlocked the gate to the exhibit and smiled when the beautifully plumed herons stalked toward her as if on stilts. "This is a serve-yourself buffet," she told them, emptying the bucket of minnows into the pond and standing back to watch the graceful dipping of the birds' long, sharp beaks. "Save some for later," she said, knowing that of course they wouldn't.

The flamingos were in the next exhibit down the Trail so she retrieved the pail of shrimp and crab from the cart and walked the short distance. It was this diet of shellfish that gave the birds their distinctive coloring. The seemingly one-legged birds' plumage ranged from muted shades of salmon and coral into pink and crimsons suitable for plastic lawn ornaments. For just a moment, Andi stood beneath the flowering jacaranda and stared. She saw the curved-beaked flamingos almost every day, yet she never tired of the miracle of them—or of any of the other birds and animals at the zoo.

She climbed over the low wall and filled the granite basins around the birds' exhibit with shellfish then paused to pick up some litter that had blown onto the wide lawn surrounding their pool. Straightening, she looked at her watch. It was early yet and she was right on schedule feeding-wise, despite calls to Dawson and Bishop Ferris.

Bidding the flamingos good-bye, Andi sat again on the low wall. Before she swung her legs over it however, she took time to look up at the sun glinting over the tops of the rock formations of Papago Park. Shadows from a few thin clouds drifted lazily across the sandstone and gave the illusion that the eons-old boulders were themselves in motion. Andi smiled. Truly, mountain-moving wasn't so very difficult when you knew how to go about it. It wasn't difficult at all.

Still, she knew that she had saved the most challenging—if most enjoyable—task for last. She had yet to call Greg and appeal to his considerate nature and genuine fondness for Clytie. If she could convince him to do her one tiny little molehill of a favor, the mountain of his resolve to "protect" her and her family with his absence was as good as gone.

CHAPTER 13

Clytie paused on her way out the front door of her house to pick a folded piece of notepaper up from the stoop.

"What's that?" her friend Kimberly asked as Clytie climbed in the front seat of her car for a ride to school.

"I don't know," Clytie replied. "Somebody must have dropped it." As usual, her brothers and sisters had left earlier for school or work. "It's probably Darlene's. She's always losing something." Clytie unfolded the paper, scanned it, and gasped in surprise.

"What?" Kimberly asked.

Dear Clytie, Clytie read silently, scarcely believing her eyes, *I have the joy of seeing you almost every day. I find you a remarkable young woman . . .*

"It's . . . it's a letter," Clytie said finally. "To me."

"Who's it from?" her friend pressed.

"I don't know." Clytie turned the paper over to see if anything was written on the back, but it was blank. "It's signed 'A Secret Admirer.'"

"Clytie, really?" Kimberly said. "That's so awesome. Who do you think it's from? Read it to me!"

Clytie shook her head. "It's a joke, Kim."

Reaching a stoplight, her friend looked over at her and said loyally, "Why do you say that?"

But the fact that she looked so quickly away again from Clytie's short legs and square figure told Clytie that Kim knew perfectly well why. She crumpled the note and pushed it into the front pocket of her backpack before firmly changing the subject.

* * *

Clytie took the mystery letter out of her bag several times during the day's classes and again when she got home from school. She looked at it now, instead of her music, as she sat at the piano. But when Andi entered the room, freshly changed from her job at the zoo and now off to a late class at Arizona State University, Clytie quickly tucked it into some pages of sheet music behind her theory book.

"Ready to go to your piano lesson?" Andi asked.

Clytie wished, as she had a hundred times before, that she could drive herself places. When would she finally convince her father that if the pedal extenders specially made for Little People were good things for pianos, they were good things for cars, too? She squirmed off the bench with a sigh. "I guess so."

Andi watched her sister fondly. "I was going to surprise you," she said with a smile, "but you look so down, I'll tell you now." It was the day's coup de grace—proof positive that with help from the right places, mountains not only move, sometimes they levitate. "Greg's going to pick you up from your piano lesson!"

Clytie's spirits rose as fast as Andi's mountains. "Greg? Don't the Diamondbacks have a game tonight?"

"Oh, yes," her sister said in her best long-suffering voice as she dug into her purse for her car keys. "Don't they always?" She opened the front door. "But Greg isn't pitching today and they've had him shooting public service ads, so he doesn't have to be at the ballpark until game time." She held the door for Clytie, then followed her sister out onto the porch. "Wouldn't you know his free time would be during the one class I can't cut?"

Clytie murmured something sympathetic but not particularly sincere. If there was one person on earth with whom she might feel comfortable consulting about the mysterious letter, it was Greg.

* * *

"Do I *have* to practice?" Darlene asked again, lugging her violin case into the living room as if it outweighed a cello.

"Darlene!" her mother admonished from the hallway.

It was Margaret's exasperated voice. Her I'm-about-ten-seconds-away-from-suspending-your-Internet-privileges voice. It was the voice that Darlene especially hated. "Okay, Mom," she called. "I'm practicing."

She removed the instrument from the case and laid it on the piano bench while she tightened the bow. Then she got out the square of rosin and ran it up and down, deep in thought. Where had she left Dawson's letter to Zona? She'd had it that morning, she knew she had. In fact, she'd been about to tear Clytie's name from the top of it when the carpool came. She remembered folding it carefully before running out to the porch and . . . what?

"Darlene!"

She dropped the rosin and picked up the violin. Tucking it under her chin, she ran the bow across the strings to make some noise while she looked for her music.

Trying to ruffle through the papers on the piano with one hand, Darlene managed to knock most of them to the floor. She bent to gather them and saw Dawson's note on the top, crumpled and worse for wear, but miraculously returned. Not being the type to wonder overmuch at miracles, Darlene stuck it hastily in her pocket with a self-satisfied grin. Then she propped *Wolfart Etude #18* over the keyboard and managed, after a minute or two, to coax sounds from the violin that even her mother might have believed were music.

* * *

"Why do you have a fly in your Jeep?" Clytie asked, nudging the inch-long rubber insect with a stubby finger.

"Good question," Greg said. He reached for it intending to open the window and toss it onto the street, but at the last second threw it onto the back seat instead. It was like the replica of his car that he'd received. He certainly didn't want it, but for some perverse reason he couldn't part with it either.

The real Jeep had been in perfect condition, according to the mechanic who had looked it over the next morning. There was nothing at all unusual about it—unless it was the large, fake fly that had been left on the dashboard.

Fly: Insect. Bug. Nuisance. Pest. Each word could be applied with accuracy to Zeke Martoni. Was that all it meant? Was calling at midnight, washing the Jeep, and leaving the bug just Zeke's way of saying he intended to pester Greg until he drove him crazy?

That was Dan Ferris' theory. True to his promise to Andi, Greg had called at last and was glad he did. It was a relief to speak with his bishop and mentor. Ferris had philosophized that Zeke was arrogant and vindictive but not stupid. Because of his mob connections, Martoni was well aware that the FBI kept pretty close tabs on him. He might try to rattle Greg's cage, but he wouldn't do anything to jeopardize his thin chance for acquittal this close to the court date. The police sergeant advised Greg to be cautious, certainly, and to keep him informed of any new developments, but suggested gently that anything beyond that—like avoiding Andi—would be agreeing to play the game by Zeke's rules.

Now Greg didn't know what to believe. He trusted Andi's alligators more than he trusted Zeke Martoni. On the other hand, he trusted Bishop Ferris more than he trusted himself. And certainly Andi was hard to resist. Her request that he pick up Clytie this afternoon had been part of Andi's "All Is Well" campaign, he knew, and with the bishop on her side, Greg had been hard-pressed to pursue his original plan. Besides, this had been one of *those* days—the ones that were best cured by a healthy dose of Clytie. So here he was, wisely or not.

"So why do you have that fly?" Clytie asked again.

"I don't know," Greg said honestly. He was relieved when, instead of pressing, Clytie changed the subject.

"Thank you for picking me up," she said. "I know you don't have much time."

He wished he could say that he had all the time in the world for her. And after this season—and this thing with Zeke—was settled, he would. He said, "It's my pleasure, Clytie. Really."

She felt the warmth rise to her cheeks because the great thing was that she knew he meant it. He'd understand her fears about the secret admirer letter, she knew he would. Still her color deepened as she began, "Greg, do you think . . ."

As the words trailed off, he glanced over at her. "Not when I can help it, Clytie. I have a reputation as a jock to maintain." He grinned back at her weak smile. "But maybe I can make an exception for just a minute or two. What's up?"

"Well . . ." She fidgeted in the seat and her smile disappeared altogether. "Do you think that . . . well . . . that a *guy* might be interested in me?" Her aqua eyes were earnest. "Be honest."

"I'm interested in you," Greg said cautiously. "And I'm a guy."

"You know what I mean, Greg." Clytie was through with banter. "Do you think a *real guy* might be interested in me?"

To his credit, Greg didn't reply at once. If he had, Clytie would have thought he was telling her what she wanted to hear—like most people do—and trying to be kind.

"Thaddeus was interested in you," Greg said finally. "And he's a guy."

"Thaddeus was blind."

"No," Greg said, "he wasn't." He slowed the car to look over at her. "Thaddeus could see better than anybody I know. He saw inside you, Clytie. He saw the only part that counts." Greg raised a hand from the wheel to halt her protest and added, "I'm not finished. Thaddeus loved you because you're compassionate and perceptive and smart enough to know that's what's important. And he sure thought other guys would be interested in you."

Tears sparkled on Clytie's lower lashes before she blinked them down her pink cheeks. "Do you know what Thaddeus told me?"

"No. What?"

"He said that Thumbelina was just as pretty as Cinderella and that she had a prince waiting for her, too."

Greg smiled. "Prince Iggy." That had been Thaddeus' and Clytie's private joke, and finally Greg, too, knew who Prince Iggy was. Clytie was silent, lost in thought. Greg gave her a couple of minutes to enjoy her thoughts before saying, "So, the answer to your original question is . . ."

" . . . yes?" she asked tentatively.

"No," he said. "The answer is, 'yes!'"

"Even though I'm a dwarf?"

Greg suppressed a sigh. Then he reached over to nudge her gently. "Come on, Clytie," he said. "I'm not blind. I knew you were a dwarf the minute I saw you. Don't you remember when we met?"

Clytie nodded, the tears increasing. The highlight of her sixteen years of life to that point had been having the famous Greg Howland come to her house for dinner and say that she was prettier than a picture.

"I think you're a beautiful girl, Clytie," Greg repeated now. "In every way. And, hey," he added, casting her a self-deprecating grin, "I think my opinion ought to count for something here. I'm 'The Most Eligible Man in America,' after all."

Clytie sniffed back the tears and beamed up at him. "You'd better not let Andi hear you say that."

"You're right." He glanced at the resized CTR ring on his finger. *Claimed, Taken, Restricted,* she'd told him more than once. "I'm going to be in enough trouble when she finds out about a contest Dawson's done," he told Clytie, amazed himself at how *fast* Dawson had done it.

Clytie smiled. "Andi already knows."

"She does?" Greg raised an eyebrow. "She didn't mention it on the phone this morning." *Odd.* "Is she, uh, unhappy about it?" *Stupid question.*

"She thinks it's a great idea," Clytie said, her eyes dancing. Andi had told her on the way to her piano lesson how she'd won the date. Clytie was proud of her.

Greg was pretty close to stunned. "Are we talking about the same thing? The 'win a date'—"

"Oh, sure," Clytie said. "Andi—" Anything else that might have spilled out about her sister's secret was lost under Clytie's high-pitched scream. Instinctively, Greg slammed on the brakes and swerved to the side of the road, his heart hammering.

"The castle's for sale!" Clytie squealed, scarcely noticing the sudden stop as she peered out the side window.

Great, Greg thought. Here he was worrying about losing his mind and his hearing had gone first. *Surely she didn't say* "castle."

"Oh, Greg, can we look?"

"At what?" He scanned the road. No carcasses littered it and a truck that had narrowly missed slamming into them had blared its horn and swung around the Jeep with a squeal of tires. Greg lowered his eyes and rubbed his forehead, hoping to avoid any visual opinion the truck driver might express about his lousy driving.

"Can we look at the castle?" Clytie breathed. "I've never been inside."

His hearing was okay, Greg realized. It must be his eyesight that was iffy. As far as he could see, both sides of the wide street were lined with trees—orange trees, he guessed. They were fairly near the Reynolds' subdivision, and Andi had said her neighborhood had been carved out of the old citrus groves. Judging by the size of the gnarled limbs, this must be the oldest part of the orchard.

Clytie bounced on her seat and pointed toward a narrow, unmarked lane. When Greg looked closer, he saw that a tall gate had been propped open with a "For Sale" sign. Just visible over the tops of the trees was a balcony that might possibly be on something that could pass for a turret. But a castle? In the Arizona desert? No way. The talk of Prince Iggy must have gone to Clytie's head.

"Can we look?" Clytie begged. "Just for five minutes?"

Greg glanced at his watch. Five minutes were about four and a half more than he had right now. But Clytie was eager and her eagerness was always irresistible. Besides, the Diamondbacks were only a few wins away from clinching the Western Division Title, and he'd pitch the key game next Wednesday night. Greg figured that made the odds of him being fired today for being a little late roughly equal to the odds of him finding Camelot at the end of this gravel driveway.

He restarted the Jeep and turned it down the narrow road. After all, Clytie *was* looking for a prince. The very least he could do for the cause was to leave no castle unturned.

HAPTER 14

Prince Charming he's not, Darlene decided as she reread Dawson's brief note to Zona May. And why did he write Clytie's name on the top of it? Really, grownups made no sense at all.

After carefully tearing off Clytie's name, Darlene smoothed and refolded the note and congratulated herself on her double dose of luck: finding the long-lost letter amid the music *and* having Zona stop by on the very same day. Lifting the flap on the worn canvas backpack her cousin had left by the front door, Darlene dropped in the paper. And not a moment too soon. She could hear Andi and Zona talking as they walked back toward the living room. Darlene giggled and slipped up the stairs.

"But it would be good for you to get out," Andi said, calling upon her best powers of persuasion.

"I'm 'out' every single day," Zona countered. "And if I were to go 'out' in the evening, the last place on earth I'd go would be to a baseball game."

Andi's hand rose then dropped helplessly to her side. This was absurd. If six months ago someone had told her she'd ask her cousin to double date with her anywhere—especially to a baseball game—Andi would have called them certifiable. And here she was practically begging Zona for a measly few hours of her time—to go on a blind date with a Dominican catcher no less. Whoever said that love causes a person to do strange things certainly knew what she was talking about.

"But have you ever been to a ball game?" Andi asked, planting herself in front of the door as Zona reached for her backpack.

"Not since I played Little League."

"See?" Andi said. But she thought, *Zona played Little League? I don't remember that. I remember she took karate and fencing . . . Really, she's the strangest girl.* With effort, she pulled herself back to the task at hand—arranging to spend tomorrow evening with Greg. "You might enjoy it," she ventured.

"Do you think so?" Zona asked, tilting her now kiwi-colored head. The green hair and bright hazel eyes made her look rather like a quizzical parrot. "Which part do you think I'd enjoy, Andi? Mingling with the crazed simpletons in the stands or watching the testosterone-driven egomaniacs on the field?"

Andi leaned against the door in defeat. Desperation alone had made her ask her cousin to go with her. Though they had been almost inseparable in the summers they spent together as children, they were virtual strangers now. "You're right, Zona," Andi said, turning to open the door and let this exotic bird fly free. "I'm being selfish and foolish. I just wanted to be with Greg so much it was all I could think about. Frankly, I couldn't come up with anybody else to ask, so—"

"All right," Zona interrupted. The single word wasn't sarcastic or put-upon or even resigned. It was matter-of-fact. So matter-of-fact that it made Andi blink.

"You mean to say that you'll go with me?"

"Uh huh." Zona turned away from Andi's happy, grateful expression with a shrug. "I spent seventy-two hours last spring in a monsoon with no raincoat and no shelter. This 'double date' of yours couldn't be worse than that." She looped a strap over her bony shoulder. "Could it?"

"No," Andi said with a giggle.

"Are you absolutely certain?"

Impulsively, Andi touched her index finger to her tongue, crossed it quickly over her heart, and held it up to Zona in an old ritual from their girlhood. With the first genuine smile Andi had seen since her cousin had come home from the South Pacific, Zona licked her own finger and touched it to Andi's.

"Double Spit Cousin Heart Cross," they said together and laughed.

Really, Andi thought as she watched Zona bounce down the stairs to straddle the three-wheeled contraption that was her preferred mode of transportation, *I don't give Zona enough credit. She's quite remarkable when you think about it. She might even like Jorge Andres—if only because he's from someplace as poor as Kiribati.* Andi's smile widened as she wondered what Greg's Dominican teammate would think about his American blind date. Hopefully he wouldn't think all American women shopped exclusively at the Salvation Army and fashioned their hair color after the hues in a roll of Lifesavers.

As grateful as she was, Andi couldn't keep her thoughts on Zona for long. She had already begun to wonder about Greg. Clytie's lesson had ended a half hour ago. Where was he? She'd cut the class lab to be home when he dropped Clytie off under the theory that even a quick hello/good-bye kiss was better than no kiss at all. She was here waiting for him—as usual—and he was who knows where—as usual.

Andi frowned. Then she looked across the valley toward Red Mountain and the smile slowly returned. *One mountain at a time, she told herself.* She had started on a small scale that morning—working on little peaks like Camelback and the Superstition foothills. But she had moved them. With patience—and practice—she could work her way up to problems as weighty as Red Mountain and the White Tanks. She knew she could.

* * *

Just as Greg suspected, the place Clytie led him to wasn't Camelot at all.

It was Dunguaire. More precisely, it was an early twentieth-century rendition of the early sixteenth-century castle on Galway Bay in Ireland. Half the structure was single story and consisted of a great room with a massive fireplace, a dining room, and kitchen with a spectacular native-stone hearth that made Clytie "ooh and ahh" with delight. The other half was three floors more of bedrooms and baths with a balcony near the top that overlooked lawns, orchards, and the Lehi Valley.

The Irish Dunguaire had been home to the likes of W.B. Yeats and George Bernard Shaw. The Arizona version had most recently been home to an eccentric elderly woman and her cats. It had been built almost a century before by the woman's grandfather—an Irishman who came to Arizona by way of Ellis Island in the late 1800s. He made his fortune planting one orange tree after another and digging one irrigation ditch after another to nurture an orchard in the arid, but climatically ideal desert.

All this had been perfunctorily related to them by a realtor who had spent the last six days of her life sitting alone in a property to which no prospective buyers had come. To which no prospective buyers would probably ever come. Not that she was surprised. Modern Southwestern design was "in." This house had gone "out" with the medieval period about 400 years before.

Greg leaned against the banister at the foot of the grand staircase, watching Clytie gaze out a window toward an algae-filled pond in an overrun rear garden. When she finally turned away from the view of the weed-choked garden, he hoped that it was to say she was ready to go.

Instead she sighed for perhaps the tenth time in ten minutes. "Isn't it . . . ?" Words failed her. "*Gorgeous*," she said finally. "Don't you *love* it, Greg?"

"It's, uh, interesting, Clytie," he said. He turned to the realtor. "Thanks for showing us."

The woman reached into her gold blazer pocket for a business card and extended it. "I have several more suitable properties," she suggested. "I'd be happy to show you any one of them."

"Thanks," he said. "Maybe in a few months. I'm getting married then."

He should never have said it. Clytie was at his side in three seconds flat, tugging on this hand. "Buy Andi this house, Greg."

Right. And a second white elephant as a pet. "A guy doesn't just buy a girl a house, Clytie," he said gently. At her clearly dissenting expression, he turned to the realtor. "Does he?"

"Not usually," she said.

"But Andi's loved this house her whole life!"

"She has?" Greg asked. "Has she ever *seen* it?"

"Well, no," Clytie admitted, "at least not really. But every year at Halloween we used to come all the way down the road to trick-or-treat just so we could look at the castle and touch the door." She didn't mention in front of the realtor that Andi had once done something more.

Instead, she looked around again and Greg rolled his eyes, waiting for the inevitable. Sure enough, she sighed.

"It's a *perfect* house, Greg," she insisted. "Every girl dreams of the man she loves buying her a castle."

"Every girl like you, maybe," he teased. "Personally, I think Andi would rather live in the townhouse."

Clytie opened her mouth to protest again, then opened it wider as a dog barked nearby and a gray, tiger-striped streak bolted in the open window, flew across a stone ledge, leaped the mantel, and hurled itself toward Greg.

"Catch it!" the realtor shrieked with none of her customary composure.

Greg, with all of his customary reflexes, caught it in flight. Holding it was another matter. The cat left three parallel gashes on the back of his right hand before dropping to his feet. It was poised for further flight then seemed to think better of it and uncoiled enough to sniff tentatively at Greg's shoe.

"Catch it!" the realtor said again.

Greg shook out his stinging hand, but kept both it and the other a prudent distance from the cat. "Uh, may I ask why?"

"I've been trying to get that darned nuisance for a week," the woman said. "The rest of the former owner's menagerie is already at the pound, but that one keeps springing the traps and getting away."

Greg couldn't help but notice that she didn't approach the cat she claimed to want so badly. He remained still as the animal apparently liked what it smelled and rubbed its head against his ankle.

"What a nice kitty," Clytie said.

Greg seriously doubted the accuracy of her observation. Still, when he saw that Clytie was about to reach for the furry flesh-shredder, he bent and scooped it up before she could. He was surprised—and grateful—when the cat lay docilely along his arm and allowed him to run his hand down its back. He could feel the animal's ribs and suspected that it had been some time since it had eaten a meal it hadn't caught for itself.

"Hold it!" the woman commanded, darting from the room. "I'll go get the cage."

Greg walked over to the window and looked out. There was no sign of the dog. He leaned outside and extended his long arms until the cat was just a few feet from the ground. "I'd beat it if I were you," he said as he let it go. It landed nimbly and looked up at him with accusing amber eyes. "You'd thank me if you knew the alternative," Greg told it. He turned at the sound of the realtor's heels on the wood floor.

"Where's the cat?" she asked.

"It, uh, got away from me," Greg said, looking convincingly sheepish, though the cause was not the deed but the fib. "And I'd like to help you look for it, but we've got to go."

"You're not going to buy the castle?" Clytie asked wistfully.

"It's quite expensive," the realtor offered as she set down the still-empty cage.

"It's not like he can't afford it—" Clytie began.

Greg made a "cut-it" motion that Clytie either didn't see or chose not to interpret, he wasn't certain which.

"He's *Greg Howland*, you know," Clytie said, waiting to see how long it would take for the name to register.

It took almost no time at all. "You're kidding," the realtor said, dumbfounded. "I know him." She turned to Greg in dismay. "I mean, I know you. I just didn't know who you were. I mean . . ."

Greg nodded and headed for the nearest exit.

" . . . *everyone* knows who you are," the woman continued, following Greg through the door and beyond to the wide stone stairs. "I mean that I just didn't know that who you are is—"

"I know what you mean," Greg said. "Thanks for your time." He motioned toward the Jeep with his uninjured thumb. "Come on, Clytie." But getting her to come, he realized, was like using boxing gloves to pull a bumble bee out of a rosebud. He'd have to offer some form of enticement himself. "Maybe you and Andi can come back and look at it again later. If she loves it as much as you say she will, I'll think about buying it."

Clytie brightened at the suggestion. So did the realtor.

"I'd be happy to show it to anyone you send, Mr. Howland. Anytime." She pulled a stack of cards from her blazer.

"You gave me your card—" Greg began.

She pressed another dozen into his hand. "Take them. Please. And I have hundreds of other properties that are more appropriate. Are you interested in Paradise Valley? Scottsdale?"

All he was interested in at the moment was getting Clytie away from the faux castle and into the car. And he'd like to take the cat, too, but he didn't see it anywhere in the yard. Why hadn't he thought of keeping it before? He should have held on to the poor creature, not dropped it out a window. Maybe he would come back for it. If, that is, he ever left in the first place. "Clytie?"

"Okay," she said reluctantly, looking back over her shoulder every step of the way to the Jeep. When she was safely buckled in the seat and on the way home, she looked up at him with her confidant, watercolor eyes. "Andi loves that castle," she said.

"I bet she does."

"She sneaked into it once." Greg's head jerked toward her, and she smiled. At least that had gotten Greg's attention.

Then he shook his head. "You're forgetting that I know your sister, Clytie," he said. "Andi is not exactly the 'breaking and entering' type."

"There's a secret tunnel," Clytie offered breathlessly.

"The realtor didn't say anything about—"

"I don't think anybody knows about it anymore," she said. "Nobody's probably used it since bootleggers back in Prohibition." She was relating what she thought was romantic ancient history, but Greg clearly wasn't suitably impressed. She rushed on with the main point of the story. "One summer when they were about Enos' age, Andi and Zona were out riding bikes, and they accidentally found the entrance in an old well or something. They didn't know where it went, but when they followed it they came to the castle!" She couldn't tell if Greg was interested or not. "Nobody would have guessed where the tunnel went," she concluded, "because the old well's all the way off the property."

Greg's only comment to the tale Clytie found so exceptional and exciting was a skeptical, "That doesn't sound like something Andi would do."

"Zona dared her," Clytie added.

"That does sound like something Zona would do, all right."

"They went all the way to some backstairs," Clytie said with obvious admiration and envy. "But then they got scared and ran back out." She twisted in the seat, trying to better see Greg's reaction. "Andi only told me about it at the reunion this year, when everybody was talking about what good friends she and Zona used to be."

"Really?" Greg said under his breath. Then, afraid that Clytie might have heard something unkind in his voice, he added, "Not that I don't like Zona."

Clytie waved it off with a small hand. "But about the *castle*, Greg—"

"Tell Andi if she wants to see it again, she can go in the front door this time." He pulled up in front of the Reynolds' house, but left the engine running. "Is it okay if I just let you off?" he asked apologetically. "I was supposed to be at the ballpark about an hour ago."

"Oh!" Clytie reached for her door handle. "Yes." She pushed open the door and slid down onto the sidewalk. "Thanks for picking me up, Greg," she said. "And thanks for spending all that time looking at the castle with me." Her pretty face brightened. "You go on to your game. I'll tell Andi all about the castle, I promise!"

"Bye, Clytie," Greg said, knowing that her telling Andi—and everyone else she saw—about that ridiculous cavern of a house was one thing he could count on.

* * *

A half block away in a nondescript car, a man stuck a finger to his ear to reposition the listening device.

"On the move," he said into the radio tucked into his cuff, then he shifted the car into gear and discreetly followed Greg to Bank One Ballpark.

CHAPTER 15

Andi had never sat in the actual stands at Bank One Ballpark so she had no idea it would be like this. She'd attended other games as a guest in minority owner Cleon Bisher's glass-enclosed skybox where the best view of the field was on a big screen TV. But tonight's front row tickets had been part of her contest prize, so she'd forsaken the quiet, enclosed tier to sit between Dawson Geitler and Zona May, just behind and above the Diamondbacks' dugout.

Everything seemed so different from down here. For one thing, the stadium was gigantic. With the roof open tonight, Andi might well imagine that she was in the bottom of the Grand Canyon—except, of course, for the din. Unlike the silent sandstone formations 200 miles to the north, these walls pulsed with the activity of almost 50,000 fans—the usual capacity turnout when Greg Howland pitched a game at home. As the Diamondbacks came out for their last warm-up before the national anthem, the walls erupted with sound.

Even Andi clapped, but Zona remained stationary, elbows on bony knees and hands clasped to support her chin. *Obviously*, Andi thought, *she's thrilled already*. On her other side, Dawson leaned toward her, clearly distasteful of the brawny, excitable man on his left. *It's going to be a long game . . .*

Then she saw Greg.

Andi had never thought she was the type to be attracted to a guy wearing a uniform, but perhaps it was only because she'd never met a man who filled out the uniform as well as Greg did his. Andi watched him jog backwards from the dugout on his way to the bullpen to warm up. But before he reached third base he stopped—and stared. Then he tucked his glove beneath his arm and reversed direction to lope over to the wall where she sat. His catcher, Jorge Andres, was only a pace or two behind.

"Andi?"

"Hi, Greg," she said softly, suddenly aware that every eye in the "walls" seemed to be on them. "Surprise."

"What are you doing here?" If he saw Zona or Dawson or the programs and balls being thrust forward by anxious autograph seekers, they didn't immediately register.

Just then a live shot of Greg and Andi appeared on the Jumbotron with "contest winner" flashing over it in neon letters. The ever-vigilant Dawson saw it immediately and leaned forward urgently. "Shake her hand," he told Greg.

"Huh?"

"Shake Andi's hand. She won the essay contest."

"She did?" Greg asked. "How?"

"Hers was the most persuasive essay in the batch," Dawson said. "I swear."

Slowly, Greg extended his hand and Andi gasped. "A bandage? Greg, what happened?"

"Nothing," he said, taking her hand and smiling artificially in an effort to get that stupid camera off them. "A moat monster at that castle Clytie dragged me to yesterday scratched me a little. The bandage is just to keep the glove from irritating it."

"Hey, man," Jorge said before Andi could respond, "aren't you gonna introduce me to my date?"

Frankly, Greg hadn't noticed he was there. "Jorge, this is Andi," he said finally. "Andi this is Jorge Andres."

Jorge took Andi's small hand in his beefy fist and pumped vigorously.

Finally, Jorge's question registered on Greg's brain. "But she's not your date, Jorge. She's . . . she's . . ." he glanced around at the dozens of people listening with interest, and the color rose beneath his tan. "She's my date. Your date is . . . *Zona May?*"

Greg's eyes were incredulous, possibly horrified, and certainly the deepest blue Andi had ever seen. Something turned over in her chest and she couldn't help but smile. He'd get over his surprise soon, she knew. By the end of dinner, he'd think this idea was as inspired as she did.

Jorge dropped Andi's probably fractured hand to reach for Zona's, and she raised both hands up near her ears, wiggling eight of the now safe fingers in a little wave. "Down, Bruno."

"Who's Bruno?" Jorge asked Greg.

"Never mind, Jorge." Greg's eyes were still on Andi as he automatically scribbled his name on a ball for a squealing little girl, accepted a hat and a pen from a teenage boy, and tried to sort this thing out.

But Joe McKay, the Diamondbacks' manager, saved him from both brain strain and possible writer's cramp. "Hey, Howland!" he bellowed from the top of the dugout stairs. "If it ain't gonna put you out none, do ya think you could get yourself ready to throw a ball sometime tonight?"

"Well, that explains what I'm doing here," Greg told Dawson under his breath as he handed the boy back his pen and autographed hat. "But you'd better be able to explain to me what *she's* doing here right after the game."

* * *

What Andi was doing was beginning to regret she'd come. Greg had a terrible first inning, and it was probably her fault for breaking his concentration. Certainly, Andi noticed, he hadn't looked at her once since the top of the second inning some two and a half hours ago. His pitching had come back, and he'd even managed to lay down a sacrifice bunt in the sixth, but every time she saw him stare down an opposing batter, she imagined him glaring at her instead and she flinched.

And as if that wasn't bad enough, she was seated squarely between Frick and Frack. On the way to the ballpark, Zona and Dawson had "chatted"—mostly about the contest and her and Greg. (And if many of Zona's remarks had carried a hint of sarcasm and most of Dawson's replies a hint of irritation, Andi had been too excited about seeing Greg to care.) On the way into the ballpark, however, she couldn't help but note that Zona and Dawson had moved on to "discussing" how Dawson enjoyed the role of a press agent and how Zona wouldn't be caught dead glorifying crass commercialism. Then they had "debated" everything from the rise of baseball paralleling the decline of American society through the nutritional merits of hot dogs, peanuts, and Cracker Jack—or lack thereof. Now they were both leaning over her, and Andi would be hard pressed to call what they were doing anything but quarreling.

Andi pushed Zona away from Dawson with her elbow. "Shh," she said. "People are trying to listen."

"To what exactly?" Zona asked in exasperation.

"To anything but you, lady," the man to Dawson's left said loudly.

Andi grasped Zona's arm to keep her from responding—or perhaps throwing a punch—and discovered to her surprise that it was Dawson who retorted.

"The lady at least has a vocabulary that exceeds the three or four crude words that comprise your own."

"I don't need you to defend me," Zona said quickly.

"I wasn't defending you," Dawson said just as fast. "I was merely pointing out to the gentleman that—"

"Shut up!" The request came from a half dozen sources simultaneously and caused Andi to sink down in her seat in mortification. Dawson and Zona, however, sat up straighter, icons of righteous indignation.

Thank goodness the Diamondbacks were ahead by two. Andi had learned enough about baseball by now to know that when the home team leads in the ninth inning, the game is a blessed half-inning shorter. One more out and she would never have to face any of these people again.

Of course, she would have to face Greg.

She watched with concern as he tossed down the rosin bag then walked back up on the mound. He pulled off his sweat-stained cap and ran an arm across his forehead. Then he pulled off his glove, shook out his hand, and stuck the glove back on.

"He's tired," Andi said anxiously to Dawson. "And his hand hurts. Why don't they take him out and let somebody else pitch?"

"Because he's Greg Howland," Dawson said.

And that explained it. Again Andi marveled at this side of the man she loved—the very public side. Somehow, she seemed to forget it existed when they were alone. Probably because he seemed to forget it existed. To Greg, baseball was a gift—what he did—a means to get out of Iowa. But to the performance-driven sports world, he was a phenomenon.

As Greg pulled back to throw the ball, Andi watched the crowd rise as one. From what she could see, Zona was the only person who remained in her seat.

The ball neared the plate almost before Andi could blink, and the batter swung. There was a loud pop and the ball sailed straight up then arced toward where they stood. Jorge Andres threw off his mask and went after it. Andi cringed as he hit the wall in front of Zona and fell backwards. The crowd stomped and cheered when he held up the ball triumphantly. The game was over and his teammates poured onto the field, but still Jorge didn't get up.

She watched Greg move as quickly as he could through the group of men to arrive at Jorge's side just after the manager and a trainer. Within a few minutes, Jorge was on his feet, but cradling his arm painfully. As his catcher and friend limped toward the dugout, Greg finally looked up.

"Take them to the wives' lounge, Dawson," he said. Then he reconsidered. "No, take them up to Cleon's suite. It's private. I'll be there as soon as I can."

Andi's heart sank. Judging from the expression on his face, Greg might as well have said, "Take them home."

CHAPTER 10

"They took Jorge in for an MRI," Greg said as he paused in the doorway of the suite. Cleon and Laura Bisher had gone, so the room was empty except for Andi, Zona, and Dawson. "But they think he's going to be okay."

Zona looked up from the floor where she'd sprawled in protest of the cruel-to-cows leather couch that she and Dawson had most recently debated. "Salutations and greetings to you, too, Ace."

When the fine lines appeared around Greg's eyes, Andi knew he was trying to control patience that must be worn very thin—not so much by Zona's snide remark as by Andi's "surprise" and his own long game.

"Hello, Zona," he said at last. "Hello, Andi. Hello, Dawson." He leaned against the doorframe. "And may I add what a surprise it is to see you all here tonight?"

He'd changed from his uniform into a suit. The ball cap was gone, but not the faint red mark that all the nervous tugging it on and off had left across his forehead. Andi wanted to go to him and caress the chaffed skin with her fingers. She wanted to kiss the newly re-bandaged hand and ask again what had happened to it. She was sorry about Jorge, but she hoped his need for treatment meant that now Dawson would take Zona home, and she and Greg could go to dinner alone.

"Sorry Jorge's accident ruined your date," he said before Andi could put her hopes into words.

"Wait a minute," she said, her Irish emotion rising before her reasonable nature. "You'd better not be thinking about canceling my date. I won your silly contest."

Greg looked over her head at Dawson and raised an eyebrow. "Fair and square, I bet."

Dawson rose from the couch. "In my opinion, Greg—and you did make me the judge—Andi's essay was by far the most persuasive."

"Yeah? I'd like to read it."

"I don't have it with me," Dawson replied slowly. He appeared unsure how Greg was taking this and seemed to wonder if he'd still have a job tomorrow. "I may, in fact, have misplaced it."

Andi didn't let out her breath until Greg laughed. Then she hurried over to him, but sensing Zona and Dawson watching her, she merely straightened Greg's tie instead of throwing herself into his arms as she wished. "You're not angry?"

"I was . . . surprised . . . on the field," he said, one strong arm encircling her waist, "and I could have done without the Jumbotron on us, but I was never mad. You don't know how much I was dreading this night until now." He grinned at Dawson. "Even if it *was* my idea."

Andi ran her fingers over his tie. The silk felt wonderful to her touch, but the desperately longed-for closeness of him was nicer still. "You never once looked at me after the start of the game . . ."

"I'm trying to win us a spot in the playoffs," Greg said with a smile. "And you saw how well I was doing it. Six batters and one home run in the first inning do not a happy manager make." He bent close so his next words would reach her ear only. "I can't chew gum and look at you, Andi. No way can I stare at that beautiful face and expect myself to throw a baseball."

Now Andi's arms slid the rest of the way around his neck and tightened. Greg's kiss told her that she wasn't the only one who regretted every moment they spent apart.

"Excuse us," Zona said, "but could you two do that later? Say, *after* dinner? My stomach's used to having all the day's food digested by now."

"Oh!" Andi said, dropping her arms and stepping back in embarrassment. It was simply amazing to her how easy it was to forget that there was anyone else in the world—let alone in a room—when she was with Greg. "Dinner?"

"Well, that's what you promised me yesterday," Zona said. She looped her battered backpack over her shoulder and scrambled to her feet. "I hope we're going someplace decent."

"But you heard Greg say that Jorge can't go," Andi began. "I thought—"

"What's wrong with *him*?" Zona asked, pointing a neon-purple fingernail at Dawson. "I mean, besides the fact that he's a microbe-brained Republican capitalist?"

"Glad to see they're getting along so well," Greg said quietly to Andi. "I'd have bet you they had nothing in common."

"Well," she murmured, "they managed to agree that a man sitting near us was of the Cro-Magnon persuasion. Besides that, they'd have debated the time of day." She frowned. "Come to think of it, they did."

"Let them argue in Dawson's car," Greg said. "You and I will meet them at the restaurant." He took her hand. "Unless we run out of gas or have a flat tire or something."

"We came in the limo, Greg," Dawson interjected. "Part and parcel of the prize."

Now Greg frowned. Beat before he started. "I hate limos."

"That, Ace," Zona said, "is the smartest thing you may ever say. After all, the earth has only so much fossil fuel."

"Actually," Dawson began, "it's fallacious to suppose—"

"I don't know what 'fallacious' means, Dawson," Greg cut in, "but suppose you call and send the limo driver home and we'll go in my Jeep?" He stepped out of the doorway to make room for Zona and her backpack. "Unless you'd rather walk to 'save' a dead stegosaurus or two."

"How far is it?" she asked.

"Back to Mesa?" He considered. "About twenty miles is all. You're in good shape, Zona. You could be there by sometime tomorrow."

"Come on," Andi said, tugging Greg's hand and wondering what had possessed her to invite Zona in the first place. Clytie would have been a better choice. *Darlene* would have been a better choice. For that matter, ninety-five-year-old Granny Reynolds would have been a better choice.

* * *

"This reminds me of the monsoon," Zona said sardonically as the restaurant lights flickered, recorded thunder rolled in the background, and spouts opened in the ceiling to send sheets of water cascading into shallow pools along the verdant walls. "And Andi assured me that this evening would be more enjoyable than a monsoon."

"It's atmosphere," Dawson pointed out. "That's why it's called the Rainforest Café."

"Ironic then," Zona retorted, "that they feel compelled to contribute to the deforestation of the real rain forest." She tapped her menu and pushed the paper napkin away in distaste.

Dawson sniffed. "The deforestation, as you call it, of the rain forest happens primarily in areas of overgrowth as a mean to curtail natural—"

"That is so not true," Zona said, leaning forward eagerly. "But I'm not surprised you would say it, given—".

Greg tapped the handle of his knife against his water glass. "And that bell, ladies and gentlemen, signals the beginning of round . . ." He looked at Andi.

"Um, thirty-seven, I think," she said wearily.

Zona and Dawson didn't notice. The rain forest controversy continued, and Zona pulled a ballpoint pen from her backpack to scribble a map of South America on the tablecloth. Dawson hastily produced a fountain pen and began to correct her geography.

Just when Andi was certain they would scribble each other to the death, or perhaps use the writing utensils to duel, the waiter appeared with their food.

"You aren't actually going to eat that?" Zona asked Greg, crinkling her nose in distaste at the hamburger on his plate.

"Zona, please!" Andi said. She tossed her fork on the table in exasperation. "Can't you fill your mouth up with that non-organically grown broccoli you complained about and leave Greg and Dawson to eat in peace?"

Zona's eyes widened in surprise at her cousin's outburst. "Of course," she said.

Andi picked up her fork. "Thank you." She had just felt the first twinge of guilt for being snappish when Zona spoke again.

"It doesn't surprise me that you eat beef," she said. "Why would a man who cares nothing about the inhumane treatment of children care about mere animals?"

"Zona," Greg said with what Andi considered Jobian patience, "what are you talking about now?"

"Kiribati."

"Then you've lost me," he said. "I have never in my life heard of a kiribati."

Zona lowered her eyes. To Andi's amazement, she thought she saw tears glistening in the corners.

"Nobody has," Zona said flatly, "because Kiribati is one of the poorest countries on earth. It's a place where children work fourteen-hour days to make those shoes you endorse, Ace." She had his full attention now and took advantage of it. "You would never believe what I saw in the eighteen months I was there . . . "

As Zona described the conditions on the island, Andi watched Greg put down his food and unconsciously push away his plate.

With it out of her system at last, Zona speared a wedge of okra. "Of course, when you're getting paid the big bucks, who cares where the money comes from? Right?"

Greg turned to Dawson. "At the risk of starting another battle of the brains, where do they make those shoes I advertise?"

Dawson shifted uncomfortably in his seat. "I don't know."

"Do you know who does know?"

"I can find out." Dawson pulled a small leather notepad from his shirt pocket and used the fountain pen to jot down a reminder to himself.

It might be her imagination, Andi thought, but after a quick glance in his direction, Zona seemed now to be leaning over to make sure Dawson wrote every letter correctly. The look on her face was queer—even for Zona. Probably, Andi thought, handwriting analysis was among her odd talents and she was gathering ammunition for their next confrontation.

Impulsively, Zona reached for her backpack, then seemed to think better of it and lowered it slowly back to the floor. She was quiet for a few moments, then put the forkful of squash into her mouth and chewed noisily, apparently back to her normal self.

If only Greg could recover as easily, Andi thought. He hadn't touched his plate since Zona had pretty much accused him of exploiting orphans. His body was at the table, but his mind was thousands of miles away—probably in the South Pacific. What could she say to bring him back?

Zona noticed too and spoke first. "Don't worry about it, Ace. Missing your meal isn't going to help the dead cows or starving kids any."

Zona, Andi knew, meant the remark as a kindness, but Greg wasn't buying it.

"I don't know anything about a cow's life, Zona," he said at last. "And I probably don't want to know." He pushed his plate further away. "And I also know I can't change the situation of every starving child in the world. But I can do something. Everyone can do something if they want to."

And Greg would want to, Andi thought with a sigh, and then felt an instant wave of remorse. She wasn't marrying Greg Howland for his money, certainly. He could give every penny he had away, and she would only love him more for it. It was just that, foolishly, she'd let Clytie convince her that he would buy her that silly "castle" she'd dreamed of since childhood. She'd come quite close to asking him for it on the phone last night. Now she was glad she hadn't. She didn't need a castle. Like Katie O'Grady, she could raise children in a cottage—or, in this time and place—a trailer or a hogan, as long as the children were Greg's.

In the meantime, she had to get him out of here. She pushed her own full plate away as the lights flickered again and the faux rain began to fall. "Well, I'm finished," she said with forced cheerfulness. "Shall we go?"

As Dawson signaled the waiter back to their secluded corner, Greg asked Andi if he could take home her mostly untouched salmon. "No, Zona," he added quickly, "I'm not going to mail it to Kiribati and call it good." He glanced down at his bandaged hand. There was little chance he could solve the problem of world hunger tomorrow or the day after, but perhaps he could at least feed a locally hungry moat monster he knew something about.

CHAPTER 17

I lied to Zona, Andi thought on the way home, *and sealed it with a Double Spit Cousin Heart Cross. A monsoon couldn't have been worse than this "date."*

As relieved as Andi was that the evening was almost over, she knew that she wasn't half as relieved as Greg. He hadn't said a word since signing autographs for the staff and a few other late-night diners before leaving the café. Of course, his silence might have been attributable to the running feud in the backseat—a battle that was interrupted only by a sudden bump and a peculiar thwump-thwump-thwumping from the rear of the Jeep.

"Oh, great," Greg muttered. "Just what I need at this precise moment." He slowed, pulled over to the wide shoulder of the Superstition Freeway and rolled to a stop beneath a streetlight.

Dawson had his cell phone already in hand. "I'll call for roadside assistance."

Zona reached for her door handle. "Don't bother. I can change a tire."

"I can change a tire," Greg said. He opened his door and had one leg on the pavement before Zona replied.

"Let she who is most qualified step forward." She opened her door as Greg slammed his.

"I don't know who you think I am," he said, "but let me tell you, I've changed more tires in my life than you have camera lenses."

"Chivalry is dead, Ace," she said blithely. "No need to sully those multimillion dollar hands of yours."

"Zona," Greg said, in a tone of voice that Andi had never heard from him, "please just step back and stay out of my way."

A few minutes later, Andi watched him remove the hubcap with a little more force than was probably needed. She picked it up from where it had landed, five or six feet away, and took it back cautiously. "Is there anything I can do?"

"Yeah," Greg said as he spun the tire iron to loosen the first lug nut. He had removed his suit coat and tie and rolled up his sleeves. Despite the circumstances Andi couldn't help but admire the way the muscles bulged in his arms and across his back as he worked. Forget the baseball uniform, he looked even better in shirtsleeves.

"What can I do?" she asked.

"You can promise me that you will not invite Zona May to our wedding."

Andi glanced over her shoulder to where Zona sat on the paved embankment with her back to Dawson. She seemed to be examining a piece of paper she'd fished from her backpack. "But she's my cousin . . . "

Greg paused in his task only long enough to cast Andi one long, baleful look.

"I promise," she said quickly.

He had just tightened the last bolt and pounded the hubcap into place with his fist when a highway patrol car pulled up behind them with its red and blue lights flashing. The young pitcher straightened. "*Now* the civil servant shows up." Before he could take a step forward, he was hit with a bright light from the top of the car. Greg raised an arm to shield his eyes. Couldn't the guy see he'd just finished changing the tire, and without the benefit of a spotlight?

"Step away from the vehicle," a man's authoritative voice said over a speaker.

Puzzled but obedient, Greg took one long step to his left. As Dawson and Zona approached, he said, "I don't know what this is all about, but for gosh sakes, keep quiet, will you?"

The trooper emerged from his car, a radio in one hand and a gun in the other. "Don't move," he commanded, approaching cautiously. When he was a few feet away, the gun lowered slowly—at roughly the same rate as his jaw line. "You're not . . . ? No, you couldn't be."

Greg started to reach for his wallet but paused immediately when the gun rose again. "My ID?" he suggested. "You want to see a driver's license or something?"

Still clearly dumbfounded, the officer nodded.

Greg removed the wallet from his back pocket and flipped it open. The license was Illinois-issued, he realized at once. It hadn't occurred to him to apply for an Arizona license even though he'd officially moved here . . . what—five months ago? But why would it? It'd been at least a year since anyone in the country had asked him for identification.

The trooper peered at the card, swallowed noticeably, and holstered his service revolver. "Greg Howland," he said. The reverently spoken words were followed by a low whistle but nothing more.

Already knowing his own name, Greg waited patiently for an explanation.

"Great game tonight," the man offered.

Zona snorted. "You drew a gun on him to tell him he played a great kid's game? What are you? A mor—"

"Excuse us," Dawson said, jerking Zona back two paces.

But the words at least had the effect of reminding the trooper why he *had* stopped. "This isn't your car, Mr. Howland," he said apologetically. "Is it?"

"Uh, yeah," Greg said. "It is. Is there a problem?"

"Do you have a title and registration?"

"Sure." Greg was glad that he'd been smart enough to see to that, at least. And he knew for a fact that he had a clear title. He'd been especially careful since he'd bought the former wreck from a sleazeball who called himself Honest Abel. "I'll get them for you."

The trooper examined the papers then excused himself to go back to the computer in his patrol car. When he reemerged a few minutes later, he was shaking his head. "Has this car been out of your possession in the last few weeks, sir?"

"No," Greg said. Then he thought of Zeke. "Yes." He frowned. "Why do you ask?"

The trooper returned Greg's documents then pointed to the back of the Jeep. "That's not your original license plate, Mr. Howland.

That plate was on a car stolen from Chandler and used in the armed robbery of a convenience store about a month ago."

Greg ran a hand through his sandy blond hair. Why was he not surprised? He hadn't had the mechanic check the *license plate,* for gosh sakes. As usual, Zeke had played him for the idiot he was. "I hope I have an alibi for the time of the robbery," he said thinly.

"Greg, don't say anything until I call an attorney," Dawson suggested, already pressing buttons on his cell phone.

"Cool it, Dawson," Greg said. "I don't need a lawyer. I can explain this."

"Actually, the Diamondbacks were in Atlanta at the time of the robbery," the patrolman said helpfully.

"Gee, thanks." Greg tried not to look at Andi. The next part would be news to her, too. "Look, Officer, my Jeep *was* stolen recently, but it was returned after only a few hours so I didn't think much about it."

Greg knew that last statement wouldn't get him past a lie detector. He'd thought about it plenty. But still, apparently, he hadn't thought about it enough to figure it out.

The officer took notes. "And you reported it, of course."

"No," Greg said. He glanced again at Andi. "I mean, yes, I did. I told Sergeant Dan Ferris of the Mesa City Police Department." Finally. Thank goodness.

The patrolman scribbled the name on his pad. "I'll need to take that plate."

Greg nodded.

"I'm going to let you take the car home tonight, but you won't be able to drive it again until you get the plate replaced." The patrolman flipped up the top of a small metal clipboard. "And I understand you've made Arizona your permanent residence?"

"Yeah."

"Glad to hear it," the officer said, scribbling on his pad. "We're gonna win the World Series with you on the mound."

"I hope so."

Finished at last, the patrolman extended the clipboard. "Would you sign this for me, sir?"

Greg took both the officer's pad and his pen. He wasn't surprised to see that he was being given a citation for driving with an expired operator's license. He wrote his name and accepted the original.

"And would you sign this, too, please?" The officer extended another sheet.

What now? Greg wondered with a sigh. Did the Arizona Department of Public Safety issue tickets for stupidity? If that were the case, he'd be here signing citations all night. He looked at the blank paper and then at the patrolman.

The man grinned sheepishly. "For my son," he said. "Could you write, 'To my biggest fan, Ben'? That kid adores you."

And you can tell him you almost shot me, Greg thought as he wrote to Ben. *What a story that'll make for the playground tomorrow.*

* * *

It was after midnight by the time Greg dropped Zona May off at her apartment and pulled up behind the car Dawson had left parked in front of Andi's house. Had the day lasted only the customary twenty-four hours? he wondered. He would have sworn that the game alone had lasted ten hours and the "date" another fourteen.

"I'll apply for a new license plate for you first thing tomorrow," Dawson said, closing his door as Greg opened Andi's.

"Thanks again, Dawson," Greg said tiredly. It was the third or fourth time the man had offered, at the same time hinting for an explanation of how the stolen plate got on Greg's car in the first place.

"But it's odd, isn't it?" Dawson persisted.

"Yeah," Greg said, "it's real strange." He didn't miss the look Dawson cast Andi but chose to ignore it. "Good night," he said pointedly, motioning toward the Volvo with his chin.

"Oh," Dawson said. "Yes. I'm leaving now. See you in the morning. Good night, Andi."

"You don't have to walk me to the door," Andi told Greg as Dawson got in his car. "I know you're tired." But she warmed with pleasure when he took her hand anyway and led her up the driveway. It clearly showed how much Zona knew about the death of chivalry.

They reached the front porch and Greg leaned on the rail while she looked for her key. "So," he said when she finally found it, "tonight was fun. When do we do it again?"

Andi dropped her keys back into her purse and reached up to run her fingers lightly along his cheek and jaw. "I'm so sorry, Greg."

"Yeah?" He rested his hands on her shoulders and moved her closer. "Then I hope it's cured you of entering every stupid contest to win a date with a celebrity that comes along."

"It has," she said, her emerald eyes softening at his touch. "I'll never date another celebrity as long as I live."

Greg buried his fingers in the silky curls at the nape of her neck. "Please tell me that the operative word in that sentence is 'another.'"

Andi meant to nod but her neck muscles wouldn't obey. She could only look up into the dusky blue of Greg's eyes and fall into the promise of forever that was in their depths.

Every day is long, Greg realized as his lips met hers, *when you're waiting to make a woman like this your wife*. Andi deserved so much more than he had to offer. What could he possibly do to show her that she meant the world to him? The world and the rest of the universe besides? He'd already resolved, of course, to marry her only in the temple. Nothing else would do, no matter how difficult it was to wait the necessary year from the day of his baptism. So what could he do in the meantime to tell her that if it were in his power, he'd make her a queen?

Andi startled as Greg pulled suddenly away. She looked quizzically up at his wide smile.

I'll buy her Clytie's castle! he thought, his mind racing with the possibilities. Sure, it was slightly more expensive than a Hallmark card, but way more convincing. And after he'd made his point, if she didn't like it, he could always do something with it: sell it or raze it or turn it into a rest home for moat monsters and retired leprechauns.

He kissed her forehead then held her at arm's length. "I have a surprise for you."

"Wasn't learning that you steal your license plates surprise enough for one night?" she teased.

"This is another kind of surprise," he said. "A good surprise."

Even the mention of the license plate couldn't distract Greg from the softness of Andi's skin and the heady scent of her perfume. He gathered her gratefully back into his arms for a final, tender kiss. The universe expanded and Greg knew that Andi was right. Nothing should keep them apart. Let Zeke Martoni play his little games all the way into prison and perdition if he wanted to. Nothing could come between Greg and the woman he loved.

* * *

"Driving without a plate, Grego? And without an Arizona license?" The chuckle on the other end of the line was silky smooth, but grated on Greg's raw nerves. "And here I had you pegged as a pillar of society. Hero to millions of little rug rats the world over—"

"Cut the crud, Zeke," Greg interrupted. He was tempted to hang up or, better yet, to throw the phone out the window and run it over with the car. As if the day hadn't been long enough, Martoni had to call the minute Andi went inside and he started his Jeep. The man had better timing than an atomic clock. It was uncanny. In fact, it was *too* uncanny.

Greg glanced around and in the rearview mirror, but the wide residential streets were still. It wouldn't surprise him to learn that Zeke was having him tailed, and it would explain how he knew about the highway patrolman, but unless the guy following him was invisible and had bionic hearing, Greg didn't know how he managed it.

"Didja like the way I pulled that little switcharooni with the plates?" Martoni taunted. "Some joke."

"Oh, yeah," Greg said. "I'm still laughing."

There were several seconds of icy silence then, "You won't be for long, kid."

The menacing words hung in the still night air. Greg didn't realize how tight he was gripping the phone until the cat scratches on the back of his hand began to sting under the bandage, and then to throb.

"Okay, Martoni," he said finally. "This has gone on long enough. Too long. I'm going to—" Greg didn't finish the sentence, but it didn't matter. The phone line was dead. Possibly it was a bad connection. Probably it was a bad sign. Greg could imagine Zeke still chuckling—knowing as well as Greg did himself that the young ballplayer didn't have any idea what he was going to do.

CHAPTER 18

This time there was no internal debate whether Greg should call Dan Ferris to tell him about the latest development with Zeke. The sergeant saved him the trouble by showing up at his townhouse just after nine the next morning.

"I brought bagels," Ferris said when Greg opened the door still winded from his morning run. There was a patrol car parked on the previously empty street with a uniformed officer in the driver's seat, and the bishop's blue compact car parked behind it. "Yeah, I know," he said, smiling at Greg's quizzical expression and inviting himself inside. "You naturally think 'policeman/donut,' not 'policeman/bagel,' but my cholesterol hit 280 last week, so what's a fat man gonna do?" He took in Greg's perspiration-stained T-shirt and flushed face. "Well, besides exercise, I mean."

"Are you here as a policeman?" Greg asked, pushing the door closed with his foot before following the sergeant through the living room and into the small kitchen. "Or as my bishop?"

The stocky, middle-aged man pushed a days-old newspaper and a couple of used glasses aside and set the bag on the table. Then he turned to Greg. "I'm here as your friend."

They both knew, however, that Dan Ferris considered Greg less of a friend than as the son he'd never had. Certainly Greg returned the affection. He gathered up the papers and moved them to the only uncluttered surface he saw—on top of the refrigerator. "I've let things go a little since Ma went back to Iowa," he confessed with a hint of a grin. "I keep thinking I'll hire a cleaning lady."

The bishop smiled as he opened the bag of bagels. "The right woman could probably whip you into shape in no time," he said. "Have you thought about getting married?"

"Yeah." Greg's grin widened. "That seems like all I think about anymore."

"That and Zeke Martoni?"

Greg pulled out a chair for the bishop and another for himself. He sank into his. "So you already heard about the license plate?"

"Oh, yeah. Me and everybody else in Arizona law enforcement." Ferris took a bagel from the bag and offered it to Greg. "If it's any consolation to you, you made Officer Ray's shift last night. He's a real celebrity over at DPS now."

"Great," Greg said insincerely. "Glad something good came out of the evening." He pulled apart the already split bagel. "Dawson was sure that Ray would be on the morning news to tell all about it." Realizing how late it must be, he glanced around the kitchen for a clock. "He wasn't, was he?"

"No," Ferris assured him, removing another bagel from the bag for himself. "And he's not gonna be. I filed a statement that you had reported your car stolen. That's the end of it."

"Thanks."

"It's pretty obvious that Martoni switched the plates." Ferris reached back into the bag and pulled out a container of sweetened cream cheese. "But it's equally safe to say there's no way to prove it. Got a knife?"

"Nope," Greg said, taking the container from Ferris' hand and tossing it over his shoulder onto an already full counter top. "But I'll get you some orange juice." As he rummaged in the fridge, he added, "If you're gonna put cream cheese on those things, you might as well eat donuts."

"Spoken," Ferris said ruefully, "as a perfect human specimen."

"Spoken," Greg said, putting the juice on the table and polishing a glass on the sleeve of his sweatshirt, "as a friend. A 280 cholesterol count is way too high." He took a bite of dry bagel himself. "And I, for one, need you. You're the only family I'll have when I go through the temple next spring."

"If you mean that," the bishop said slowly, meeting the younger man's eye and trying to hold it, "why won't you let me help you?"

"You have helped me," Greg said quickly. "You do help me."

"I want to, son."

Greg took another bite of bagel to avoid responding immediately and chewed for a moment in silence. When he felt the bishop's eyes still on him he finally swallowed and asked, "What kind of help do you think I need?"

"I think you need to learn to trust the people who love you," Ferris said.

When Greg crossed his arms, Ferris leaned forward. "Let me try to put this the right way. First of all, it's normal for people to unconsciously ascribe to Heavenly Father attributes they've seen in their earthly father." Greg's face registered his revulsion, and Bishop Ferris reached out to grip his wrist. "It's human, Greg. *You're* human. I wouldn't have believed how far you could have come if I hadn't seen it for myself, but a childhood full of betrayal and loneliness can't be healed overnight. It takes a lot of hard, spiritual effort."

"I've forgiven my father . . ." Greg began.

The bishop inclined his head. "I know you have. And that's the first step. But there are others. You need to know that your Heavenly Father will always be there for you—no matter where 'there' is. And you need to believe that the people who love you—like me and Andi—won't let you down."

Greg frowned. "I know that."

"Maybe you know it in your head," the bishop said quietly. "But you're never going to fully heal, son, until you know it in your heart."

Greg turned the remainder of the bagel over in his hand. He'd like to say that Bishop Ferris was wrong. Failing that, he'd like to claim at least not to know what the older man was talking about. Unfortunately, he did know. He knew all too well. When he finally raised his face, it was open and earnest. "What can I do, Bishop?"

The big man smiled. Knowing Greg as he did, he'd come prepared. He removed a single sheet of paper from his shirt pocket. "You can read these scriptures, Greg." As the young athlete's fingers closed on the paper, Ferris covered them with his strong, warm hand. "More, you can ponder them. Pray about them. Christ taught that there are some things that are healed only with fasting and prayer." His fingers tightened. "And you're not alone anymore, Greg. Remember that."

Nodding, Greg glanced down at the paper. The list of references was brief. He knew that as a convert himself, Dan Ferris was an advocate of searching out truth for oneself. Greg looked up with a half smile. "If you've taught me anything in the last few months, Bishop, it's that no matter what my question is, the answer is always found in the scriptures and in prayer."

"Now I'm going to teach you another concept that's just as important," Ferris said with a smile. "It's called '*application* of the principles you learn.'" He looked down at his cranberry bagel, glanced wistfully at the cream cheese, then leaned back in his chair, resigned to his plain-breaded fate. "You can start applying the lesson right now—by telling me everything there is to tell about what you've heard from Zeke Martoni since he got out of jail."

Greg did. Besides relating again the little he had so reluctantly told the sergeant a few days earlier, he told him about the call last night and how Zeke had seemed to know exactly where he was and what he was doing. He even went out to the garage and brought in the plastic fly and die cast miniature Jeep and placed them in front of his bishop with a shrug. "That's it. All of it."

"Nothing to bring Martoni in on," Ferris observed. "Not even for questioning." He tapped a single finger on the table while he thought. "I could run your Jeep and these toys through the lab, I guess, but dollars to donuts we'd come up empty."

"Forget donuts," Greg said. "You're betting with bagels from here on out, remember?" It amazed him that merely sharing everything with the bishop had already made him feel better. "I think you were right the other day," he added. "All Zeke wants to do is get to me. I'm not going to let him."

Ferris was suddenly the one with less confidence now in his previous advice about Martoni. "Considering the phone calls you've been getting—and Martoni's rap sheet," he said, "we ought to have enough to put a tap on his phone and a tail on his rear." He smiled thinly at his own pun, then pushed back his chair and fished a set of keys out of his pants pocket. "I'll promise you this, Greg—if Martoni *is* up to something, we're going to nail his oily hide to the wall. In the meantime keep your head up." He jangled the keys and forced a grin. "You can use my car until you get your plate replaced. And may I suggest—as a policeman this time—that your first stop be Motor Vehicles for a valid driver's license?"

Greg grinned and caught the keys when Ferris tossed them. "Thanks, Bishop," he said. Then he picked up the short list of scriptures from the table. "Thanks a lot."

* * *

Trust in the Lord with all thine heart; and lean not unto thine own understanding. In all thy ways acknowledge him, and he shall direct thy paths.
It sounded like something you'd write on a poster, Greg thought at first. No wonder it came from a book in the Bible called Proverbs. He pulled the heavy quad off the end table and into his lap and reminded himself that he wasn't supposed to be *reading* the scriptures Bishop Ferris had given him, he was supposed to be *pondering* them. There was a difference, and Greg knew it.

He leaned back on the couch, read through the words again, and considered their application in his life. Who *did* he trust more—the Lord or himself? Who *did* he turn to first? And of the two of them, he asked himself ruefully, who had a better grasp of the overall game plan?

Trust in the Lord with all thine heart, Greg read again, *and lean not unto thine own understanding.* This time he knew that they weren't words to write on a poster so much as they were words to etch on one's heart.

He consulted the bishop's list again then flipped back to the first few pages of scripture. Greg wished, as he often had lately, that he'd had enough religious training in his youth to know if Deuteronomy and Joshua were books in the Old or New Testaments. At least, he thought with some satisfaction, he'd read the Book of Mormon, Another Testament of Jesus Christ, often enough in the last few months to know that they weren't found there.

Both scriptures were in the Old Testament, Greg discovered, and not very far apart.

I will not fail thee, nor forsake thee, he read and saw that this was a promise the Lord had made to Moses. Turning a few pages, Greg found the same promise made to Joshua and, just four verses down from it he found this:

Have not I commanded thee? Be strong and of a good courage; be not afraid, neither be dismayed: for the Lord thy God is with thee whithersoever thou goest.

Greg knew that—knew it in the core of his being. The words were so similar to what his brother had told him that day last spring when Greg had almost died from a baseball injury to the head. He felt the blood rise warm to his ears and the tiny hairs prickle along the back of his neck. *How had he forgotten?* Or, if not forgotten exactly, how had he let that sacred experience be pushed from the very front of his consciousness? Jim's words echoed in his mind: "For He is with you always, Greg. He always has been. He always will be."

Greg closed the scriptures and held them, feeling foolish and ashamed. Was there anyone less worthy than he of the Lord's continued care? Anyone who questioned more and trusted less?

At last, still clutching the scriptures in his strong hands, Greg knelt at the side of the sofa and poured out his heart to his Heavenly Father. When he finally rose at last, it was to turn to the final one of the bishop's scriptures, in D&C section 121. In it Joseph Smith had cried out to the Lord and received this response:

My son, peace be unto thy soul; thine adversity and thine afflictions shall be but a small moment; And then, if thou endure it well, God shall exalt thee on high; thou shalt triumph over all thy foes. Thy friends do stand by thee, and they shall hail thee again with warm hearts and friendly hands.

Greg sat back with a contented sigh. What miraculous law of the universe was it, he wondered, that allowed for a heart poured out in care and repentance to be so immediately refilled to overflowing with gratitude and love?

None of the circumstances of his life had changed after reading the scriptures and seeking his Father in prayer. But *he* had. He felt better. No, he felt wonderful. It was a beautiful day. A perfect day— and he still had several hours of it to himself before he had to report to the ballpark and, later, to the plane for the D-Backs' road trip.

It was such a perfect day in fact that it ought to be put to yet another perfect use. Greg laid his scriptures reverently aside and stood. He couldn't think of anything he had to do at that moment than was more important than feeding a hungry cat. And—as long as he was in the neighborhood—maybe he'd just buy Andi Reynolds her very own castle.

CHAPTER 19

She never should have let Clytie talk her into this, Andi thought as she drove up the narrow, tree-lined lane that led to the "castle." True, she'd wanted to see inside practically all her life and this would probably be her only chance, but she simply wouldn't show any enthusiasm no matter *how* wonderful it was. Andi knew that if she so much as sighed, Clytie would tell Greg that she wanted this beautiful, rundown estate, and he would feel obligated to buy it for her.

So she wouldn't sigh. She wouldn't stare. And she most certainly wouldn't covet—at least not overtly. She'd walk calmly and noncommittally through the place with Clytie and Darlene and Enos, and then she'd leave.

And probably dream about its charm for the rest of her life.

There were two cars parked in the wide driveway that encircled the fountain, but Andi took no notice of them. "A fountain!" she exclaimed, then glanced nervously at Clytie. "How impractical."

"I think it's beautiful," Clytie breathed. "It's all beautiful. Oh, Andi, wait until you see it!" She looked unhappily at the two cars. One she recognized as the realtor's, but the blue one might be somebody looking to buy. "I wish you'd brought Greg," she said.

"He's already seen it, silly," Andi said, trying to keep her eyes from the balcony and her mind from imagining herself sitting there with him, watching the sun set every night for the rest of their lives.

"I wanna see the lake!" Enos announced from the backseat. "Can we see the lake first?"

"I told you, it's a pond," Clytie corrected. "And I'll walk around to the back with you so you can see, but you have to leave the ball and bat in the car."

Enos dropped his Jeff Jensen autographed bat but only tightened the grip on his Greg Howland autographed baseball. Surely his sister couldn't expect more. Everybody knew that Enos temporarily parted with the ball on only two occasions: bath time and sacrament meeting. The rest of the time it was in his backpack (if he was in school) or in his hand (if he was anywhere else). The same ball had, in fact, been autographed almost a dozen times now just to keep the name on it. Enos wore off a lot of ink with his constant stroking.

"I'll go inside with Andi," Darlene decided.

Andi was relieved. Darlene wouldn't watch her reactions the way Clytie would. In fact, she probably wouldn't notice a wistful sigh or two at all. "Good," she agreed, "but just ten minutes, then we have to go."

As she stood at the base of the wide stone stairs, Andi watched Clytie and Enos walk across the lawn toward the weed-entangled side garden. Then she looked up at the miniature Dunguaire Castle and caught her breath. She couldn't say exactly what she so loved about it, only that she always had loved it, even in her childhood. But, why? It wasn't practical. It wasn't even pretty in the classic definition. But, oh, it was grand!

Andi's copper curls cascaded over her shoulder as she leaned her head to the side and listened to herself say the words aloud. "But, oh, it is grand!" What did it remind her of? Suddenly she knew and smiled at the knowledge. It was a classic Granny Reynolds expression, said ever-so-often with the Irish brogue that had clung to her tongue for almost a century. *Dunguaire of Galway*. Her roots.

"It looks kinda old," Darlene observed, pulling Andi back to the present. "And how come the windows look so wavy?"

"The ones in front are leaded glass, Darlene," Andi said, scarcely believing it herself. She almost ran up the stairs. She'd said ten minutes and she didn't want to waste a single precious one.

The realtor met them in the hall. "No sightseers," she said with a smile. "The estate is sold."

"Sold?" The word caught in Andi's throat. She didn't care, of course. She'd have never mentioned buying it to Greg in a million years, but she had hoped to make believe here for just a few minutes before giving up the dream. Now it had been yanked away faster than she could blink. "It's . . . sold?"

"Yes!"

The way the realtor said the single word made Andi suspect that she wanted to shout it. Sing it. Rip off her prim gold blazer and twirl it over her head while she danced for joy. Maybe, Andi thought, it wouldn't be too wicked to take advantage of that scarcely controlled elation.

"Would it be all right if we looked for just a moment?" she pled. "There's nothing here we could harm, surely."

"Well, the buyer's in the next room," the woman said hesitantly. "But maybe you could go upstairs—only for a minute, though."

A minute was better than no time at all. At least she could stand on the balcony for a moment and perhaps peek in at the claw-footed tub Clytie had told her was in the master bath. Clytie and Enos forgotten, Andi grasped Darlene's arm and pulled her toward the stairs. "Thank you," she said over her shoulder. "You won't even know we're here."

* * *

"I know it was good," Greg told the gray tabby that nosed his hand hopefully. "But too much salmon isn't good for you." He ran his bandaged hand over the cat's back. "Especially when you haven't been eating regularly." He nudged a new dish of just-purchased kibbles closer. "This is better. Trust me."

"May I assume you're planning to keep the cat, Mr. Howland?" the realtor asked.

"Uh, yeah," Greg said, turning at the sound of her voice. "I guess." But he hadn't any plans, actually, beyond feeding it.

"Since financing obviously isn't a problem," the realtor practically purred herself, "and since the property is vacant, you can take occupancy immediately."

"You mean, uh, live here?" Greg asked. The idea frankly hadn't occurred to him.

"You're buying it as an investment, then?"

How could he tell her he was buying it in lieu of a greeting card? "I, uh, don't know." He looked from the stone fireplace in the kitchen to the windows, which showcased an ancient rose garden beyond. Whoever had built this "castle" hadn't been true to the original Dunguaire's design for fortification, or even the architectural conventions of his own time. He, like Greg, had apparently liked sunlight and open spaces and lots of both. Greg grinned. Even if Andi hated it, he could stay for the few months before they were married. It would solve the problem of what to do with the cat, there would be plenty of room for his nephews to visit, and fixing the place up would give him something constructive to do when baseball season ended. He nodded to himself. "I think I will move in."

The realtor extended her hand to shake her famous client's. "Then I hope you'll be very happy here."

* * *

It had been easy to *say* she'd be happy in a cottage or a trailer or a hogan, Andi thought. She trailed her finger along the exquisitely carved banister as she walked reluctantly down the first stair. But now she feared that despite herself she'd always secretly long for this impractical, dear old monstrosity of a house.

She and Darlene met Clytie on the first landing. How had she forgotten them? "Where's Enos?" she asked.

Clytie's eyes widened. "I thought he was with you."

"Clytie," Andi said, "he was with *you*. You took him to the pond—"

"And he managed to toss his ball in the mud," Clytie broke in, "and of course he waded in after it so I made him take off his shoes and socks. He said he was going to come find you while I tried to clean them off." She held up the soggy shoes. "I'm sorry."

"We have to find him, Clytie," Andi said. "Fast. The house is sold and the new owner doesn't know we're all here."

Clytie stood stock still, her diminutive form blocking the stairs. "Sold? Oh, Andi! The castle *can't* be sold."

"Well, it is!" Andi regretted the note of despair in her voice, but she couldn't very well recall it. "Now come on. We have to find Enos."

Crash.

Andi took the stairs as quickly as she could, knowing instinctively that when she found the mess, she'd find Enos.

* * *

"Don't move!" Greg commanded.

Enos froze except for pushing his glasses up the bridge of his nose to better see the gaping hole in a high skylight, the sparkling glass shards around his bare feet, and Greg entering the room at a run.

A step behind him, the realtor froze herself. Then she shrieked at Enos before beginning to apologize profusely to Greg. "I don't know how he got in here, Mr. Howland, I really don't. But I'll see to it that—"

"Never mind," Greg said over his shoulder. He crossed the glassy floor in two long strides. When he picked Enos up, the little boy wrapped his thin arms around Greg's neck. "Enos, are you okay?"

"Greg!" Enos wailed. "I broke the castle!" His body began to shake. "And I lost my ball!"

"It's okay," Greg said soothingly as he lowered the child enough to check his rusty hair for glass shards. "Shake your head, Enos," he said. "Really hard."

Enos did as instructed and almost managed to lose his thick glasses in the process.

Reassured that no glass had landed on Enos, Greg patted his back and carried him across the room and away from any danger of cutting his feet. "Don't cry, pal," he said. "Everything's okay now." He would have set Enos down but the little boy was as firmly attached as a tourniquet, his face buried in Greg's broad chest.

"You know this child?" the realtor asked.

Greg nodded as he looked around the room for any sign of Enos' prized baseball.

"What is he doing here?"

Now Greg froze. "You know," he said, turning to her slowly, "I have no idea."

"Enos!" Clytie and Andi called in unison from the hall.

Greg grinned. "I have a better idea now."

The three Reynolds sisters entered the room at a run. "Enos!" Andi said, then slid to a stop. "Greg?"

"He's not hurt," Greg assured her. "Just scared."

"I broke the castle!" Enos cried into Greg's collar. "And I lost my ball!"

"Your ball's over there on that window-seat-thingie," Darlene said, waving vaguely toward an alcove. Nothing surprised Darlene.

"Greg?" Andi repeated. "What are you doing here?"

This wasn't exactly the way he'd planned to tell her he'd bought her a castle. He had planned to . . . Well, he had to admit to himself, he hadn't actually planned anything yet. But this wouldn't have been it if he had planned something. "What are *you* doing here?" he countered.

"I broke the castle!" Enos wailed.

Greg laughed. "We know what you've been doing here, Enos."

"We were just looking," Andi said. "Clytie wanted to—"

"I'm sorry, Mr. Howland," the realtor interjected before she could finish. "I never should have let them in since you'd already purchased the property."

Clytie shrieked and even Enos raised his head in interest.

Andi's eyes were wider than Greg had ever seen them, and her cheeks were pinker, but there were no dimples in sight. "You *bought* the castle, Greg?" she whispered.

Okay, he thought, *dumb idea. Next time you stick with Hallmark.* He shrugged lamely. "Well, it wasn't broken when I bought it."

"I broke it," Enos repeated, but more quietly this time. His lower lip quivered. "I'm sorry I broke your new old house, Greg."

"Don't worry about it, Enos," Greg said. He peeled the boy off and set him gently down. "I'm gonna need a lot of help fixing this place up. You can come over and work off the price of that window."

Enos' eyes glowed. "Every day?"

"Every day I don't have a game," Greg agreed.

Enos let out a whoop. "Then I'm glad I broke your castle!" He was immediately repentant. "I mean—"

"I know what you mean, pal," Greg said fondly, ruffling his hair. "We'll have a great time."

"You bought the castle for us, Greg?" Andi asked, her voice still so soft he scarcely caught her words.

But Darlene heard her. "You did?" she chimed in. "You bought this place for us?"

Greg pointed a finger at Andi and then at himself. "I, uh, bought it for *us*, Darlene." Andi's fingers, he noted, were now covering her lips. In horror? His brows knit. "You hate it," he ventured.

She shook her head no.

His hopes rose. "You like it?"

She shook her head no again, more vigorously.

He turned to Clytie. "Is there another option here that I'm missing?"

"Yes!" Clytie exclaimed. "Greg, she *loves* it!"

"She does?" He turned back to Andi. "You do?"

She nodded, her luminous eyes filling with happy tears. *So*, he thought, *this might work out after all*. He took a couple of steps toward her and tripped over the cat that had come out of nowhere, begging for salmon.

Greg managed, but barely, to right himself instead of toppling into Andi. "Do you like cats?" he asked hopefully, stooping to disentangle the tabby from around his ankles.

"Not particularly," Andi said honestly, "but, oh, Greg, how I love *you*!"

* * *

When Greg arrived back at his townhouse a couple of hours later, Dawson Geitler was there with a vacuum cleaner. Greg watched him work for a couple of seconds, then jerked the plug.

"Dawson," he said when the noise had abated, "it isn't your job to clean up around here."

"Apparently," Dawson said dryly, "it isn't anybody's."

"I'm, uh, going to hire somebody," Greg said, wondering where he'd lost the phone book and when, if ever, he'd have time to look for it. "Sometime."

"I already took the liberty," Dawson said. "They'll be here this afternoon."

"Great," Greg said. As usual, Dawson was way ahead of him. "Then why are you cleaning?"

Dawson wound the cord carefully around the machine. "To keep the crew I hired from fleeing in horror. Or selling the story to a tabloid: Greg Howland's Home Ransacked by Reincarnated Huns."

"Very funny," Greg said sarcastically, but he couldn't suppress a grin. "I'm glad they're coming, though. I need to get everything in shape here so I can move when I get back from San Francisco."

"Move?" Dawson asked incredulously. He'd last seen Greg at 12:37 A.M. this very morning. How much could have happened in the last eleven hours and forty-eight minutes?

"I bought a castle," Greg said.

Apparently quite a lot. Dawson pulled out a chair and sat down. "A castle?"

"Well, Clytie calls it a castle," Greg said, looking around the room to see where Dawson might have stashed his duffel bag. He had to head out to the ballpark before too long. And he had to leave from there for the West Coast. Beforehand, he needed to pack. "But it's more of a big barn of a house," he continued, opening the coat closet hopefully. "Really old." He found the bag, pulled it out, and unzipped it. "Kinda run-down," he concluded.

"It sounds lovely," Dawson said. "May I asked *why* you bought it?" This was Greg, after all. It could be another homeless shelter— this one for Kiribatian refugees—or, since it was so big, perhaps he intended it to shelter doomed bovine. Heck, he might be planning to have his shoes manufactured there from here on out.

Greg removed six pairs of dirty socks from the duffel and tossed them back in the closet. Five pairs of clean socks remained and it was only a four-day series. Good deal, he was packed. He zipped up the bag. "I bought the castle for Andi," he told Dawson. "But I want to live there now myself so I can start fixing it up."

So he *was* going to move. His press agent wondered if Greg knew that he didn't own any furniture since the townhouse he leased had come furnished. Dawson doubted it. Greg was a good guy, and plenty intelligent, but organization and attention to detail were not his long suits. He sighed. One thing at a time. He reached over to an end table to collect the fruit of his first morning mission.

"A license plate!" Greg said admiringly. "That's great, Dawson. How'd you get it so fast?"

"It helps to work for Greg Howland."

"It's legal, right?" Greg asked cautiously, then shook his head. If Dawson had it, it was legal. Besides, he reflected, sometimes it even helped to *be* Greg Howland. He'd not only been taken to the front of the line at Motor Vehicles this morning, he'd been whisked straight into an office. Of course, it was probably less in deference to his "status" than it was an effort to keep state property intact. Greg had walked into the licensing building after buying the castle and taken #128 from the peg. Since they were then serving #16, one hundred and eleven people were suddenly more interested in meeting him than they were in whatever business they had originally come for. Chairs scattered in every direction and Greg was behind the counter almost before he knew that a security officer had taken his arm.

Whatever the reason for the quick service, Greg was grateful. And he was grateful to Dawson, as well. "Good job," he said, clasping his publicist on the shoulder. "Come out to the garage with me and I'll tell you all about the castle while I put the new plate on the Jeep." He grinned. "Unless you'd rather stay inside and wash the windows."

Dawson followed, hoping to hear not only about Greg's new residence, but to finally learn why his friend had needed this new license plate in the first place. That the stolen plate had something to do with Zeke Martoni, he had no doubt. That Greg should be facing the problem alone, well, that he doubted seriously.

HAPTER 20

The temperature had reached triple digits by noon and peaked a few hours later, but still Clytie stood at the end of the Reynolds' driveway, resolutely watering the already drenched gazanias. It was the fifth day this week she'd watered the desert flowers at precisely 4 P.M., and the poor things were limp and yellow from the unaccustomed, unneeded moisture. But what else was there to do at the end of the driveway besides water the gazanias—and wait for the paperboy?

Right on cue, a white VW beetle chugged up the quiet street. Clytie turned the nozzle from "spray" to "off." The battered car rolled to a stop in front of her, and Ian Lansky extended a *Gazette* through the open window.

"Hi, Clytie," he said, brushing a lock of dark hair back from his flushed forehead. "Here's your paper."

"Oh! Hi, Ian!" she responded cheerily.

Ian Lansky was her secret admirer. Ever since Greg had reassured her that she might actually have one, Clytie had known Ian was it. After all, who else saw her every day in algebra? Who else looked at her in the lunchroom *(that way)* when she thought he wasn't looking and then turned away instantly when she caught his gaze from the corner of her eye? It had to be Ian.

Every afternoon since the revelation, Clytie had stood at the end of the driveway, watered the drought-resistant flowers, and acted surprised to see Ian deliver the newspaper to which her father had always subscribed.

Every afternoon Ian Lansky acted surprised to see Clytie waiting for him.

Only one of them wasn't acting.

"The paper looks really, um, interesting today," Clytie said.

"Yeah," Ian replied nervously. "There's sure lots of, uh, news in there."

"It's so neat the way you put it in the plastic bag," Clytie continued. "It, um, keeps it really clean."

"Well," Ian said, "your driveway's usually pretty wet."

Clytie's pretty face colored and she pointed to the gazanias. "This kind of flower needs lots of water."

Gripping the steering wheel, Ian leaned further out the window to look the plants over. "Yeah, they don't look like they're doing very well." Now the color deepened on his already ruddy face. "Not that you don't take real good care of them, Clytie, you do. I-I like them," he stammered. "I-I like them a lot. They're my favorite kind of flowers."

Clytie considered the pathetic orange and ochre spikes. "They're my favorite flower, too."

Ian took note of his ink-stained hands and snatched them into his lap. "Well, I guess I better deliver the rest of these papers."

"I guess so," Clytie said reluctantly. "See you, Ian."

But probably not tomorrow. There was only a morning paper on Sunday, and he brought it at 4 A.M. That wasn't a very believable time to be out front drowning gazanias, even for Clytie.

"So, uh, I guess I'll see you at school Monday," he said.

"In algebra," she agreed, standing with the paper in one hand and the hose in the other until he turned the corner and disappeared from sight.

So maybe it *wasn't* exactly a scene from any romance novel she'd read, Clytie thought as she carried the newspaper up the driveway and into the blessedly cool house, but it *was* sort of tummy-twisting in a pleasant sort of way. Admittedly, Ian was no glib Thaddeus, but that was one of the best things about him. Besides, If she'd loved Ian desperately—or only to distraction—she might have felt disloyal to Thaddeus. This way she felt sure that she was just doing what Thaddeus wanted her to. Besides, she genuinely liked Ian.

The problem, though, was how to get him to admit on something besides paper that he liked her, too. Homecoming was just around the corner, and Clytie needed an admirer who wasn't quite so secret.

* * *

If there was one thing she didn't need, Zona thought plopping down on the floor in her apartment on Monday night, it was a secret admirer who looked like Bill Gates, dressed like Al Gore, and talked like Pat Buchanan.

She pulled the note from her backpack for the sixth or eighth time that day. It was obvious last week at dinner that Dawson Geitler had written it, though she didn't know how he had sneaked it into her backpack the day before. And she didn't know where he had seen her "almost every day" either, unless he was following her. But it had to be him. The paper was the same he'd used to make that notation for Ace. The neat penmanship was the same. Heck, the blue ink was even the same. Who else in the Western Hemisphere used an indigo fountain pen? The Canadian prime minister?

Zona pushed a pile of dirty clothes and a stack of overdue library books out of the way, then lay on her back and held the note up in front of her thin nose. *I am often struck by your individualism, sweetness of nature, and determination,* she read. *I find you an exceptional young woman.*

Well, she couldn't fault Geitler for his taste. Nor for his perception. He had clearly described her to a T. And he was smooth. He'd got Andi to persuade her to go on the stupid date, and then he and Ace had arranged that convincing little act with Bruno so Dawson would be the one to take her out to dinner. Definitely smooth.

Zona chewed her full lower lip and tried to force down growing feelings of respect for the guy. Obviously, Dawson's infatuation with her hadn't overcome his natural adversarial inclination. She admired that as much as anything about him.

Refolding the note carefully, Zona wondered again what had kept her from confronting Geitler with her discovery as soon as she had made it. Perhaps only the suspicion that it, too, was part of his smooth master plan. Why *else* would he have pulled out the fountain pen and, when she failed to recognize it immediately, the notepad? He had clearly wanted her to know that he was her secret admirer, and she wouldn't give him the satisfaction. If Dawson Geitler thought he was going to run this whole dog-and-pony show, he had another thought coming. She wasn't some weak-minded maiden to be wooed and won with fancy words. She was a latter-day woman, wise in the ways of the world and privy to the privations of men.

Zona rolled to her stomach and rooted among the haphazard piles of junk until she found a spiral notebook and well-chewed, stubby pencil. She licked the dull tip.

Dear Mr. Geitler, she wrote, then ripped out the page. No, he'd started this anonymous little charade; she'd play the game on his terms. She started again: *To Whom It May Concern . . .*

* * *

To Whom It May Concern? Dawson unfolded the note and pushed the glasses back up the bridge of his nose. It had been on the windshield of his car after leaving the Reynolds' house just now, so it must concern him. He'd come over this Tuesday afternoon to get Andi's approval on a rug he intended to purchase for the living area of the "castle." The furniture he bought yesterday and today would be delivered tomorrow, and everything would be ready for Greg to move in when he came home on Thursday night. Most things he'd purchased hastily and at wholesale with the idea that Andi would replace them. The hand-knotted Aubusson, however, was too ideal too pass up and too expensive to purchase unless she liked it. She did.

With this mission complete but dozens still ahead, Dawson read through the note quickly. Puzzled, he read through it once again, slowly.

Though I don't see YOU almost every day, I wouldn't mind if I did. You are rather unique yourself. I might even go so far as to call you exceptional and determined. What do you plan to do with that determination?

What? Dawson thought. He looked around. Then he looked down at the note and read it once again. This time, he had a better question: *who?* Or, specifically: *who* had left the note on his car, and *what* did it mean?

In his typically well-organized modus operandi, Dawson began mentally listing "prime suspects."

Those with opportunity: Andi, her sisters, and perhaps her cousin Zona May, who had been there when he arrived and left, fortuitously, soon after.

Those with motive: He drew a blank. Not Andi, certainly. The only time she wasn't thinking about Greg was when she was dreaming about him. And the only person less likely than Andi to have written him this kind of note was Zona May. That left Andi's sisters.

Darlene, Dawson suspected with a wry smile, couldn't spell "exceptional," let alone define it and Clytie . . . Suddenly, Dawson tapped his fingers to his forehead. *Clytie! Of course.* This note had a ring of familiarity about it because it wasn't dissimilar to the one he had written her. *Motive.* And the teenager wasn't thirty feet from his car at this very moment—right at the top of the driveway watering the flowers—probably waiting for him to come over to talk to her. *Opportunity.*

Dawson considered the note in his hand carefully. What to do about it? A young woman's first crush was a delicate thing. He'd have to be tactful.

He refolded the note and stuck it in his pocket, then approached Clytie cautiously. The caution, certainly, was twofold. Besides giving him time to gather his thoughts, it helped ensure that not a droplet of mud splattered onto his polished leather wingtips.

"Good afternoon, Clytie," he said formally. He knew it would be unwise to raise her hopes up by seeming too familiar. That would only make it further for the poor girl to fall when he let her down.

"Oh, hi, Dawson," she replied, looking resolutely up the street.

Avoiding my gaze, he thought. *Poor, sweet Clytie.* It touched him to watch her pretend interest in a beat-up old Volkswagen. Clearly she hoped he wouldn't note how deeply she had colored at his approach.

But . . . how to broach the subject at hand with just the right amount of finesse? After all, he smiled to himself, it was only natural for a young thing like her to be flattered and delighted to think she had caught the attention of a mature, urbane gentleman like himself. He had apparently erred in writing her the note; he must now see that he did not compound the error by breaking her heart.

Dawson straightened the impeccable Windsor knot in his tie. "Clytie, about your missive . . . "

"What's a missive?" she asked.

"Your note."

"What note?"

Playing innocent, he thought. *And the girl is a natural actress.* He'd never seen eyes so wide and guileless as the ones she turned on him.

But he didn't see them for long. The VW pulled to a stop a few feet away, and a somewhat disheveled young man opened the car door.

Clytie abruptly dropped the hose.

Dawson learned two things in the resultant shower:

1. Clytie probably didn't write him the note, after all.

2. He had worried about his shoes when he should have worried about his suit.

CHAPTER 21

"A package came for you, Mr. Howland," the clubhouse attendant said meekly and from a respectful distance.

It was Wednesday evening and Greg Howland would take the mound in about ninety minutes, hoping to win the Western Division Title. This put him right in the middle of the "do not disturb" portion of his game-day ritual, and the clubbie knew it. He'd been around baseball a long time.

Anyone who says that baseball players—particularly pitchers—are not creatures of habit probably hasn't met one. And anyone who says that baseball is a physical game more than a mental one probably hasn't played it. When it came to pitching, Greg Howland was as superstitious and set in his ways as the next guy. His routine was always the same. He ate the same food and wore the same hat, and though of necessity he sat on different benches in different stadiums around the country, it was always the same position: turned away from his teammates and everything going on in the clubhouse.

Tonight, as always, he held a new ball in his hand—one to which the traditional Delaware River mud had already been applied—and silently counted every one of the 108 Haitian hand stitches. Then he counted them again—as many times as it took to focus his mind on nothing but that little round baseball.

And it worked. Although his strong left arm and tall, well-proportioned body was largely a gift of genetics, the greater part of his success on the mound was due to his ability to concentrate well enough to command it. The concentration, paradoxically, was based on the ability to will himself to relax before he climbed the mound in the first place. Somehow, he had to make the pressure of being Greg Howland disappear, and take with it the crowds and the cameras and the radar guns. Only when throwing the ball became as automatic as throwing stones back home in Iowa did he have the power and accuracy and endurance that made him almost unbeatable on the field and almost a legend off.

When Greg turned, the clubbie took a step back. "I wouldn't have bothered you," he said quickly. "We'd have put it in with the other stuff fans brought you and shipped it to your agency, but it came special delivery from Arizona and it's marked urgent."

Greg turned the ball over in his hand. "What did you do with it?"

The man appeared hurt that Greg had felt he had to ask. "We had security open it, of course."

Greg nodded. "And?"

"It's just a little castle," the man said. "I brought it in 'cause we thought maybe it was a good luck charm from your family or something." When Greg motioned him forward, he advanced far enough to extend his arm to drop the small pewter object into the pitcher's open palm. Then from a jacket pocket the clubbie produced a square of brown paper. "Here's the wrapping it came in, sir. But there's no return address." He took a step back. "And there wasn't a card or anything."

Despite having been in the clubbie's hand, the metal felt cold to Greg's touch. He set it on the bench.

Concerned at the celebrity pitcher's unhappy expression, the clubbie almost reached for the castle. "You want I should forward it?" he asked.

"No," Greg said, berating himself for the first thought that had come to mind. He had to stop imagining that Zeke Martoni lurked in every dark hallway. "I'll keep it. Thanks." But even after the man turned to leave, Greg didn't touch the castle or the paper it had come in.

It's paranoid to assume it came from Zeke, he told himself. Dan Ferris had a tap on the phone and a stakeout in the hotel. Martoni didn't seem to talk to anybody but his attorney, and he didn't leave the hotel except to pick up alcohol, cigars and other "necessities" at a nearby strip mall. *There's no possible way he can know that I bought a castle. And he couldn't have mailed this himself without the police knowing.*

He shook his head to clear it. Probably this was Dawson's way of telling him everything was set for when he got back to Mesa late tonight. The Great Geitler had struck again. The power and water were on in the castle, and all Greg's things had been delivered. Presumably, there would even be a couch to sleep on.

Still, Greg had never known Dawson to be anything but straightforward, so maybe Andi had sent him the trinket to wish him luck in the big game. Perhaps her note had been lost. The lack of message was really the only strange thing—that and the timing. Everybody who knew him knew that he had to think nothing but baseball before he pitched an important game.

Everybody knew it. Even Zeke Martoni.

* * *

Andi hadn't sent Greg the castle.

Dawson hadn't sent it either, but when Greg asked his press agent about it on the phone after the game, he was sorry. Dawson wanted to call the police—if not the FBI, CIA, and Air National Guard. Greg never should have explained the license plate thing to him, he thought now, or shared his concerns about Zeke Martoni. Dawson Geitler was a consummate worry-wart.

Like you're not? Greg asked himself sarcastically, turning his Jeep onto the freeway exit just before 3 A.M. on Thursday morning, on his way home from the airport. *No, I'm just tired*, he answered himself.

What a game. The Diamondbacks had taken the first major step toward the World Series by clinching the Western Division Championship on Giant soil. Despite the disruption to his warm-up routine, Greg had struck out fourteen men and, thanks to his teammates, worked only eight innings to do it. With the team ahead by three runs in the top of the ninth, Greg was pulled from the game so a pinch hitter could be sent to the plate in his place. Nothing could have made him happier.

Except, perhaps, to be similarly excused from the media frenzy and team party in the clubhouse afterwards—a party that continued onto the private plane and was still going on in numerous spots downtown, thankfully without him. As it was, he reeked of a champagne shower and had one heck of a headache.

Part of the headache was from the smell of liquor. Part was tension left over from media interviews both in San Francisco and back home in Phoenix. But the largest part of the headache had another name: Wes Westen. If some of the guys had been a little drunk after the game, Westen had been drunker. Of course it was no secret that the veteran pitcher often got a head start in the clubhouse before games, and tonight had been no exception. Consequently, Westen hadn't been called out of the bullpen once during the series, and though it was in no way Greg's fault, the way Westen ragged on the young ace, it seemed clear that he thought it was.

Greg, who had thought on the way to San Francisco of giving Wes the biography he'd been reading on Satchel Paige (a 1940s fastballer who pitched successfully into his fifties), had felt more inclined tonight to shove it down the man's throat. He'd resisted the urge. But barely.

The stupid thing about the whole deal in Greg's eyes was that he knew perfectly well that Westen's problem was his attitude, not his arm. They'd often shared a bullpen on Greg's third-day warm-up, and he'd seen for himself that while Wes wasn't the flamethrower he'd admired growing up, he was still a pitcher with timing and skill that Greg honestly envied. He told Westen that, and found that it was like making the acquaintance of a junkyard dog. You could try it once— maybe even twice—but after that you'd run out of hands to extend in friendship.

Well, Westen could *have* the game of baseball for all Greg cared at that moment. He yawned and glanced at his watch, grateful to be almost home and to have the next thirty-three hours off except for a lousy team meeting, batting practice, and media interviews. What a luxury.

And what a life. Play baseball. Get on a bus. Get off a bus. Get on a plane. Get off a plane. Get on a bus. Get off a bus. Get in your car. Go home. Sleep. Begin again. *Baseball players may well be overpaid*, he concluded, *but we keep worse hours than Dracula.*

He shuddered involuntarily at the thought—not of the vampire, but of the small pewter castle and what it could mean. *Speaking of the undead*, he told himself, *you'd better not start thinking about Zeke*

Martoni again or you won't sleep tonight at all. Already the idea of going "home" to that empty, unfamiliar house gave him a case of willies more often felt by scrawny eight-year-olds than good-sized adult athletes.

Maybe I'll get Enos to help me plant garlic around the place, Greg thought. *If it works on vampires, maybe it'll work on Zeke.* Although, when he stopped to think about it, a wooden stake through Zeke's heart was even more appealing. For a blood-sucking creature of the night like Martoni, it just might work.

After a moment, Greg told himself firmly to stop thinking and keep driving, but in less than ten seconds, the voice in his head was at it again. *No way could Zeke know about that castle,* it said. *Think about it.* And, despite himself, Greg did.

Even if Zeke was having him followed and was receiving the reports by—Greg didn't know . . . carrier pigeon?—Martoni still couldn't have known it was a "castle" Greg had purchased. Only the Reynolds girls called it a castle. It didn't make sense. Zeke wasn't omniscient.

But he knew *everything.*

Zeke knew Greg didn't drive his Jeep home after it had been "washed," for example. And he knew the very night that a highway patrolman approached him. Greg gripped the wheel tighter. *And he even knew when I got back in the car outside Andi's house, for gosh sakes. The guy must have a crystal ball. Or is a fly on the wall?*

Dazed, Greg didn't stop at the next red light. He didn't even see it.

A fly on the wall? As in a *bug?* Greg thumped a fist on the steering wheel. Hard. *I don't believe it! Here Martoni came right out and told me what he's doing and I was too stupid to get it. I'll bet he laughs himself to sleep at night.*

Unbelievably irritated at himself and Zeke, Greg took the only revenge he could devise at the moment. He hit a button to switch the radio station from jazz to hard rock then turned up the volume as loud as he could stand with his head pounding as it did. Then he turned the radio a little louder.

Greg took advantage of the last streetlight before the turnoff to his new house to slow the car and glance around the interior of the Jeep. His chances of finding the bug, or bugs, that Zeke must have had planted when he switched the plates were slim, he knew. But the police would find them in no time. Maybe Zeke wouldn't be quite so smart when he didn't have Greg himself to tell him everything he wanted to know.

Zeke had overheard the trooper, of course. And he'd learned about the castle not only from Greg's conversation with Clytie, but from what he'd heard him tell Dawson while he put on the new license plate.

Stupid. Stupid. Stupid.

Greg turned onto the lane in front of his new house and was surprised to see that the gate had been left open. He was even more surprised when it closed automatically behind him, and through the trees he saw lights burning on the bottom floor. He hoped for a moment that the little pewter castle had been a tip that Martoni would come calling. He hoped that he was there right now, as a matter of fact. Nothing would give him greater pleasure at this moment than to wipe the smirk off that man's face once and for all.

But it was only Dawson. The worrywart had invited himself to a sleepover.

"You sure picked an odd time to feed the cat," Greg observed, dropping his duffel so he could pick up the tabby that had appeared between his ankles almost the minute he stepped through the door.

"I haven't seen that cat until now," Dawson said, yawning and laying aside the book he'd been reading. "But I know he eats because his bowl is always empty."

Greg did a double take. The book Dawson had been reading was an old Book of Mormon Greg had once bought at a used bookstore. He raised an eyebrow, then another as he took in the rest of the marvel. This wasn't a cavern anymore. It was a room. And a nice one. "Wow," was all he could say.

Dawson interpreted it as decorating approval. "I didn't know what bedroom you'd want to use so I had them set up the two closest to the main living area." He motioned. "They're just down the hall on this level."

"I have a bed?" Greg asked.

"Two of them," Dawson confirmed. "Take your pick."

"That's great," Greg said. "I just kinda figured I'd sleep on the couch—if I had a couch, even."

Dawson shook his head in resignation. "That's what I figured you'd figure. That's why I ordered the beds."

"I don't know how to thank you—"

"About that." Dawson pushed up his glasses and cleared his throat. "I got a paycheck from your accounting office today." He glanced at his watch. "Yesterday."

"Yeah?" Greg said, releasing the restless cat. It apparently didn't think he smelled any better than he thought he did himself. "Does that mean you're buying breakfast?"

Dawson frowned and said perfunctorily, "The pantry's stocked, of course."

"Of course."

Then he added flatly, "I don't need a raise, Greg."

"You got one?" Greg asked in mock surprise. "Good for you. You're definitely buying breakfast." He looked around. "But we'd better make it lunch. I'm beat." Three hallways led in different directions. "Now where did you say those rooms are? And please tell me that I've got hot water. Or cold water. I really don't care at this point what I shower in as long as it isn't champagne."

"You paid me well before," Dawson continued doggedly.

Greg sighed and gave up trying to talk around the issue. "Dawson, look. I hired you as a publicist and press agent. You work on that about eight, ten hours a day, right?"

It was more like twelve, but Dawson said, "Yes."

"And in your spare time you track down license plates and cleaning ladies and moving vans." Greg motioned with a sweep of his arm. "And now you're furnishing castles and feeding cats. Dawson, I owe you big time." He picked up his duffel and headed toward the hall he hoped was most likely to lead toward a sleeping area.

"Has it ever occurred to you that I do some things only because I'm your friend?"

Greg stopped abruptly. *Like babysitting me tonight?* It was a moment or two before he responded. "Yeah, Dawson," he said when he finally turned back. "It's occurred to me."

Dawson waited silently but his eyes were faintly accusing.

"I'm not very good at friendship," Greg admitted honestly. "I haven't had a lot of practice." His own eyes lowered. "As you know, my two best friends . . . died."

"You're forgetting that I handle your press conferences," Dawson said quietly. "And I once dated Zona May Reynolds. I think that means I'm indestructible."

"You know," Greg said with a slow grin, "I bet it does." He knelt to scratch the cat behind the ears, then he looked up. "So how does a guy say thank you to a friend?"

"The words themselves suffice," Dawson said. "Or you could ask him to be the best man at your wedding reception."

"I'll take both suggestions," Greg said warmly. His eyes fell on the Book of Mormon Dawson had left on the end table. "You know, there's nothing I'd like more than to think my friend might someday be there at the temple with me."

Dawson followed his gaze. "It's an interesting read," he said. "But Christianity is a pretty far stretch for a Jew."

"I don't know," Greg said. The grin lingered. "From what I've read myself, it wasn't such a stretch for Lehi. Or Peter. Or—"

"Point taken." Dawson picked up the book of scripture. "Now if you're planning to whip up one of your inedible omelets before I buy you lunch, you're headed in the right direction. But if you're going to go rinse off the after-effects of a highly successful game before you get some sleep, you'd better veer left."

Left, Greg decided. *Definitely left.* He needed to shower. He needed to sleep. He needed to be fresh at some point tomorrow so he could think how he might eventually drive that wooden stake right into Zeke Martoni's black heart.

CHAPTER 22

Greg had slept roughly three and a half hours before the gong sounded for Judgment Day. There was no other explanation for the sound that reverberated through the rooms of the empty house and had Greg standing in the hall before he felt his feet touch the floor.

"What the heck was that?" he asked Dawson.

"That," Dawson said calmly, "was your doorbell."

Greg ran a hand over his unshaven face. "Disconnect it."

"Done." Dawson distastefully looked over the bleached gray sweat shorts and somewhat shrunken red T-shirt that Greg had pulled on before bed. Dawson, despite the early hour, was already wearing a suit and tie. "I'll answer the door," he said quickly. "I opened the gate earlier. We're expecting another delivery."

"Sure," Greg agreed. "Good. I'm going back to bed. Wake me when we make the World Series." He'd walked most of the way back to his room when he heard the feminine voice, and his curiosity got the best of him. He turned back to join Dawson at the open doorway.

Zona May had brought her bicycle—or tricycle, to be more accurate—right up to the porch. Her cameras were slung over her shoulders because her bike basket was full of a box. And the box was full of kittens.

"Zona?" Greg asked from over Dawson's shoulder. "Do you know what time it is?"

"Yes, Ace, it's 7:30," she said apologetically. "I know it's late in the day, but I was sidetracked by kittens."

"Kittens?" Dawson repeated.

"Don't even ask about the kittens," Greg cautioned. He didn't yet know that this had anything to do with him, but feared it might if he wasn't careful.

"Kittens," Zona repeated. "Three of them."

Her hazel eyes were wide in her fresh-scrubbed face, and her hair, Greg observed in surprise, not only wasn't spiked, it wasn't purple or green. It was yellow. Banana-yellow, to be sure, but the closest color to actual human pigmentation he'd seen on her.

"You're photographing kittens today?" Dawson asked politely.

Greg resisted the urge to kick him. How had Geitler managed to learn every rule in life except the most important one? *Never make eye contact with a person who has a box of kittens.*

"No," she said quietly.

It amazed Greg how sweet and innocent Andi's cousin could look when she put her mind to it. But he wasn't buying it.

"I found them in a garbage dumpster," Zona continued, "where some moronic monster devoid of compassion and decency must have left them."

"I see," Dawson said sympathetically.

Unbelievably, Greg saw that Geitler *was* buying it.

"The Humane Society is, I believe, on Thunderbird Road," Dawson offered helpfully. He considered for a moment then added, "It's some distance, but perhaps I could drive you."

"The Humane Society?" Zona asked, her own kitten-wide gray-green eyes narrowing slightly. "An oxymoron if I ever heard one. Do you know the percentage of kittens adopted out by the 'Humane' Society?"

"No," Dawson began, "Or, yes, approximately. But—"

"And do you know what happens to the kittens not adopted?"

"Yes," Dawson said. "Yes, I do. But you need to understand . . ."

Good, Greg thought. Things were getting back to normal. This game could well go into extra innings, which meant that he could go back to bed. He took a single step in that direction before Zona called him back.

"Not so fast, Ace," she said clearly over Dawson's first point of argumentation. "I brought these kittens to *you*."

How had he known? He'd been in the castle four lousy hours and Zona was already at his door with a welcome wagon full of cats.

"Thanks," he said. "But I just moved in myself. I'm not taking in boarders right now."

"What's the matter?" she asked, pulling up a flap on the box. "You can't afford to feed them?"

"It's not that . . ." Greg began patiently.

The first kitten Zona pulled out was white and hardly bigger than a softball. "You can honestly say that you could look this poor little thing in the eye and then send her straight to death row?"

"I . . ." Why, Greg asked himself now, had he come to the door in the first place?

Zona handed the white ball of fuzz to Dawson and took out a black one with one white front paw and a spot on the top of its head that Greg thought was shaped something like a baseball cap.

"Zona . . ." he began, but what could he do when she pressed the little thing to his chest and let go? He couldn't very well drop it. He stroked its head with his finger and willed it not to purr.

The third kitten had four white feet and a mostly white face. Zona nuzzled it with her chin. "Congratulations, Ace," she said. "It's another boy."

That was an idea. "Satchel wouldn't like them," he said hopefully.

Dawson turned. "Satchel?"

"You know," Greg said. "That tomcat that lives here." The one that was smart enough to stay on Greg's bed when the doorbell rang—right where Greg should have stayed himself.

"You mean *your* cat?" Zona asked sweetly.

"He's not my cat," Greg said.

"You named him," Zona countered. "And probably fed him that forty-dollar-a-pound salmon." She looked around. "And you bought him a house."

"I bought the house for Andi," Greg said. "But the cat does think he owns the place and—" he extended his furball, "—he won't like kittens. He might hurt them, even."

Zona took a step back to avoid the kitten and looked up at the castle. "How many rooms have you got here, Ace?"

"I don't have any idea, but—"

"Twenty-seven," Dawson supplied.

Greg shot him a "thanks-a-lot" look.

"So if they don't get along, you give the kittens their own suite," Zona said. "Toss 'em a blanket and a litter box and a few cardboard boxes to play in, and they'll be in feline heaven."

"But I'm gone a lot," Greg pointed out. "Who'd feed them when I'm on the road?"

She turned her huge eyes on Dawson. "What about you?"

Greg waited confidently for Geitler to refuse. To back him up. To do what friends did for friends.

"As a matter of fact," Dawson said, "I was going to talk to Greg today about renting out a room and some office space here. With the playoffs and World Series coming up, and some contract renewals to work out, I'd like to save myself the daily commute from Phoenix."

Greg's chin dropped toward the cat that was now trying to scale his broad chest. *Save a commute? Right.* Dawson intended to keep right on babysitting. Even though Greg didn't figure he needed a 150-pound "bodyguard" any more than he needed the Three Little Kittens, he knew he wouldn't get rid of Dawson very easily until he got rid of Zeke. Geitler was loyal, he'd say that for him—but at least he could mount one more attempt to stave off the kittens and limit his roommates to one press agent and only one pussycat.

"Andi doesn't like cats," he told her cousin.

"Andi doesn't live here yet," Zona said. "And I'll be successful enough in my new career to have a place of my own to take them long before spring."

"I can arrange for the litter box, of course," Dawson told Greg.

Greg looked at him incredulously, but before he could speak Zona said, "While you're at it, you can make the appointment at the vet." She pressed the third kitten on Greg and bent to scratch Satchel behind the ear. "Let me know when you have this big guy fixed," she told Dawson, "and I'll take some time off to stay with him."

Dawson seemed genuinely impressed. "That's very kind of you, Zona."

"Wait a minute—" Greg began.

Zona drew herself up to her full height—an imposing five foot three inches, give or take a half inch. "You don't believe in responsible pet ownership, Ace?" she asked.

"I do," he said, "but—"

"Zona will bear the greater responsibility," Dawson inserted, "since she'll have these three cats to provide for once she gets her own place."

Greg shook his head. "You don't believe she's coming back for these cats, do you, Dawson?"

"When her career is established, I'm sure she'll—"

"What career?" Greg interrupted. "Have you ever seen Zona take a picture? Have you ever even seen a picture she's taken?"

Zona raised one of the cameras looped around her neck to her eye, pointed it at Greg, and clicked. "Now *that's* a picture, Ace," she said with a smile. "Do you smell a Pulitzer?"

All Greg smelled was trouble.

"Dawson," she continued, "you're his press agent. Tell him what you figure a picture like that's worth on the tabloid market."

Dawson appraised Greg's tousled hair, the too-small shirt stretched across his muscular chest, and his bare legs. Then he raised one thin shoulder. "Offhand, Greg, I'd have to say it's worth quite a lot more than three stray kittens."

CHAPTER 23

"You let Zona May talk you into taking three kittens?" Andi asked incredulously. She removed the phone from her ear as if staring at it would make what Greg had said make more sense.

"It was actually more like letting her blackmail me into it."

Greg was across town in the Diamondbacks' clubhouse, Andi knew, waiting for a team meeting to begin. He'd probably have to hang up any minute, and she didn't want to spend precious time talking about cats. She sighed. "Besides that," she said, "how was your day? Did you see Bishop Ferris?"

"Yeah," Greg said. The police had found three bugs in his Jeep. And left them there at Ferris' suggestion. From here on out, Greg thought with satisfaction, Zeke Martoni would hear only what they wanted him to. "I'll tell you about it, Andi, as soon as—"

"I know," she interrupted. "As soon as I see you. Any idea when that will be?"

"I don't have to be at the ballpark until two tomorrow," he said. "Do you have to work?"

"Only until noon," she reported happily. Imagine being ecstatic over two short hours! But it would be the first two hours she'd spent with Greg in the last seven days. And maybe, with luck, she could almost double it. "You could come to the zoo," she suggested. "I'm driving the train from ten on."

"Save me the seat with the best view," he said. Then his voice lowered. "You know the one I like, where I can see the driver's face in the rearview mirror and almost touch her hair when I lean forward."

"'Please keep your hands and feet in the train compartment at all times,'" she recited, then laughed. "And what disguise are you going to wear? I don't want to mistakenly flirt with the wrong passenger."

"See that you don't," Greg told her. "Let's see. I kinda liked that little old lady thing Dawson dreamed up when I left the hospital after my accident. I look pretty good in flowered skirts and support hose."

"Oh, Greg," Andi said, suddenly missing him almost more than she could bear. "Isn't baseball season over yet?"

"Almost," he assured her. "We've just got to get past the Mets, then probably Houston, and then we're on our way to the World Series."

"Do you have to keep winning?" she asked impatiently. Even she knew that if Greg Howland would lose a few of his games for a change, the Diamondbacks might get a whole extra month off. Let someone else's fiancé or husband pitch in the World Series. She'd like to see her love's face occasionally off the TV screen.

He chuckled. "Making the World Series is the general idea."

"Be at the zoo by ten tomorrow morning," she urged. "No later."

"I'll be there at 9:30," he promised. "I'll meet you in the swamp. I've missed the alligators. It's about time I drop by for a visit."

"I miss you, Greg," Andi sighed.

"Yeah," he said, his voice quiet. There was noise now in the background and Andi guessed that he wasn't alone in the room any longer.

"I love you," she said.

"Yeah," he said again, confirming her hunch. "Me, too."

It was the story of her life of late. Greg always called, but often from a public venue, so she heard "yeah" and imagined, *I miss you.* Heard "me, too" and imagined *I love you.* Heard "talk to you soon" and imagined *I need you.* It wasn't enough to go on forever, but it had to be enough for now.

"Bye, Greg," she said.

"Greg!" Rufus shouted, startling Andi so that she almost dropped the phone. "That was *Greg?*"

Andi looked down at her little cousin with a smile. "Yes, it was Greg."

"Is he coming over?" the little boy asked eagerly.

"No, Rufus," Andi said. "Not today."

Rufus whined, "But Enos said he comes over every day."

"Enos exaggerated," Andi said. "Unfortunately."

"But I'm only stayin' a week or two," Rufus continued.

Only? Andi thought. Rufus had been here for two days now while his mother was at a computer technology convention, but it seemed as if his visit had lasted a month or more already. "I hope you'll get to see Greg before you leave," she said. "Now why don't you go play with Enos?"

Rufus shook his head. "He's sortin' out his baseball cards, and I'm not allowed to touch any of them."

"Well, play with Francie then."

"Francie doesn't like me."

"Of course she likes you, Rufus," Andi said. "She's your cousin." Besides, to the best of her knowledge, her littlest sister liked everybody.

"Well she doesn't like me as much," Rufus insisted, "since I bit her."

"Rufus!"

"It wasn't real hard," he said quickly. "No blood, even." He scraped a small sneaker along the tile floor. "But she still doesn't want to play with me."

Andi glanced out the front window. "Maybe Clytie needs help watering the flowers." Her green eyes narrowed. What was up with that, anyway? Just yesterday, her mother had replaced what little was left of the gazanias with pansies. But she should have replaced them with water lilies by the looks of things. And Clytie was only watering the cement now, as she dropped the hose and ran toward the street.

Andi watched a VW beetle chug to a stop a moment later. A disheveled young man extended the evening *Gazette* through the open window, and her sister accepted it as she might a dozen American Beauty roses.

"Come on, Rufus," Andi said. "Let's go meet that paperboy."

* * *

"Head of the class," Wes Westen sneered, motioning toward Greg's seat in front of the room as he ambled in and slouched into a chair on the back row. "As usual."

Greg's lips tightened into a thin line. He'd had enough of Wes Westen to last him into retirement and beyond. So what if the guy had been Greg's idol when he picked up that first rock and chucked it across the field in Iowa? That didn't mean he had to like him now. And he didn't. Decidedly.

Let it go, he told himself. *Baseball is baseball.* Besides, Westen probably wasn't the only guy around who hated him; he was just the only one with the opportunity to be so vocal about it. It was too bad that his arrival on the team had bumped Wes to the bullpen, Greg thought, but somebody in the bullpen had then been bumped to Triple A, which meant that a Triple A pitcher would have gone down to Double A, where somebody had probably left the game altogether. The domino effect was the toughest aspect of a tough sport. But leave it to Westen to make it tougher. Mostly on himself.

"Hey, man," Jorge said, pulling back the chair at Greg's side, "don't let him get to you." Andres' injury, fortunately, had been only a bruise, and the catcher had started the next time Greg did. "When you can't throw big, you gotta talk big!" The last remark was made loud enough to carry throughout the room, and most of their teammates snickered.

Greg didn't crack a smile. "I wish he'd take a swing at me and get it out of his system," he muttered to Jorge. "I wouldn't swing back. I wouldn't tell McKay. Heck, I wouldn't even duck. It'd probably make us both feel better."

"Never happen," Jorge said, jutting his elbow into Greg's side with such force that it almost knocked him from the chair. "To get to you, man, Westen'd hafta go through me." The catcher's dark face broke into a wide grin. "And we both know that don't *nobody* go through me."

"Yeah," Greg said, shooting him a quick grin. "The league won't steal a base on you; they're still afraid to pitch to you, and you're the only guy who can fool the umpires into thinking my slider's over the plate." He extended his fist to bump against Jorge's. "I guess that what makes us the dynamic duo."

"You betcha."

The meeting was long and fairly routine. Greg had stopped listening long before the time they were finally released to suit up for batting practice. But he was standing too close to McKay not to hear the manager shout Westen's name as the lanky veteran made his way out of the room.

"One more thing, Westen," McKay said. "You've gotta be at that car expo tomorrow. Noon. And try to look sharp for a change."

Wes paused in the door, his face grim. "I told you already—I can't do it."

"And I'm telling you," McKay said just as grimly, "you're up. "

"Look," Westen began, as close to meek as Greg had ever seen him, "my little girl's got a soccer game. It's her championship. I haven't seen a game all year and I . . . I promised."

Another reason to get out of baseball, Greg thought, *before you end up with two kids, no wife, and no child custody like this guy.*

"Sorry," McKay said. And to his credit, he seemed sincere. "But there's nothin' I can do about it. This is a corporate sponsor and they want a 'name.'" He shrugged. "That's you. Management's saying to tell ya to show up or ship out."

At the same moment Wes offered an expletive, Greg impulsively offered to go in his place.

The room was suddenly still. "You say something, Howland?" McKay asked.

"Yeah," Greg said, feeling sheepish now. "I said I'll go to the . . . whatever."

The stillness was replaced by a buzz, and Greg realized that as usual he'd opened his mouth before turning on his brain. He'd probably just made things twice as bad.

"Not that I think I've got a name in baseball like Wes Westen," he added hastily. "I'm just saying that I don't have a daughter who needs me tomorrow and, well, I could go to the thing if you think the sponsor might take me instead of Wes."

McKay ran his fingers along his grizzled chin to wipe away any threat of a smile. "Oh, yeah, Howland," he said finally. "I think they'll probably take you."

Greg stayed in the room a while to get directions to the Expo and generally stall as long as he could to give Wes time to suit up and head out for the bullpen before going out himself for some much-needed if equally dreaded batting practice. But he didn't stall long enough. He'd just opened his locker door when he heard the too-familiar voice from behind his back.

"Howland."

Greg turned reluctantly.

The older man was clenching and unclenching his fists.

Remember, Greg told himself. *Don't duck.*

"Thanks," Westen said, extending a hand that was decidedly unclenched.

Greg shook it. "No problem."

Except for Andi, he suddenly remembered as his teammate walked toward the tunnel that led to the field. He'd just given away the few hours he'd committed to her. He shook his head ruefully before pulling on the cap. He ought to have time for a brief visit to the swamp, at least. Hopefully she wouldn't feed him to those crocodiles she tended.

CHAPTER 24

"Hey, Al! How's it going? Howdy, Croc! Long time no see."

Andi looked up, looked again, and smiled. Greg was finally here. Well, either him or Steve Irwin from Animal Planet.

The ballplayer wore a safari outfit that ill-concealed his muscular build, but the wide Panama hat and sunglasses did obscure most of his famous face. Well, that, Andi thought, and a five-day growth of beard. The end result was that nobody would recognize Greg Howland this morning if he stood next to a life-size poster of himself. Nobody but her, of course. She'd recognize those broad shoulders in any crowd; she certainly couldn't miss them in a mostly empty swamp. She felt her knees weaken as he leaned over the rail.

He said, "And how is the Phoenix Zoo's most beautiful creature this morning?"

How, Andi wondered, could he always make her believe that she was beautiful—even when she knew that her nose was freckled and her hair a mess? She brushed self-consciously at some mud on her knee and only managed to smudge it down her leg. She gave up finally and wiped the residue of swamp silt on her shorts before looking back up at him.

"That's some costume," she said, leaning on her rake for support. She was engaged to this man, for goodness sake. How long would it be before her heart stopped racing and her knees stopped turning to gator mash every time he was near?

"Dawson dug it up somewhere," Greg said. He looked down at the khaki shirt then flipped the brim of his hat. "Probably at an archeological dig, by the looks of it."

"Did he glue the beard on for you, too?"

Greg scratched his chin. "No, it's mine, unfortunately. We had a five-game winning streak going, you know, so . . ."

"But you're not a superstitious ballplayer," Andi teased.

"Nope," Greg said. "Just a slob." He raised his chin. "Pretty good disguise, don't you think? I walked right in the front gate and over here without one person stopping to stare."

"I wouldn't say that." Andi laughed. "There's a group of Japanese tourists staring at you now. They probably think you're the Crocodile Hunter."

"Me?" Greg said. "No way. I'll leave that to you and the Croc guy. Kittens are more than I can handle." He held up an arm that was well-marked by the effects of a romp with a passel of baby cats. "Those little guys may look soft and cuddly, but they have some real sharp edges on them."

"Three kittens did all of that?" Andi asked.

"Uh. . . there are seven of them now."

Andi almost dropped the rake. "Seven? How did you get four more kittens since yesterday?"

"Maybe they're like tribbles," he suggested with a grin. At her blank look, he shrugged. Obviously she had better things to do while he was on the road than watch old reruns of *Star Trek*. He wished he did. "Ask Zona where they all come from," he said finally. "She attracts cats faster than a fish fry." He rolled his eyes. "And Dawson just keeps taking them in."

"If Dawson's taking them in," Andi asked, "why are they all at *your* house?"

"I didn't tell you that Dawson's moved in with me?"

"No," Andi said, thinking that this was growing odder by the minute. "You haven't mentioned it." She looked down at the engagement ring sparkling on her soiled hand and considered her next question. She shouldn't have to ask, but with Greg's soft heart, you never really knew. "Is Dawson, um, is he going to move out before next spring?"

"Yes," Greg said with a tender smile at her discomfiture. "Absolutely."

"*And* the cats?"

"They'll move out, too," he said. "Honest. It'll just be you and me and Satchel."

"Satchel?"

"The tomcat," Greg said. "He kinda owned the place before we did, you know."

Well, it wasn't as though she hated cats, Andi thought. She could tolerate Satchel—perhaps even come to like him since Greg apparently did. "One cat might be nice," she said. "But only one, okay?"

"Scout's honor," Greg agreed, holding three fingers up to the brim of his ridiculous hat and making Andi laugh. "The rest of the 'kitten caboodle' are up for adoption even as we speak. Think Clytie might like one?"

"Clytie has a duck," Andi reminded him. "Cats and ducks do not interact well socially." But the mention of her sister reminded her of something. She looked up at Greg suspiciously. "Did you by any chance write Clytie a secret admirer note?"

The expression on Greg's face answered the question. Then he grinned. "Did somebody?"

"Well," Andi said, "I don't know, really. She says that someone did, but she also says that she's lost the note."

"Does she know who wrote it?" Greg asked.

"She thinks she does," Andi said. "She thinks it's our paperboy."

Greg studied her face. "But you don't think so?"

"I don't know him very well," Andi admitted. "I've only barely met him. But he doesn't seem like the type to notice a girl, let alone write to one. And from what Clytie said about it, it doesn't sound like something a seventeen-year-old would write in the first place." She tilted her head. "I hoped maybe it was you—to try to make her feel better after Thaddeus. Otherwise, I'm afraid it might have been Darlene."

"It wasn't me," Greg said. "And if it doesn't sound like a teenage kid, how could it have been Darlene?" His lopsided grin widened. "My money's on the paperboy." He moved away to make room along the bridge for two women with Jeep-repro strollers full of preschoolers.

Andi lifted her rake and motioned with the handle toward the food prep area. Greg met her at the door.

"I have to clean up and go drive that zoo train," she said. "And I know you need to go get ready for the car show."

"I'm sorry about that," Greg said. "I know I'm not very reliable—"

"If I had wanted 'reliable,'" Andi interrupted, "I could have married Sterling Channing three months ago."

"But you held out for an undependable jock who has to dress like Indiana Jones just to go out in public," Greg said with a grimace. "Good call."

"I held out," Andi said, running a finger along the golden stubble on his jaw line heedless of anyone or everyone who might be watching, "for the nicest guy on this animal planet. I'm willing to live with the consequences."

Greg captured her swamp-stained fingers and brought them to his lips. "I don't deserve you."

"No," she said feeling an electric current pass down her arm and into her heart and marveling how it was that when a certain man merely takes your hand it can mean more than an embrace, and connect you more deeply than even a kiss. "But you're stuck with me. Forever."

Greg's back was to the crowd. "Can I kiss you hello and good-bye or are there too many people watching?"

Andi glanced past him at the knot of Japanese tourists, a teenage girl, and an older guy in a green polo shirt. All were looking on with some interest. "I don't see anybody," she said, closing her eyes and raising her lips to Greg's. "Kiss me."

* * *

"Darling?" Dawson repeated, unsure that he had heard the young woman correctly. "Your name is Darling?"

"No," the girl sighed, clasping her hands beneath her chin as she gazed at Greg with starry eyes while waiting her turn in line. "But you asked who I want him to sign the picture to and I want him to write 'Darling.'" She shot a glance at her friend and the two girls giggled.

Dawson popped a couple of aspirin in his mouth and chewed as he wrote the word on a small piece of paper and passed it dutifully to Greg with a photo. The young ballplayer was on automatic pilot, Dawson noted. He didn't pause for a second. He glanced at the paper, signed the picture, and offered it to the girl with a smile he had plastered on more than an hour ago and still managed somehow to maintain. Dawson stepped forward and took the girl's elbow to move her along before she swooned and blocked the line. Then he turned and did a quick double take.

"Mr. Howland will take a three-minute break," he announced to the crowd. "Right after . . ." he pretended to consider then stepped up to Andi, "you, miss."

When Andi's turn came, Dawson held his ground in the line, effectively providing a privacy barrier of three or four feet. Andi smiled back at him, wondering why she had ever thought Dawson Geitler was anything but wonderful. Then she slid the photo onto the table.

"Your name?" Greg asked without looking up.

"Andi," she said. "With an I."

He had written the first two letters before the name and the voice registered. He looked up.

"D, I," she prompted.

"Huh?"

"Finish writing my name." When he didn't, Andi reached down to jiggle the picture in front of him. "I've stood in that line for more than an hour, Howland. I want my autographed picture."

"What are you doing here?" he asked as he glanced over at the long, impatient line, then obediently scribbled.

"Well, I found out last night that I'd have some time to kill this afternoon," she said with a smile, "and I've never been to a car show."

Greg glanced around the civic center. The show consisted of aisles and aisles of shiny cars, half-dressed women, and has-been celebrities who should have had somewhere—anywhere—better to be than here. He raised one eyebrow. "So, see anything you like?"

She looked down into his handsome, newly shaven face and was barely able to resist the urge to touch it. Caress it. Kiss it. "I do now," she said.

He grinned and held up his left hand with the back out. Then he pointed to the CTR ring. "Sorry, miss," he said. "But I'm Claimed, Taken, and Restricted." He motioned across the aisle with his cleft chin. "But MoJoe over there might be available."

Andi looked over her shoulder at the professional wrestler, then froze.

"I was kidding," Greg said when she didn't turn back to him after several seconds. "I hear he's got a wife and six kids."

"Greg," Andi said. The breath caught in her throat. "I saw that man at the zoo this morning."

"I don't think so, Andi," he teased. "MoJoe doesn't wrestle alligators, he wrestles other actors."

"No," Andi insisted, her voice growing low and her face white. "The other man. The one in the green polo shirt." She glanced back over her shoulder. "He's gone."

She watched Greg's blue eyes narrow as he stood and scanned the crowd. "I don't see anybody in a—"

"It's the same man, Greg!" Andi insisted. "I know it is. He must be following you."

Greg continued to search the crowd, his face contemplative. But when he looked back at Andi a few moments later, the contemplation was gone—replaced by apprehension. "Or following you," he said tightly.

When Dawson approached in concern, Greg took his arm and spoke into his ear. "Call a security company," he said. "I want somebody with Andi before she leaves the building. And twenty-four hours a day after."

"Greg—" Andi began.

"Sit down," he commanded, pulling out his chair for her. He looked at the long line of fans that had approached with Dawson and quickly circled the table. "Stay there where I can see you," he added over his shoulder. "I'll get through this thing as fast as I can." He accepted the next photo and pulled the cap off his pen with his teeth. "Dawson, don't just stand there with your mouth open," he said around the cap. "Call somebody."

The bodyguard arrived at about the same time as the security detail that had been assigned to get Greg out of the building and on his way to the ballpark. As their group neared the rear exit, Andi paused and placed a hand on Greg's arm.

"This is silly," she said, looking from him to her brawny new escort and back. "I don't need a bodyguard."

Greg took her shoulders and pulled her close. When he spoke she could feel his warm breath on her ear. "Look, Andi," he said. "I can't play baseball—I can't even breathe—if I have to worry about you. Just put up with it until Martoni goes to jail and we know for sure you're safe. Please?"

"But what about you, Greg?" she asked with wide, anxious eyes. "What if that man's following you?"

"Don't worry about me," he said with a forced grin. "If it's anybody but MoJoe, I think I can take him." Then he indicated Dawson. "Besides, I've got Killer there to back me up."

"Take care of yourself, Greg," Andi whispered as he bent to kiss her good-bye once again. "Please take *good* care."

A minute or two later he walked out to the car with only Dawson Geitler at his side and Andi closed her eyes. She closed them tightly and said a prayer that God would protect a certain sweet, stubborn ballplayer with a knack for taking in kittens and looking out for everybody but himself.

CHAPTER 25

"So are the bodyguards taking care of you all right?" Greg asked into the cell phone. He had turned the Jeep's radio down low so that Zeke Martoni wouldn't miss a single bugged word. It was a full week later but he wanted the slimeball to know that Andi was still guarded and would stay that way if it took employing an entire U.S. Marine Corps Special Task Force to do it.

"Well," Andi replied, "the guy on the last shift left about ten tonight. The next one is sitting in a car outside my house right now."

"Good," Greg said.

"But I'm thinking about inviting him in for cocoa," she continued, a smile slipping into her voice. "And if he's as good-looking as the one who went to school with me this morning, I think I might run off with him to a tropical island paradise. One," she added meaningfully, "where they don't play baseball."

"Think again," Greg said, but he sounded distracted.

"Greg?" Andi asked quickly. "Greg, is something the matter?"

"No," he said. "No. I just thought that Dawson would have left the gate open and the lights on." He glanced at his watch. It was about 11:30—an early night for Greg, but a late one for Dawson. "He must have gone out, I guess."

A few weeks ago he wouldn't have thought a thing of it. He wouldn't think a thing of it now except for the stupid pattern. Martoni sent him a miniature Jeep then switched the plates on the real one. He gave him a rubber bug then left him to figure out that it represented the other, electronic ones. Then he gave him a castle. Greg had spent the days since just as Zeke had probably intended him to— wondering what would happen next. It had been long enough now that he was almost convinced that the miniature castle was merely a long-distance attempt to throw off a crucial game. Almost convinced.

"Are you all right?" Andi asked in his ear. "Don't go in there alone if you feel any apprehension at all, Greg. Listen to the Spirit."

"It's okay," he said. "I've made myself paranoid is all." He shifted the Jeep into park. "Andi, I'm sorry, but I didn't bring the automatic gate opener. I'm going to have to get out and use a key. I'll see you at church in the morning, okay?"

"But—"

"Everything's fine," he said. "I can't wait to see you. I love you."

He tossed the phone on the seat as he climbed from the Jeep. Clouds scudded over the moon, throwing the orchard into pitch darkness. Greg had to stand away from the headlights to avoid casting a shadow over the lock so he could see. He fumbled with the ancient key, but finally the wide, iron gate swung open on its rusty hinges. Greg's skin crawled at the sound and he returned hastily to his car. The blackest of the clouds moved on, and the round, yellow moon shone once again. Greg looked down the narrow lane at the jagged, eerie outline of the castle.

What? he asked the skeletal trees. *No vampire bats? No howling werewolves? What kind of creep show* is *this?* Only the kind, he thought with a shrug, that he had built it up to be in his own imagination.

Sure enough, when he pulled into the circular drive he saw that Dawson's Volvo was gone. Greg took the wide stone steps two at a time then fumbled again with his keys to unlock the massive front door which, he soon discovered, wasn't locked in the first place. Dawson was really slipping.

He flipped on the light in the front room and was surprised to find that it was conspicuously unoccupied by cats. Even Satchel.

"Hey guys!" he called. "Kitty, kitty?" From the corner of his eye, Greg caught a flicker of movement along the balustrade. Amber eyes gleamed from the deep recess where the railing met the wall. "Satchel?" Greg said. "What are you doing up there? Where's the rest of the team?"

The eyes didn't flicker. "Are you hungry?" Greg asked, taking two deliberate steps toward the kitchen. It was an action guaranteed to bring Satchel running from anywhere, anytime. Still the cat crouched, unmoving. "Suit yourself," Greg said. "But I'm going to make a sandwich. Tuna, if you're interested."

Greg's footsteps echoed in the big, empty house and caused an involuntary vibration of apprehension to run up his spine. *I'm tired,* he decided. If Satchel could survive one night without a midnight snack, so could he. He veered left toward the bedrooms instead.

As he passed Dawson's room, Greg flipped on the light. Immaculate, of course. And no sign of kitties. As if by some primal instinct, the cats seemed to know better than to shed on Dawson's militarily made-up bed. Chances are they were all down in Greg's room nestled among the tangled sheets. Then he heard a tiny mew. And another.

Puzzled, Greg walked into the room. "Kitty, kitty?" There was no visible sign of them, but the audio signals intensified. Finally, he dropped down on his knees and pulled up the bedspread. At the very back of the bed next to the wall was a fuzzy pile of tails and paws and round amber eyes. "What are you guys doing?" he asked. Only the fluffy white female—the one Greg called Christy after pitcher Christy Mathewson—finally approached his wiggling fingers. Greg pulled her out and held her in the palm of his hand while he stood.

"What's with all those scaredy cats?" he asked the kitten as he exited Dawson's room, leaving the light on in case the rest of the crew were afraid of the dark. He ran a finger down its ear and under its soft chin. "You want to play, don't you?"

The kitten mewed as Greg reached for the light switch in his room. He jiggled it twice, but nothing happened. As his eyes adjusted to the dark, Greg blinked. And then he stared.

He might leave his room in disarray from time to time, but it had never looked like this. His clothes were strewn across the room, and most were shredded or covered with red paint. His bed had been all but destroyed and his dresser stood empty. Like the desk, its drawers had been pulled out and used to shatter the light fixtures and even the window panes. Glass and bits of wood lay atop the piles of torn fabric

that had once been his wardrobe, and the foul words splashed
haphazardly across the wall showed the primary use for all the paint.

Greg took a step back and willed himself to swallow, then to
think. The first was hard, but the latter was harder. There had been a
cold calculation to this destruction, and the recognition of it made
Greg's heart pound in his ears. There was more than a mess here;
there was a message. But Greg didn't, at least at that moment, want to
know what the message was.

Christy mewled in protest and Greg realized he was holding her
too tight. He strode back to Dawson's room, knelt to release the
kitten, and closed the door on the way out. The kittens were better
off where they were. Safety in numbers and all that.

Resisting the sickening urge to look in his room again, Greg
strode back down the hall toward the living room. Satchel met him
halfway. "You've had some night here," Greg said, slowing his steps to
avoid tripping over the tabby. "And it isn't over yet. You might want
to hunt up another hole. I'm going to have to call the police, you
know."

He picked up the cell phone from the back of the couch where
he'd left it. Nothing in this room was out of place. Nothing in the
entire house outside of his room was out of place. Greg's lips formed a
grim line. "Glad they don't want me to take this thing personally," he
told the cat.

* * *

"Must be a slow night for crime," Greg observed to Dan Ferris as
the sergeant came back into the living room from the back part of the
castle. "I'd swear every police officer in town is right here."

"They're wrapping up," Ferris said. "For tonight, anyway." He
lowered his bulky frame into a chair recently vacated by a detective
who had taken Greg's statement. "That's quite a mess."

Greg nodded. "And I only saw it in the dark."

"You don't want to see it any better than you did," Ferris said
grimly. "Anyway, we're going to seal it until we've got everything back
from the lab." He sat silently for a minute, then added, "Funny about
that dream catcher being the only thing not mutilated."

Greg lifted an eyebrow. "Dream catcher? What's that?"

Ferris frowned. "Circular thing. Looks kinda like a spider web."

Greg shook his head and Ferris called to one of the technicians. The man went out then returned a few minutes later with a sealed plastic bag, which he handed to the sergeant. Ferris passed it to Greg.

"I've never seen this before," Greg said, turning the small thing of leather cord and feathers over in his hand. "What did you say it is?"

"It's called a dream catcher," Ferris said slowly. "It's a Native American handicraft that you find now in tourist traps more than anywhere else." He took a deep breath. "It was hanging from the light fixture in the middle of your room, Greg. Some folks believe that dream catchers filter out nightmares."

"More like cause them," Greg said. Not being able to bear holding it any longer, he tossed it on the table between them with roughly three times more casualness than he felt.

The bishop noticed. "Look, if this was Martoni, he's finally crossed the line."

"If?" Greg repeated. He crossed his arms. "You and I both know that there's not gonna be one darn thing in that room linking him to me."

"Still, we'll leave a unit here tonight—" Ferris began.

"For what?" Greg said. "Martoni delivered his message loud and clear. Whoever the messenger is won't be back." He looked at the dream catcher on the table and grimaced. "Tonight."

Ferris hit the arm of his chair with a fist. "Okay, I've got another idea. Be right back."

As he opened the door, Dawson rushed in. His eyes darted around the room.

"He's my press agent," Greg explained to the officers who moved to block Dawson's way. "And my roommate." He ran a hand through his hair and glanced at the clock. "It's about time you got home."

Dawson scanned his friend quickly. "You're all right?"

"Yeah," Greg said. "Me, the cats, everybody." He watched Dawson draw a deep breath and search his coat pocket for Tums. It was the first time Greg had seen him frazzled, and he had seen Dawson in some difficult situations. When Geitler cleared his throat three times in succession, Greg managed a thin smile.

"The, er, police?" Dawson asked finally.

"Somebody came in and redecorated my bedroom tonight," Greg replied.

"Re—?" Dawson paused. "May I look?"

"Suit yourself." As he entered the hall, Greg called, "Your room's fine, Dawson. But all the kittens are in there."

And without a litter box, he realized with a bemused shake of his head. "Fine," in this case, was a relative term.

CHAPTER 20

"So where were you last night?" Greg asked Dawson before swallowing two aspirin with his morning orange juice. He hoped the pain reliever would be enough to get him through sacrament meeting and Sunday School. The drawn look on his face and dark circles under his eyes would surely get him out of batting practice—if not the dugout—later.

Dawson made great work out of straightening his tie and avoiding Greg's gaze. "I was out."

"I know that," Greg said. And he was glad of it. The last thing he would have wanted was Dawson around when the "redecorators" came. But his gratitude for his friend's absence didn't make him any less curious about it. "Out where?"

Dawson picked up his suit coat. "Out with Zona Reynolds."

"Out on a date?" Greg asked, choking on the last of his orange juice. "Or out of your mind?"

"What do you think?" Dawson walked out of the kitchen.

Greg grabbed his suit coat from the back of the chair. "Believe me, Dawson, I have no idea." Though, if pressed, he would lean toward Dawson being out of his mind. He followed him into the living room. "What were you doing 'out' with Zona Reynolds?"

It had just occurred to Greg that he was not Dawson's mother when the other man said, "If you must know, we went to a movie festival."

"You're kidding."

"They were gritty foreign films," Dawson said tersely. "And we each paid our own way and bought our own popcorn."

Greg backed off. "It's none of my business."

"Correct."

Greg contained himself for seven and a half seconds more then exploded, "You and *Zona May Reynolds*? You must be kidding."

"No." Dawson put on his coat and pulled a small lint roller from the pocket. After using it to remove nonexistent fuzz from his lapel, he offered it to Greg.

"That's okay," Greg said slowly. He'd been so curious about where Dawson had been up to this point he hadn't thought to ask him where he was going now. "But—"

"You've been playing with the cats again," Dawson said with a nod toward Greg's pant leg. "Hurry up and use the roller. It's a quarter to. It will take us twelve minutes to drive to the chapel, and I imagine that your arrival creates enough of a stir without us going in late."

"Us?"

"I do believe," Dawson said briefly and with only a glance to gauge Greg's reaction, "that every Church of Jesus Christ of Latter-day Saints church building I have ever passed has a sign that reads 'Visitors Welcome.'"

Greg could only nod. "Just a minute," he said finally. "I'll get my hat."

When he reentered the room from the kitchen a few seconds later, he had his scriptures and a white Diamondbacks ball cap in hand. It was the one Bishop Ferris had given him the night before.

Dawson did a double take. "A variation on the yarmulke?" he asked dryly.

"I don't have to wear it wherever I go," Greg said. "I just have to take it. Ready?"

"As I'll ever be," Dawson said.

* * *

Chances were good, Greg thought, winking at Clytie as he shifted Rufus to his other knee, that no sacrament meeting pew had ever held a stranger assortment of people. Besides three Primary children, a prospective elder, and a clearly devoted dwarf Laurel, it held a Beehive who spent most of the meeting turned backwards, passing notes, and a smiling Relief Society president with her long-suffering high councilman husband. Rounding out the group was a celebrity convert, his born-in-the-covenant-and-sticking-to-it fiancée, her burly Catholic bodyguard, a slightly confused Jewish press agent, and, next to him, the pièce de résistance: a who-knew-what-she-believed young woman with a long, flowered skirt and short, butterfly-bedecked hair. Greg leaned back and crossed his arms over Rufus for the closing prayer. *God is no respecter of persons,* he thought, *as this group proves beyond a doubt.*

Bishop Ferris came down from the stand after the meeting to shake hands all around. When Greg stuck the ball cap under his arm to extend his hand, Ferris smiled. "Doing okay?" he asked quietly, clasping Greg on the arm.

"Fine," the athlete responded—so quickly, though, that it made Andi's green eyes narrow. "Great," he added under his breath.

"Glad to hear it."

"Just a minute," Andi said, reaching for Greg's elbow as he started down the hall toward the Gospel Essentials class. "Something's happened."

"I'll say," Greg whispered back. "Dawson and Zona have not only come to church together this morning, they were out on a *date* last night."

Andi stopped abruptly, causing an immediate bottle neck of deacons. The boys always followed Greg down the narrow hall like a pack of adoring puppies.

Greg pressed his palm against the small of Andi's back. "Keep moving," he said with a grin. "Those guys'll run you over. Besides, you know that Sister Jorgensen doesn't like to be kept waiting." He smiled at the Scouts as he held open the door to the classroom. Andi, Dawson, Zona, and the bodyguard filed in and thus almost tripled the average class attendance.

"Where were you last Sunday, Brother Howland?" Sister Jorgensen said by way of welcome.

"I don't know," he said sheepishly. "San Francisco, I think."

"Did you partake of the sacrament?"

As he did every Sabbath after he'd been on the road, Greg dutifully pulled a paper from a pocket inside his suit coat. Then he unfolded the church program from whatever ward he had found in whatever city he had been in and gave it to Sister Jorgensen.

The elderly woman examined the cover carefully before nodding her approval. "And today I see that you've brought friends." She looked from stiff, uncomfortable Dawson to colorful, slouching Zona, and then toward the big man in the corner. Even inside the stake center the bodyguard wore sunglasses and sat with his burly arms crossed and his face alert. Sister Jorgensen removed her glasses and left them to dangle from the gold chain around her neck. "How nice," she said finally. "Shall we begin with prayer?"

* * *

"We have to go," Greg told Andi regretfully after class. "I have to get to the field and Dawson has some, uh . . . things . . . to take care of." Like finding him some clean socks and other clothes, he thought. Thank goodness neatness wasn't his best quality. If it had been, the suit and shoes he now wore would have been destroyed with everything else in his room. As it was, he'd kicked the shoes off in the kitchen and left the suit in the laundry room with a few dress shirts he'd been meaning to ask Dawson to send to the cleaners. They comprised all the clothes—with what was on his back last night and six or eight uniforms in his locker downtown—that Greg possessed.

"What kind of things?" Andi asked suspiciously. She moved against the wall to make room for a passing Primary class but took hold of Greg's tie on the way. "Listen, Howland," she said, wrapping it once around her slender fingers, "you're not going anywhere until you tell me what you're not telling me."

Since he'd borrowed the tie from Dawson, Greg figured he'd better come clean before Andi destroyed it. "One room at the house was kinda messed up last night," he said. He glanced at Zona. "The cats are fine."

Andi's eyes flicked from Zona to Dawson and back to Greg.

"What do you mean 'messed up'?" she asked. "Do you mean ransacked?"

"More like demolished."

"Which room?" she pressed, the sprinkling of freckles across her nose growing more prominent by the moment.

"My bedroom."

"Greg!"

"Andi, it's all right," he assured her. He couldn't help but notice that the small hand that held the tie—the same hand that fed toothy reptiles on an almost daily basis—was now trembling. *And she wonders why I don't like to tell her everything.* "Really," he continued, covering her hand with his own, "it's no big deal. I called the police, but it was probably random. A bunch of kids out to tear something up."

"That's what the police said?" she asked hopefully.

Lie, he commanded himself. He gently untangled Andi's hand from Dawson's tie. "Yeah. That's all it was."

She braided her cold fingers into his strong warm ones and pulled them close. "You're a terrible liar, Greg Howland," she said softly. "You know that?"

"It could be true."

"Take my bodyguard with you," she urged.

"Not a chance."

"Then hire another." She looked up at him with large, liquid eyes.

He shifted his grip on the brim of the cap that, with his scriptures, was in his other hand. "It's okay, Andi," he said. "I'm safe. I promise."

But how could he promise? she wondered as he held her close. How could he promise her he was safe any more than she could make herself believe it?

 CHAPTER 27

Dawson walked down the hall from his office, paused in the doorway to the spacious living area, and shook his head. Greg lay on his back on the floor, covered with kittens. Dawson didn't know where he got the Eau de Catnip Aftershave that he must surely use, but he sure hoped Greg would keep it to himself.

Dawson liked cats well enough in moderation—and even admired Zona Reynolds in a nebulous sort of way for her dedication to the cause of saving every feline in the Phoenix metropolitan area—but this was getting out of hand. Ten cats, to his way of thinking, was *not* moderation. Fortunately, Greg hadn't noticed the most recent population explosion.

The young ballplayer held up an orange tabby with one hand. "I've never seen this cat before, Dawson," he said.

On the other hand, maybe he *had* noticed. "We've had it a while," Dawson said vaguely.

"Since when?"

"Sunday. But you've been a little, er, distracted this week." And who wouldn't be after having his car stolen, his house invaded, and all his personal possessions destroyed?

Greg stroked the kitten's soft, white underbelly with his thumb until even Dawson could hear the purr. "What's its name?" he asked.

Dawson shrugged. He had felt it incumbent on him to take in the kittens, although he did so reluctantly. He fed them and saw to it that they had fresh water. He tried not to step on them. He even wrote the checks to buy their litter boxes and have those boxes cleaned three times a week. But he didn't name them—nor often remember the names Greg attached.

"But if you're naming," he said now, "you might as well come up with three since that's how many more there are."

"The two orange ones," the pitcher guessed. "And who else?"

Dawson looked around the room. "The calico in the far corner, I believe."

"How about Tinker for you?" Greg asked the contented kitten in his hand. "And your friends can be Evers and Chance." He looked toward Dawson for approval.

Again Dawson shrugged.

"You don't know who they are, do you?" Releasing Tinker and clearing his chest of Shoeless and Addie, Greg sat up. "They were only the greatest triple play trio that ever lived." He grinned and quoted, "'These are the saddest of possible words—Tinker to Evers to Chance. Trio of Bear Cubs and fleeter than birds . . .' Ring a bell?"

"No," Dawson said. But he was pleased to see Greg almost smile again. It was something his friend honestly didn't do much lately. And maybe he could make him feel even better. "But I came out to tell you that 'something' you wanted to do—in Kiribati—is taken care of. I just got off the phone with the Peace Corps officer responsible for the area and—"

"He doesn't know?" Greg interrupted.

"No," Dawson said quickly. "He doesn't know who's building the school, only that it's being built." He paused because Greg wasn't smiling anymore. "I wish you'd have talked to him. He says one can't imagine the impact the school will have on the island. That and the supplies for the clinic will—"

"I only gave them money, Dawson," Greg said before the other man could finish his sentence.

"Money is what they need."

"No," Greg said. "What they need is teachers. They need doctors. They need missionaries. They need people who are willing to sacrifice the things that really count—time and ability. Money is nothing." He sat up, crossing his legs, and three kittens scrambled into the now available lap. "At least it's nothing when you have a lot of it."

Dawson didn't know what to say. Greg Howland not only had money, he had fame, good looks—everything most men could desire. But it meant little to him because he also had one thing many men lacked: perspective. Geitler stood for a moment and considered his friend. There was a lot to learn from him and he was grateful for the crash course. Greg's example—and the Book of Mormon they often now discussed—were certainly changing his life.

Dawson wanted to give Greg something in return and thought he knew what. For a guy with great eternal perspective, Greg spent a lot of his temporal life on baseball. "What time do you have to be at the ballpark?" he asked.

"One," Greg said. "Two."

"Do you have plans until then?"

Dawson knew the answer, of course. With Andi at school or working almost all the hours Greg was free, his plans would be the same as they were every day he didn't pitch or have contractual obligations. He'd kill the few hours between getting up and reporting to the clubhouse by entertaining the cats, reading, and worrying about Zeke Martoni. It wasn't much of a life for the "Most Eligible Man in America." It wasn't much of a life for anybody.

"What do you have in mind?" Greg asked Dawson, his interest clearly fluctuating between little and none.

"I'm going to the zoo with Zona Reynolds this morning," Dawson said. "Andi arranged for her to submit a freelance photojournalistic piece to the *AriZoo* magazine, and I'm going to write the text."

Greg's sandy eyebrow rose, but he didn't ask how this odd collaboration had come about.

"I saw Zona Sunday night at the Reynolds'," Dawson explained anyway. "They, er, invited us both over for dinner. When I drove Zona home I had a chance to see some of her work." *Not to mention her apartment,* he didn't add. To Dawson's orderly eye, it very much resembled Greg's room after the vandalism. But, always a gentleman, he didn't mention it then or now. "Actually," he concluded, "Zona's quite a good photographer."

Greg's only comment was a slightly amused, "Huh."

"Anyway, why don't you come with us this morning?" Then, knowing that a little Zona went a long way with the man she called

"Ace," Dawson modified the invitation. "Or meet us there. You can surprise Andi and maybe have lunch together before you have to go downtown." He was pleased to note that Greg was at least considering it.

"You know I lost that costume you got me along with everything else in my closet," Greg said finally.

"That's the good thing about going with Zona May," Dawson said. "Who's going to look at *you*?" He was encouraged by the slightest hint of a smile. "Besides, it's a weekday." He motioned toward the window at the uncharacteristically gray Arizona sky. "And not even a nice one. There probably won't be a hundred people there. I've seen you sign that many autographs in ten minutes when you have to."

Finally the smile was wide and authentic. "Thanks, Dawson," Greg said. "That's a great idea."

* * *

Greg swung his Jeep into a parking space near the front of the Phoenix Zoo and wondered if this had been such a great idea after all. He couldn't get the thought of Zeke's latest calling card out of his mind. The "dream catcher" had to mean something. And it was something he didn't want to have anything to do with Andi—or with Dawson or Zona for that matter. Something that increased in menace with each "gift" Zeke sent.

Something.

Greg leaned on the steering wheel and gazed at the long bridge that led over a lagoon and to the zoo entrance. *So what are my options?* One, he could continue to try to spend most of his time as far away as possible from everyone he cared about. But who was to say that even that drastic measure would do anything to protect them from Martoni? And maybe that was the real objective of Zeke's game in the first place—to isolate and depress him.

And it's working.

But only if he let it. The other option, of course, was not to let Zeke get to him. Assuredly, he'd have to trust not only in the Lord, but in metropolitan law enforcement and the eventual triumph of justice. (And of the three, Greg had real confidence only in the first.) Still, he'd read every book he had at least twice by now, and you can get only so much conversation out of kittens.

He pulled his white ball cap more firmly over his head and resolutely opened the car door. Then he reached up to the visor for his dark glasses and slipped them over his famous face, squinting in the artificial twilight. Between these shades and the gray, overcast sky he'd be lucky if he didn't trip over an elephant on his way to meet Andi for lunch. He only wished he was sure this was a good idea.

* * *

It was almost twelve hours later when Greg pushed open the steel door to the parking garage at BOB to finally go home for the night, and he was still smiling. Love could do that to people. And he loved Andi more than he would have believed possible only a few months before. Before he found God and the gospel. Before he knew what it meant to believe in an eternal commitment—and to want your promises to the one you love to last even longer. He loved Andi Reynolds for her goodness and her courage and her trust in the Lord. And he loved her for loving him enough to put up with baseball and bodyguards with the same grace and good humor she showed the crocodiles and alligators at the zoo. Going to the zoo had been a great idea. If forty minutes were all they had today to stroll through the lush aviaries hand in hand, they had still been the best forty minutes Greg had spent in a very long time.

If only he didn't have to pitch tomorrow, he thought on the way to his car, he'd go back to the zoo or over to ASU or anywhere else Andi was. What a difference it had made to be strengthened by her closeness today and to touch each of the precious dimples in her cheeks and be reassured that she was real.

Greg pulled open the door to his Jeep and the smile dissolved from his face. Hanging from the rearview mirror was another hoop of leather and thread and feathers. This dream catcher was smaller than the one that had been left in his room and later confiscated by the police—but otherwise it was identical. It was black and teal, the very colors, Greg realized with a start, of the uniform he would don to pitch tomorrow night. Woven into the spiderweb-like threads in the center was a single white bead, and attached to the bead was a note.

A little good luck charm for my favorite pitcher. Sweet dreams. Zeke.

The thong broke as Greg snatched it from the mirror and threw it onto the concrete at his feet.

"Howland?"

He spun in surprise. He hadn't heard anyone follow him into the garage.

Wes Westen paused on his way to his car. "You okay?"

"Yeah," Greg said. He saw the veteran pitcher's eyes move questioningly toward the dream catcher so he bent to pick it up. "I just can't seem to hold on to anything tonight," he added lamely, wondering if people like Martoni went to school somewhere to learn to lie convincingly.

"Hope you don't have that problem with the ball tomorrow night."

It was the closest to amiable that Greg had heard Westen except, of course, for the time he'd thanked him for going to the car show in his place. He nodded. "But if I do blow it, at least I know you're there to save my skin." He extended a hand. "Great game tonight."

Westen shook it gratefully. "Yeah, well, maybe I've got a little stuff left after all."

His hero had been his old sober, easy-going self for more than a week now, Greg had noted with a little surprise and a lot of satisfaction. Tonight McKay had finally noticed, too, and called Westen out of the bullpen in the sixth to face the heaviest hitter in the Mets lineup. Wes stayed in the game until the closer came in to finish off the visitors in the ninth. He had pitched three flawless innings of baseball, and nobody had been more pleased than Greg. He said, "Hey, from where I was sitting it looked like you had a whole lot of stuff. I sure wouldn't want to face you."

"Howland," Wes said without missing a beat, "you couldn't get a hit off my grandma."

It was said not only without an audience, but without a hint of malice. It was also, Greg thought ruefully, probably true. He laughed.

Westen chuckled too, but sheepishly. "Howland, I shoulda told you before now, the team's lucky to have you and I, uh, I owe you a—"

"A few pointers before the Series," Greg finished for him. "I'd be grateful, Wes, for anything you can teach me. Right now I throw hard and hope for the best, but I always wanted to be a real pitcher, like you."

Westen examined the face of the famous southpaw—the youngest man to throw a perfect game in a World Series—for a trace of ridicule. Finding none, a slow smile creased his face. "Well, okay then." He hit Greg lightly on the shoulder. "My first advice, kid, is to take that rubber arm of yours on home to bed. It's a big game tomorrow. You need a good night's sleep."

Involuntarily, Greg's fingers tightened on the dream catcher. The threads of the web dug into his fingers, cutting off the circulation, but he didn't notice.

Dream catcher.

It meant something, Greg knew. He feared that all too soon he would find out what that something was.

CHAPTER 28

Focus.

Greg sat at his locker in the Diamondbacks' clubhouse the next night, his back to the rest of the room, turning the small leather orb over and over in his hand.

Focus on the ball.

He stretched his fingers along the rows of red stitching, felt a slight give in the leather at the pressure he applied, then relaxed his fingers, and let the ball roll to rest in his open palm.

Squeeze. Release. Squeeze. Release.

The Diamondbacks were closing in on the National League pennant and could already smell victory in the air and taste it on their tongues. If the electric company could have harnessed the emotional current coursing through the clubhouse of the Western Division champions, they could have used it to light up not only the cavernous Bank One Ballpark but most of the surrounding metropolitan area.

The starting pitcher, who seemed the most immune to the commotion of press, players, and management, squeezed the ball again until his knuckles ached.

Focus.

He could do this. Still, tuning out the commotion of fifty men in a clubhouse, and even a thousand times that many people in the stadium above, was simple compared to escaping the one voice left in his head. Zeke Martoni's voice saying "dream catcher" over and over again. Dan Ferris had called to tell Greg that Zeke was in the stands tonight.

There was no law against that, of course, though there should have been. Despite the disconcerting news, Greg was on the mound and the National League Pennant was coming down to the line. If he and his teammates wanted to watch the World Series from a dugout instead of an armchair, he'd need to forget about Zeke for at least a couple of hours.

Focus.

He almost had when a door slammed and a loud, off-key rendition of "Via Con Dios" startled him almost off the bench. It sounded like—though he knew it couldn't possibly be—Jorge Andres. Greg gripped the ball tighter but glanced over his shoulder to see the cause of all the whistles and snickers.

It *was* Jorge, fully dressed in his catcher's accoutrements but little more. Only the white towel knotted around his thick waist hung precariously between him and indecency. When he caught sight of Greg on the far side of the room, one thick arm shot up in an expansive wave. *"Hermano!"*

Greg dropped the ball.

"There you is!" Jorge called, pushing his way across the room and ignoring, or not noticing, his teammates' jokes and the media's flash bulbs. When he reached Greg, he brandished a mitt-sized palm for a high five. "This be our day!"

Reaching up quickly, Greg grabbed Jorge's elbow and pulled him down onto the narrow bench as he rose himself. Looking down into Andres' dark, sweaty face, he said, "What's with you?"

"I'm there," Jorge said eagerly. "I'm ready, man. Let's go."

Greg drew a long breath. "Aren't you forgetting something? Like, say, your clothes?"

Jorge laughed and banged a fist against the rubber and plastic of his chest protector. "Oh, man, I tell you I'm on. We gonna play today like no mens ever played before. Right, Greg? You and me. We's on? Right?"

Greg looked into his friend's glittering black eyes and tried to glean from them the information he wasn't getting from his words. The brightness seemed artificial, but familiar somehow. Greg's own eyes narrowed as he tried to connect Jorge's expression with a vagueness flitting just this side of surety. The exuberance and unnatural confidence reminded him of something.

"We's on, I tell you!"

On what?

Suddenly, Greg could almost hear his heart as it slammed against the wall of his chest. Of course. It wasn't some*thing* it reminded him of—it was some*one*. It was his father when he was drunk and on top of the world before the inevitable plunge into meanness and despair. And it was Jim, after the undiagnosed cancer had begun to make life a nightmare, and Zeke Martoni had fed him crack cocaine as an antidote.

His heart beating rapidly, Greg bent forward and put his hand on Jorge's shoulder, not sure if he wanted to help him, or hold him in place, or just quiet him for a minute or two so he could think.

Perhaps he was partially successful. When Jorge spoke, his voice was very low and conspiratorial. "I used the stuff, Greg. Just like you say."

"What?"

Jorge nodded, his face glistening and his breath coming ragged and fast. "My momma, before I left the island, she made me promise I'd stay away from all that." Doubt flickered momentarily across his broad, honest face, then he brightened. "I wouldn't trust nobody but you. But you right about the stuff, Greg. You the man."

Greg's heart no longer beat as rapidly. Most likely, it didn't beat at all. Gravity, and weakness from a sudden lack of circulating blood, pulled him onto the bench next to Andres. "What are you talking about?"

"You know," Jorge grinned, "in the garage. You tossed me that little bag and said it's our day, man. I just did what you say."

"Jorge," Greg said carefully, "you couldn't have seen me in the parking lot. I came early. Besides, you know I'd never . . ." Judging by the look on Andres' face, the catcher wasn't going to buy a word of it. And as guileless as Jorge was, Greg wasn't sure he believed it himself.

He shook his head as his eyes sought out the baseball he had dropped. Focusing on it was pretty much out of the question. Greg felt cold. And ill. This must be the "dream catcher." But how in the world could Martoni have pulled it off?

Greg stuck out his foot to nudge the baseball toward his locker. *Someone who looks like me? Is that how Zeke got a lackey in the parking lot and the clubhouse? Is that how he stole my Jeep and got the dream catcher in it last night? Could there be somebody who looks enough like me to fool even Jorge?*

Suddenly, and with great clarity, Greg remembered an actor Dawson had hired for a press conference months before—on the day Greg had left the hospital after his injury in spring training. He nodded slowly. *From a few yards away, that guy looked enough like me to fool me.*

Greg knew he might yet spend hours if not days trying to convince Jorge—and probably the Commissioner of Baseball and the Phoenix Police Department—that he had a double. But he'd have to worry about that later. Right now he had to worry about Jorge.

He put his hands on Andres' shoulders and tried to steady them enough to reassure his friend. "Listen, Jorge, we're gonna have to sort this out, you and me. But first we've gotta get you to see the doc."

"I feel great!" Jorge insisted. "I'm on, man!"

Greg shook his head and tightened his grasp. "That stuff you took could hurt you, Jorge. It could kill you."

"You gave it to me, man."

The hurt and conviction were so sure Greg winced. "It was somebody who looked like me," he began. "You've gotta listen—"

Greg didn't have a chance to finish. McKay had arrived with the batting coach and a trainer. The latter had Andres by the arms and on his feet almost before Greg could blink. The media had mysteriously disappeared, and the rest of the team looked on, now eerily quiet.

Only McKay's mustache twitched as he watched the young pitcher watch his catcher being dragged from the clubhouse all the while howling Greg's name. The other players had turned away, as if from the site of a horrific accident, and were gathering up batting gloves and hats as they headed for the tunnel that led to the dugout. McKay's bushy eyebrows rose. "You pitching tonight, Howland?"

Greg raised his eyes, wondering if his manager was deaf or dumb. Then it dawned on him that McKay was merely determined. Jorge had clearly indicted Greg Howland for something—everyone in the clubhouse knew that—but it could have been for bludgeoning baby seals or murdering a nun, and most of his teammates would still want him to pitch before turning himself in. The gas chamber would wait. In this society, the pitching mound was the immediate and important thing.

McKay motioned toward the field. "Connoly's waiting to get you warmed up."

Greg glanced around for his hat, realized he was wearing it, then scooped up his glove as he rose from the bench. "Right."

"And Howland," McKay called as Greg reached the door, "we need this game."

Focus, Greg repeated as he entered the tunnel. *Yeah, right.*

CHAPTER 29

Greg moved away a stray kitten as he reached across the table for milk to pour over his oatmeal. Even that small effort hurt. In fact, he hurt all over. He'd dug himself such a deep pit in the first three innings of the playoff game last night that it had taken him the next six innings to get himself back out of it. They had finally won the game, but it had taken great hitting by his teammates, and 142 of the hardest pitches Greg had thrown in his life to do it.

And he could prove it by the way he felt this morning. Pitching, at its best, is an unnatural act. As the arm passes the ear, it gains tremendous speed and then changes direction, comes down, and stops sharply. Muscles stretch and tear and bleed. And that's when he did it right.

He would be expected to do it "right" all over again on Friday. It was unusual to pitch on three days rest in the majors, but not unheard of. Especially not if you were Greg Howland, and the National League Pennant was still up for grabs.

Dawson tapped twice more on his laptop computer keyboard before raising a hand to push the glasses back up the bridge of his nose. "The BBC is reporting—" he began.

"As in British Broadcasting?" Greg interrupted dubiously. "This stupid thing is being picked up in *England?*"

Dawson's eyes didn't leave the screen. "It wouldn't surprise me to learn that they're reporting it in Bangkok," he said. "Shall I check?"

"No!" Greg exclaimed. He gulped a bite of cereal just seconds ahead of a cat and then peeled a banana. He had to leave for the airport in thirty minutes. The next three games would be played in Houston. Friday's game, if necessary—and it probably would be, with two teams as evenly matched as the Diamondbacks and Astros—would be back in BOB.

That was the game Greg would start—if he hadn't been suspended by the Commissioner of Baseball first or fired by the D-Backs over all the lousy press.

"What about my statement?" he asked Dawson between bites of banana. "Those guys are reporting my statement with the story, aren't they?"

"Well, yes . . . "

"Why am I not relieved by your tone of voice?"

"Nobody's exactly leading off with it," Dawson said.

"But they say that the police believe I have a double, don't they?"

At least the police believed it, thanks to Ferris' idea to put a microphone in Greg's ball cap. The police not only knew where Greg was, they knew where he wasn't—specifically they knew he hadn't been in the garage to give drugs to Jorge. It hadn't hurt his case any either that they had pursued the lead from Dawson and learned that the actor he had hired to impersonate Greg had left his agency about the time Martoni got out of jail and dropped out of sight soon after.

"Everybody's taking their lead from CNN and Reuters," Dawson tried to explain to his frustrated young employer, "neither of which have mentioned the detail that you have a double." He looked quickly back down at the website to avoid Greg's disgusted look. "They're all reporting that you deny dealing drugs, of course."

Greg ran a hand over his face. "Great. Zeke denies dealing drugs too and he's guilty as sin."

And that had been the worst part of the whole, rotten night. Even after he heard the report in the top of the fourth that Jorge would be okay, Greg couldn't seem to keep himself from looking up in the stands at Martoni's smirking face. It was all he could do not to hurl a baseball 100 mph right into the center of the sneer. And this morning, even after an all-nighter of damage control on Dawson's part, Greg was taking such a beating in the press that he quite sincerely wished he had.

When the doorbell rang, Greg dropped the banana.

"I mean to disconnect that," Dawson said. Greg waved it off as he stood, toppling the chair without seeming to notice.

Dawson quickly summed up his friend's state of mind, factored in the likelihood that a reporter had somehow gained entrance through the gate, and concluded that he had best answer the door himself. He jumped to his feet.

"No, I'll get it," Greg replied to the implied offer.

"That's probably not a good idea," Dawson said hastily. "It could be a member of the press and—"

"I'll get it," Greg repeated in a tone of voice that had the desired effect of returning Dawson immediately to his chair. He had foolishly passed up the opportunity to kill Zeke last night, but maybe decking a reporter this morning would help him blow off a little frustration in a pinch.

Greg dutifully pulled the white ball cap over his head and picked up his cereal bowl on the way out of the room. He managed to down three or four spoonfuls of oatmeal on his way to the front door. Then he set the bowl down on a table and walked across the room to pull open the door, more than ready for a fight.

But not with Andi.

He took a step back in surprise. "Don't you have classes this morning?"

"Yes," she said. "And work tomorrow morning and classes the next day and both on Thursday. But I want to go to Houston with you instead."

"You do?"

Andi tossed back her copper curls as she nodded vigorously. "The last time you needed support—when your brother's wife said those terrible things about you—I . . . I wasn't there for you, Greg," she said. Her full lips trembled and her eyes were moist. "I swore to myself then that it would never happen again." She reached for his hand. "Never."

Though she had certainly never intended her words as an indictment, Greg couldn't help but wince at the remembrance of all he had put her through—and was putting her through again—just by being himself. He leaned against the doorjamb. "I'm sorry about all this, Andi."

She let go of his hand to raise her fingers to his lips. "It's not your fault, Greg. Everybody knows that—everybody who matters." She reached into the back pocket of her jeans and pulled out two sheets of saffron-hued paper adorned with sunflowers. "These are from Clytie," she said.

Greg unfolded the papers. His eyes softened as he read Clytie's note of love and encouragement. It was nothing he hadn't already heard from her, but it was everything that he needed to hear again. He refolded it with a smile and looked at the next paper.

> *Our share of night to bear,*
> *Our share of morning,*
> *Our blank in bliss to fill,*
> *Our blank in scorning.*
> *Here a star, and there a star;*
> *Some lose their way.*
> *Here a mist, and there a mist,*
> *Afterwards—day!*

He passed the verse to Andi to read. "Emily Dickinson, I presume." Dickinson was Clytie's favorite poet and this wasn't the first time she'd come through for Greg. Talk about a person with perspective. When Andi handed the paper back to Greg, he folded it also, then placed it with Clytie's note and carefully tucked them together in his pocket. "Thanks for bringing it," he said sincerely. "It means a lot to know that I can always count on you and Clytie and Emily."

"I have something else," she continued, "from yet another Reynolds woman who loves you." From the front pocket of her skirt she removed something small, but heavy, wrapped in worn tissue. "This is from Granny," she said. "She sent it to me after the reunion with a letter saying to give it to you at our wedding. But then she called this morning and told me to give it to you now."

Andi pressed the bundle into his hand. "Granny's fit to be tied, as she puts it," she continued with a smile. "She wants me to find her the number of that 'traitor' Matt Lauer so she can call him personally and set him straight about her future great-grandson-in-law."

Greg grinned. "I'll see if Dawson has the *Today* show's number to give her." He took a corner of the paper in his right hand and let the gift fall into his left palm. It was a gold pocket watch with a crest engraved on the back. The face on the front was yellowed with age, the crystal pockmarked and scratched. It was unbelievably old and unbelievably magnificent.

"It belonged to Aidan Reynolds," Andi said softly when Greg didn't—couldn't—speak. "Kathleen gave it to him when they were married. The family legend says that her father stopped the hands at the hour she left home and slipped it into a pocket of her traveling bag. She never found it until she reached America. It doesn't work anymore, but the hands are supposedly set to the same time they were 150 years ago in Galway."

"I can't take this," Greg said huskily, his eyes deepening to indigo.

"You'd better," Andi said as she curled her fingers around his to press it more securely into his palm. "Or else Granny will never forgive you. Open the back." When his thick fingers seemed too clumsy, she stuck her own small nail into the groove.

Greg looked down at a cameo of a beautiful, porcelain-skinned girl with emerald eyes and burnished red-gold hair.

"It used to have Kathleen's picture in it, of course," Andi explained, "but the family took it out years ago to preserve it." She raised her eyes to Greg's. "But everyone says I look like her, so I suppose you'll have to make do with me for the next hundred years or so."

"I'll . . . manage . . . somehow," he said thickly.

Andi felt the watch press against her shoulder blade as Greg took her in his arms and kissed her tenderly, heedless of the bodyguard looking on from the driveway or the kitten climbing up his pant leg. "Tell Granny I said thank you," he whispered finally.

Andi's head still spun moments after he released her. "I'll tell her it was the best thank you she ever got," she murmured.

Greg smiled down at her. "Now get Conan the Barbarian out there to drive you to school."

"But—"

"There's nothing for you to do in Houston," he said, finally noticing the kitten and moving it from his thigh to his shoulder. "You don't like baseball, remember?"

"But I love you."

"And I love you," he said. "I'll be back on Friday. Hopefully, the police will have found that guy who looks like me by then and some of this, at least, will be over." His brows came together in concern. "I'll bet your father's as 'fit to be tied' as Granny is, what with me on the news and Conan in his front yard."

"Actually," Andi said, frowning slightly at the kitten, which was rubbing its head against Greg's neck, "he's taking it all surprisingly well. Raving at the morning headlines put him in such a good mood that he invited this morning's bodyguard in for breakfast and scriptures." She tilted her head. "That reminds me, is Dawson still reading the Book of Mormon?"

"He's analyzing it," Greg said, "the way he analyzes everything. So far he's told me that plates resembling the brass plates described in Nephi were actually in use in the sixth century B.C. and that several books contain chiasmus, an ancient Jewish form of poetry that Joseph Smith could not possibly have known." Greg grinned. "Among other things. I've tried to tell him that he only has to *believe* the Book of Mormon, not single-handedly prove it beyond a shadow of a doubt—but you know Dawson."

"I'm glad he's reading it," Andi said. "And I think he has Zona reading it again, too, if for no other reason than to claim she knows it better than he does." At the mention of her cousin, Andi's eyes wandered past Greg and his mewing neck wrap into the living area. "How many cats did you say you have?" she asked.

"Uh, eight, maybe," he said, "or nine. Not more than ten, I don't think."

"Greg!"

"Zona's finding homes for them."

"Sure she is." Andi's frown deepened. "Are the cats *supposed* to be doing that?"

"No," Greg said, knowing the answer immediately if only by the tone of Andi's voice. He turned to look. "What?"

"Eating out of the cereal bowl," she said distastefully. "Climbing the curtains. Sharpening their little claws on your new furniture."

"I'll, uh, talk to them about it," he said.

"And they'll listen to you?"

"Not a chance."

Andi put her hands on her slender hips. "Greg Howland, you simply must get rid of those cats!"

"I'll put it at the top of my list," he teased. "Drug charges, World Series, Zeke Martoni—nothing takes higher priority from this moment on than getting rid of those rotten kitties."

Despite herself, Andi smiled. And moved closer. "Take me to Houston with you."

"I have a better idea." He held up the pocket watch. "I'll take your picture and your prayers, and you stay here and help Zona find homes for the cats."

"The pound?" she asked hopefully.

"Homes," he repeated. "Not cages."

"All right," Andi conceded, moving closer still. She was puzzled when Greg suddenly seemed to remember his hat. He took it off and tossed it as far as he could, then he nudged the front door closed with his foot.

"Have I ever told you I love you?" he asked.

"Mm, hmm," Andi nodded blissfully.

"Yeah?" he said. "Then I'll just have to tell you again."

CHAPTER 30

Zeke Martoni had enjoyed last night's game more than he had enjoyed anything in a long time. It was a stroke of genius to attend. He enjoyed walking confidently ahead of the two supposedly undercover FBI agents who were now as familiar to him as his own reflection. He enjoyed taking his seat, reveling in the knowledge that just as he settled in, chaos broke loose for young Howland in the clubhouse below.

He imagined the scene again now as he had many times in the past few hours—and in the days of planning before that. Stupid Andres with enough stuff in his system to send him higher than the ballpark's famous roof, insisting repeatedly that the irreproachable Greg Howland had given him the drugs. The parking lot attendant was brought in to back him up; he had seen Howland himself in clothes he'd worn before—clothes "borrowed" from the star athlete's own closet.

He imagined Howland's face: confusion and shock at first then finally revulsion as he finally began to realize that as long as he continued to play those same tired cards of his—faith, hope, and charity—wiser men than he would always hold the upper hand.

Nor had he missed a glance that Greg's teammates had exchanged when they came out of the dugout at last. Zeke had reveled in the tension, confusion, and suspicion they so obviously shared. But seeing Howland himself enter the field from the bullpen—watching the kid struggle to hold himself together under the gaze of a hundred thousand eyes and failing miserably at first—that was worth ten fortunes more than they charged for admission.

He never took his own eyes off Howland, to be sure. He basked in the young pitcher's scarcely controlled anger near the end. He felt his hatred and fury as a palpable thing and drew it in like a tonic.

But even that hadn't been the best. The best had come first, like a fine wine before a sumptuous meal. Howland had stood on the mound before the first pitch and their eyes had met: tormentor and tormented. It had been all he could do to keep his seat, to show no more than a sly smile of recognition when he had at last seen that one emotion he had so long craved—and repeatedly failed—to put upon Howland's candid face.

Fear.

A man who didn't have a price most certainly had a breaking point—and he, fortuitously, had stumbled upon Howland's.

To be sure, the fear that he saw upon the young ballplayer's face had not been for himself. It disappeared, to be replaced with anger, as soon as it became apparent that no lasting harm had been done to his worthless friend. And that moment of transition was the one in which Zeke Martoni realized that he had been wrong. Knew at last that he had been searching for Howland's weaknesses in all the wrong places.

It wouldn't be necessary to change the plans that were laid, of course. Dismantling Howland's spotless reputation piece by piece while destroying his credibility on the witness stand would be both pleasurable and profitable. But he knew now that he could take it a step further. He could prick that area of raw compassion again—and more exquisitely this time—and produce perhaps the most delicious reaction of all: to have the indomitable Greg Howland completely in his power.

CHAPTER 31

Besides passing drugs to his catcher before leaving Phoenix, "Greg Howland" had been drunk in Metropol, obnoxious to a group of school girls in Seabrook, and involved in a brawl at a sleazy strip joint on the wrong side of Houston. And all this without leaving his hotel room and Enron Field.

"I don't know how that guy is doing it all," Greg said to Dawson over the phone on Wednesday evening. He kicked his shoes toward the bathroom and lowered himself onto the hotel bed. "It wears me out just to hear about all the hours I supposedly devote to acting like a creep."

"It's over the top now, Greg," Dawson said. "That's in our favor. The TV networks aren't buying it anymore. The major papers are going to follow suit in the morning. You'll see."

"They might not buy it themselves, but they'll sure as heck keep selling it as long as there's a market," Greg predicted. He tiredly stretched his long legs out on the bed. "Be sure to tell me when I start to turn into a cynic, Dawson."

"It isn't without cause," his friend said.

"I'm already there, huh?"

"I only meant to say—"

"How bad are the repercussions?" Greg interrupted.

"I managed to contact most of the ad agencies before they heard it from the press," Dawson reported. "You might lose the shoe account, though."

"Good," Greg said. He thought about their overseas factories and added under his breath, "Like those guys oughta be throwing the first stones." He reached up over his head to scrunch the pillow more securely under his neck. "Have we heard from the Commissioner?"

"Yes!" Dawson said, glad of some decidedly good news. "He wisely chose not to investigate."

Greg was silent while he considered whether or not this was good news. He'd watched the Astros tie up the series tonight. That meant that if the Diamondbacks won tomorrow, he'd be on the mound Friday and expected to win the pennant. If they lost tomorrow, he'd be on the mound Friday and expected to save the pennant. A good old-fashioned suspension from baseball right now just might be the lesser of three evils.

Dawson chuckled. "And I guess you know that Jorge Andres is swearing on a stack of Bibles that the guy who gave him the drug didn't look *anything* like you."

"Yeah," Greg said, "but I don't think Jorge really believed it wasn't me until we passed through the lobby a few minutes ago, and he saw the other guy live on the eleven o'clock news."

This, apparently, was news to Dawson. And he wouldn't have let the broadcast slip past, he suspected, if Arizona had gone on daylight savings time with the rest of the nation instead of insisting on their own little time zone to confuse people. He grabbed a pen. "What did the double do now?"

"Bit the heads off live chickens." There was a stunned silence on the other end of the line, and Greg shook his head. "I was joking, Dawson. I don't know what he did. I didn't pay any attention. Does it matter?"

"No," Dawson said quickly. He'd pick up the broadcast again off the Internet. "Zona found a home for one of the kittens today," he said, hoping to end the conversation on a relatively positive note.

"Oh?" Greg said. "Which one? Not Christy, I hope."

"Koufax, I think." Dawson considered. "Or maybe it was Cy or Maddie."

"So I can tell Andi we're down to nine cats?"

"Twelve."

"Your math's a little off there, Dawson," Greg observed. "You're multiplying instead of subtracting."

"No," Dawson said calmly. "It's your fiancée's cousin who's a little off. Zona's bringing in cats roughly eleven times faster than she's taking them out."

Greg let out a low whistle and glanced guiltily toward Andi's picture in the open pocket watch next to his bed. "If I'm lucky, maybe that guy will keep on making me look bad enough to distract Andi from asking about the cats."

In another minute Dawson heard Greg yawn and knew he must be exhausted. He said, "I guess that about covers it for tonight. Sorry I haven't been able to do more to contain this thing for you, Greg."

"Dawson," Greg said, immediately more attentive, "thanks. I'm sorry I don't say it more often. Nobody could do any more than you." He sat up again before he fell asleep on top of the bed instead of in it. "That reminds me, I got a call today at the ballpark from some guy at *Newsweek*. I didn't call him back because I figured he just wanted to quote me saying something stupid." He paused when Dawson remained strangely silent. "But the odd thing was that the message said he'd called about you. Got your name right and everything." There was still no response. "It was nobody I've heard of," Greg said finally. "If you think I should, I can scrounge up the number and give him a call tomorrow."

"No," Dawson said quickly. "No, Greg, you've got enough on your plate. Let me call him back."

Greg had dressed for bed, brushed his teeth, and just knelt to say his prayers when he realized that Dawson hadn't asked the name of the caller from *Newsweek*. How was he going to call the man back if he didn't know who he was? Greg made a mental note to call Dawson in the morning. Unless, of course, Dawson got a hold of him first with an early report from Bangkok on the further escapades of Greg Howland, Celebrity Cretin.

* * *

When Greg at last fell asleep, he dreamed he was in a hall of mirrors.

He didn't recall how he had come to this place of endless reflections. Worse, he didn't know how to get out of it. Everywhere he looked were images of himself distended, distorted or diminished. He stood before the latter, and saw himself as a child again, small and powerless and at the mercy of a persecutor who ought to have been a protector, a father not a fiend.

He managed to tear himself away from the reflections that mocked his tenuous hold on size and strength, but turned immediately into another. In this mirror Greg appeared larger than his actual self, larger than he ever had a right—or hope—to be.

He turned away again and saw himself distorted and unreal, a self he recognized by his features but could not control by his movements. He frowned, and the image sneered. He extended an open palm, and the image extended a clenched fist.

He turned again and then again, but there was no entrance and no exit and no end to the mirrors. He was by turns large, small, powerful, frightened, bewildered, enraged. All the reflections were true and all the reflections were false. He spun wildly from one to the other and could not seem to stop.

Until he heard the voice and was suddenly still.

It was Andi, calling to him as she had in another dream—in the coma after his accident where he had been lost in a world of twilight and shadow from which only her beloved voice made him summon the effort that was required to return. She called again and his heart pounded in his chest. He knew suddenly that if he answered Andi it would bring her to this nightmare place, but if he remained still, they both would die.

Sweat rose on his brow as her footsteps echoed down an unseen hall. He willed her back, but she came forward. He couldn't see her, yet he felt her nearness and was gripped by panic. He had to get to her—to get her out of here. He raised a fist and sent it crashing into the nearest of the mirrors. Glass shattered and began to fall. Greg fell with it, and as he did he heard Andi scream.

* * *

Greg sat up in bed, gulping for air and trying to get his bearings. He'd heard Andi scream, heard it as surely as if she'd been in the room.

Which, of course, she wasn't. The room was empty except for him and dark except for the dim, artificial light that spilled in through a window he had opened before going to bed. He ran a hand across his face and into his hair and reached for a water glass on the table. As he did, his cell phone rang.

Greg let out a breath. Perhaps the phone rang once before and his brain, lost and twisted in the nightmare, interpreted the shrill sound as a scream. He reached for and fumbled with the tiny electronic thing before finally finding the right button with his thumb. But as he raised it to his ear, he discovered that the dream had twisted more than his brain, it had twisted his vocal cords as well.

"Yeah?" he managed finally.

"I hope I didn't wake you from your sweet dreams, kid."

Zeke? It couldn't be. Didn't Martoni know by now that his phone was tapped? Or did he know and not care any more than he had cared about being followed to the ballpark and watched every moment he was there? Another possibility, Greg realized, was that his former publicist had a cell phone the police knew nothing of. Zeke managed to contact the actor and have his little messages delivered to Greg somehow.

He reached for the white ball cap that was on the table by the bed, then made himself settle back onto the pillow. "I was awake."

"You oughta get more beauty sleep, kid," the silky voice replied. "You don't look so good. I saw you on the news tonight and said to myself, 'That Howland just ain't as pretty as he used to be.'"

"This game of yours is wearing real thin, Martoni."

"You think so?" Zeke asked, affecting injury. "I'm just starting to enjoy myself." When Greg was silent, he asked, "Did you get the little token of affection I sent you today?"

"I got it," Greg said tightly. He realized now that it had probably been the impetus behind the nightmare. "Too bad I dropped it." Then he'd used a cleated shoe to smash the mirror into a million sparkling shards.

"Tsk, tsk," Zeke chuckled. "Didn't your mother ever tell you that breaking a mirror is seven years' bad luck?"

Despite himself, Greg swallowed.

"And you're gonna need luck, Grego," Zeke concluded. The chuckle was replaced by a rasp. "You're gonna need it real bad."

Greg's hands were cold. He stuck the one that he wasn't using to hold the phone under the bedcovers. Then he remembered the minimizing mirror of his dream and not only pulled his hand back out, but threw off the sheets and blankets altogether. If some law enforcement officer somewhere *was* listening, he had to get Zeke to say something better than this drivel.

"Wasn't that mirror a little stale?" Greg asked. "I'd known long before it came that you'd managed to hire a double to give Jorge the drugs."

"You're slipping, Grego," Zeke said. "Or are you just too big a man to think maybe you oughta step back and take another look at yourself? A real long look."

Greg sat up. "What do you want, Zeke?"

"I wanna be your friend, kid," Zeke said. "Like always."

"You were never my friend." Greg said. "You used me. You lied to my family." His voice was dangerously low. "You killed my brother."

"You've got it mixed up, kid," Zeke responded calmly. "I always looked out for you, Grego. I tried to help Jim even, but he was too far gone. I feel bad about it. You gotta believe that." He let out an audible breath as if sighing under the burden he'd been forced to bear. "Maybe that's why I put it all on the line for you, kid. You might not appreciate it now, Grego, but Uncle Zeke here's your guardian angel."

"You?" Greg scoffed. "Name one thing you've done for me."

"I made you a god," Zeke whispered. "And I've kept you alive."

The room seemed to darken and recede. Greg leaned involuntarily back against the headboard, glad to feel the shock of the cool, hard wood along his spine. It meant that his body hadn't gone as numb as his mind.

"But that could change, Howland," Martoni said, his voice still as smooth as glass and his meaning transparent. Before the line went dead, he added, "But that could change in a heartbeat."

CHAPTER 32

The problem with leaving the curtains open to combat claustrophobia, Greg learned, was that in Texas the sun comes up too big, too early, and too bright besides.

He rolled out of the square of light and pulled the pillow over his head for good measure. Then he lay there, wide awake. Every time he closed his eyes, he saw Zeke taunting him from the stands of Bank One Ballpark. Or, worse, he saw himself in the hall of mirrors and heard Andi scream.

Greg glanced at the clock as he swung his legs over the side of the bed. No more thinking—he'd do something physical. Rising this early at least meant that the streets would be clear enough to go for a run. His hotel wasn't far from Enron Field and he'd never had more than a glimpse of the new stadium from the outside. Besides, there was no place he'd rather be than outdoors when he was troubled. Running was his preferred therapy and he often used it as a time to talk to God. This morning, with the many versions of his mirrored self still fresh in his mind, there was a lot to talk about.

Greg nodded at the doorman on his way out of the building and was pleased to see no recognition in the man's eyes. In baggy sweats and mirrored shades, Greg looked like most of the young businessmen who had already passed through this door on their way to run Houston's almost empty downtown streets.

Out on the sidewalk, he stretched tentatively, swung his arms, and was pleased to discover that his previously achy muscles were well on the way to recovery. He'd throw a few dozen balls this afternoon to loosen up, then ice down his arm during batting practice. If there was one perk to abusing your body every fifth night, Greg thought as he began to jog, missing a batting practice once in a while would have to be it. He liked to throw balls, but he hated trying to hit them.

The day was cool and clear and the city seemed to glisten in the morning sun. Greg ran with vigor, enjoying the stretch of his muscles and the feel of the air on his face. When he reached the beautiful new Enron Field, he ran in place for a minute to admire the high clock tower and full-sized locomotive that adorned the back of the outfield wall. This field and Bank One Ballpark were a far cry from the comparatively ancient, ivy-covered walls of Wrigley Field, where he'd first played with the Cubs, and an almost quantum leap from the uncultivated soybean field where he'd got his start by throwing rocks.

As always, Greg was humbled and amazed. And grateful. Drawing in a deep, cleansing breath he realized how often he'd petitioned his Father in Heaven of late, and how seldom he had thanked Him for the blessings he'd already received. Clytie was right. Andi was right. Bishop Ferris was definitely right. Nothing could come into his life that he—and the Lord—couldn't handle. Greg expressed his gratitude as he ran and found his spirits lift with each footstep.

Reaching the end of a particularly long stretch that he had taken full speed just to prove to himself that he could, Greg stopped for a passing city transit and bent to grasp his knees while he recovered his breath. Glancing between his legs, he saw a large man halfway down the block looking steadily up at him. The man continued to stare until he realized that Greg's eyes were on him, then he turned casually away.

Too casually?

Even as he berated himself for jumping at shadows and seeing suspects in strangers, Greg turned and loped back down the street he had just run to see what, if anything, the man would do. The big, athletic man stepped back as Greg passed, then slipped a couple of coins into a box to buy a copy of the *Houston Examiner.*

Greg jogged another block and around one corner then slowed the pace before he reached the next. Sure enough, the guy was matching him almost step for step, and somewhere along the route he'd lost his newly purchased paper.

Greg kept going, but more slowly, as he considered. It could be a coincidence. The man could be one of Zeke's goons or a savvy fan. There was no way to know for sure. Greg didn't have his cell phone, so his options were limited. He could keep running until he ran into a policeman, he could jog back to the hotel and ask the doorman to call the police, or he could turn and confront the man himself.

Funny, he thought, *how the option that makes the least sense is often the most appealing.*

A service alley lay just ahead and to his right. Greg entered it as if it was part of his normal route. His pace slowed but his heart accelerated as he suddenly realized he'd picked a dead end. *Well, if you're gonna do the stupidest thing, you might as well do it in the stupidest spot.*

He wouldn't have more than a minute before Mr. Tall, Dark, and Ominous arrived. His eyes darted from the cracked pavement to the brick walls and back before lighting upon the only real hiding spot there was. A stray cat meowed its displeasure over being joined for breakfast as Greg swung himself up and into a large garbage dumpster.

"Sorry," he told the cat, dropping the lid and trapping them both in the dark. "I don't like this any better than you do."

Within thirty seconds, Greg heard the heavy footfall on the pavement. He knew, by the slowing of the man's steps as he passed the dumpster, that the man was confused. Greg let him move another fifteen or twenty feet down the alley, then came partway out of his crouch and poised his fingers against the heavy metal lid. It was now or never. He pushed it open.

With a last yowl of outrage, the cat was two blocks away before the agile ballplayer had catapulted himself back over the side and onto the asphalt. Then he spread his legs and crossed his arms. *Kinda like Superman*, he told himself with a grin. All in all, it was pretty smooth. He was on the outside of the alley now, which clearly gave him the upper hand.

Unless, of course, the other guy has a gun.

Which he did. Greg caught the glint of metal in a holster beneath the man's jacket as he spun toward the sound. *You've had some stupid ideas, Howland*, he told himself now, the grin replaced with a grimace, *but thinking you're the Man of Steel is about as smart as—*

"I apologize, Mr. Howland," the man said, holding his hands out, palms forward.

"You—" Greg's own arms dropped to his sides in disbelief. *"What?"*

"Sorry if I made you uncomfortable," the man said, taking a step forward. "I screwed up."

"Uncomfortable?" Greg repeated. He'd probably be able to handle this better, he thought, if the man would just shoot him. At least he *expected* that. He struggled to regain his composure. He didn't know who this soft-spoken titan was, but he apparently wasn't an assassin. Or, at least, he was a really *polite* assassin.

"Uncomfortable?" Greg said once again. "You mean because I jumped in the trash can? Nah, I always do that. It's part of my morning workout."

The man smiled politely and reached for his gun. Greg didn't breath again until the guy produced a slim leather wallet instead and flipped it open to reveal an ID and a silver shield. "Steve Van Wyck," he said. "FBI."

"FBI?" Greg said. He was going to have to stop repeating every word this man said, and he knew it. *"The* FBI?"

"Federal Bureau of Investigation."

"Look," Greg said quickly, "that guy who's been posing as me all over town—he isn't me." *And that,* Greg thought ruefully, *made as much sense as you thinking you're Superman.*

"We know all about him," Van Wyck said calmly.

"Then why aren't you following him instead of me?"

"I was assigned to protect you, sir."

Greg shook his head in disbelief. "How long have you had this, uh, assignment?"

"Me?" Van Wyck said. "Only since you got to Houston."

"Why all of a sudden?" Greg asked. "And whose idea is this?"

"I need to check in," the agent said suddenly, stepping a few feet further into the alley. Greg watched him stick a finger in his ear as he bent his head to speak—apparently into his shirt sleeve. He resisted the urge to step closer to hear at least one side of the low conversation. The guy was an FBI agent, after all; he could probably still shoot him.

"Mr. Howland," Van Wyck said as he finally lowered his arm, "we need to talk."

CHAPTER 33

"Does Zona May seem different to you?" Darlene asked Andi as the older girl hit a button to print one more page of research from a website before leaving for her first class.

A loaded question if ever she'd heard one, Andi thought with a smile. She said, "Different in what way, Darlene?"

Darlene shrugged. She was still in her slippers and nightgown because she was staying home today with a cold. The virus had made her too sick for school but too restless for bed, and she hoped to use the computer as soon as Andi vacated the chair. "Different than she was before."

"Before what?" Andi asked, although she suspected that Darlene meant "before Dawson." If Andi had ever thought that her love affair with Greg had been a case of opposites attracting, she thought the two of them were practically identical twins compared to the bohemian Zona May Reynolds and punctilious Dawson Geitler. Andi was surprised, however—and somewhat alarmed—that Darlene knew anything about the budding romance. She leaned forward anxiously. "You shouldn't mention it to Zona," she said.

"Mention what?"

"You know," Andi said, "anything about her and Dawson. She's probably sensitive about it right now. You need to leave her alone and let—" *Oh, no!* she thought suddenly as her sister's eyes widened. She'd guessed wrong. As usual, she hadn't known what Darlene was talking about. But she could almost see the antennae rise on the top of Darlene's tousled head. "I mean—"

"Zona likes Dawson?" Darlene asked in wonder.

"No," Andi said. "Yes." She bit her bottom lip. "No. Darlene—"

"I did it," Darlene whispered to herself.

"Did what?" Andi asked. "And whatever you did," she continued in dismay without waiting for an answer, "don't ever do it again, okay?"

"It must have been the secret admirer note," Darlene said. "But how did Zona know that Dawson wrote it?"

"Secret admirer note?" Andi repeated slowly. "Darlene, I told you not to write that note."

"I didn't write it," Darlene said patiently. "Dawson Geitler wrote it."

"*Dawson* wrote a secret admirer note to *Zona?*"

"He put Clytie's name on it," Darlene admitted.

"Dawson wrote a secret admirer note to *Clytie?*"

"Yes, but I tore off her name," Darlene explained with satisfaction. "And I gave the note to Zona. How do you think she found out it was from Dawson?"

"I have no idea," Andi said with a sigh.

Since her sister was now slumped in the chair that Darlene had hoped to appropriate, the younger girl prompted, "Don't you have to go to school?"

"In a minute." Andi put her palms together and interlocked her fingers—although she suspected that she didn't have an actual prayer of straightening this mess out. "Let me see if I understand." She raised one tapered finger. "Dawson Geitler wrote a secret admirer note to Clytie."

"Yes," Darlene said, then added helpfully, "but he was supposed to write it for Zona."

"He was?"

"That's what I asked him to do," Darlene said. "It was your idea, remember?"

"It was *not* my idea!" Andi said firmly. "Darlene Reynolds, I *told* you—oh, never mind." She took a deep breath before starting again. "You asked Dawson to write a note for Zona, but he wrote it to Clytie instead and you don't know why. Right?"

Darlene nodded.

So far so good. "And Clytie got the note and thought it was from Ian?"

"She did?" Darlene asked in amazement.

"She didn't?"

"You just said she did," Darlene said. "Do you know what you're talking about, Andi?"

"No," the older girl admitted. *But isn't it too much of a coincidence for two secret admirer notes to surface at the same time in the same house?* Still, she'd better take this one step at a time.

"Never mind Clytie," she said. "You took Clytie's name off what Dawson wrote and gave his note to Zona?"

Darlene's head bobbed up and down. "I put it in her backpack."

"And that's the last you've heard of it."

"Until you just told me that Zona and Dawson are in love!"

"They're not in love!" Andi exclaimed for what it was worth.

Which wasn't much. Darlene pushed her tangled mane back from her glowing face. "I'm amazing, aren't I?"

"Oh, yes," Andi sighed, gathering up her papers from the desk. She might as well go to class. There was nothing left to do here but pray for the best and, failing that, apologize for her unwitting part and hope for everybody's understanding in this life or the next. "You are easily the most amazing person I have ever known." She stood and offered her seat. "Next to Zona May, of course."

If Andi thought she was amazing now, Darlene thought, wiggling comfortably into the chair as her sister left the room, wait until she saw what else she could do!

Her best friend had told her about an Internet site yesterday that they had giggled about all through lunch. Using four fingers in a hunt-and-peck method that was faster than many people type using standard fingering, Darlene called up one of the most remarkable sites on the web. It was the Love Letter Generator, "brought especially to her by The Number One Online Romance Site"—at least according to the web page.

The instructions were easy enough. She had only to click her way through six simple steps, and she would have the type of letter she should have given Zona in the first place. A real love letter. A love letter dripping with all the neat things that Dawson Geitler should have put in his but didn't.

Subject. Darlene considered the choices carefully. "Words from the Heart" sounded pretty good, so she chose that.

Greeting. Did she want "Sweet Pea," "Sweetie Pie," or "Snugglebunny"? This was a little harder, but she selected "Sweet Pea" at last.

First Line. She didn't even understand the first choice, but the second: "I know we don't know each other well, but I am stuck on what I do know about you" was perfect, so Darlene clicked on it without looking at the third option.

She laboriously chose a dazzling *Second Line* and a hopelessly mushy *Third Line,* then paused to twirl her hair around her finger as she considered the three *Closings.* "Thinking of you" was what Grandmother Phillips wrote on birthday cards and Valentines, so that couldn't be very romantic. "Completely Yours" was better, but "All My Heart" was probably the best. Darlene clicked on it then typed "Seceret Admioror" in the *Sender* box. Finally, she leaned back to read the finished version.

> *Sweet Pea,*
>
> *I know we don't know each other well, but I am stuck on what Ido know about you. Your eyes are as bright and intriguing as stars.Words aren't enough to express all the tumbling, frenzied, wonderful feelings in my heart!*
>
> > *All my Heart,*
> > *Seceret Admioror*

In a word, Darlene thought, it was a masterpiece. In another word, she was amazing. And in a short time—maybe even before the end of next week—she would probably be the maid of honor at Zona's wedding.

She chose the most passionate color available—a garish purplish-pink—to highlight the letters, then pointed to and clicked on *Print* as she imagined what she would wear to Zona's reception—something with lots of lace and maybe some sequins and definitely yellow. Yellow was Darlene's favorite color. Besides, it would match Zona's hair.

The printed result was perfect. Almost. It had her family's e-mail address at the top and the website's address at the bottom. Darlene frowned over it for a moment before she realized that she could fix it with only a pair of scissors. She had just finished when she heard her mother call from upstairs to ask why she wasn't in bed.

"Coming, Mom!" she called. But her voice was too hoarse to carry and in moments she heard her mother on the stairs.

She looked around for a place to put the letter for safekeeping, but no place seemed right. Why don't nightgowns have pockets anyway? she wondered. When she heard Margaret Reynolds only a few steps away, Darlene hastily stuck the note in the only place readily available: between the pages of last night's newspaper. With Greg's picture right there on the front, surely no one would throw it out. She would have plenty of time later to retrieve her masterpiece.

"Darlene, what are you doing out of bed?" Margaret asked.

Darlene giggled. Her mother would find out soon enough to stitch the sequins on her lacy yellow dress. She was going to be a bridesmaid. And when word of what she'd done got around, she might even be famous. Maybe she'd have a column in the news-paper—or on the Internet—and maybe people from all over the world would ask her for help and advice with their love lives. Maybe—

"Darlene," Margaret said with more amusement than exaspera-tion, "you can daydream in bed."

"Okay, Mom," Darlene said happily. As she made her way up the stairs, her mind raced faster than the speed of cyberspace communica-tion. Life was wonderful. She was a romance diva at thirteen—how could anything be more exiting than that?

 CHAPTER 34

Some people thrive on excitement to the extent that they stir up tempests in their teapots. Other are dismayed and overwhelmed at the slightest ripple in their teacups of life. A third group of people stand on the pier, gaze into the gathering storm, and grit their teeth.

Greg gritted his teeth. Then he brushed what he could of the dumpster remnants off his sweats and said to the FBI agent, "So let's talk."

Van Wyck motioned up the alley toward the street. "Shall we do it on the way back to your hotel?" As the two men fell into step, the agent began to explain. "This morning was the first I've been assigned to you, Mr. Howland. And probably the last," he added with a self-deprecating shrug. "But someone from the agency's been on you all along."

Talk about observant, Greg thought. *Here some guy's been watching me lace my cleats, and I'm too dumb to notice that the shoe's on the wrong foot.* "How long is 'all along'?" he asked. "Since Martoni managed to get himself out of jail?"

"Since you came out of the hospital," Van Wyck said. "And to be accurate, sir, we *let* Martoni out of jail."

"You what?" Greg stopped abruptly. He pulled off his cap, then seeing that the streets were now full of pedestrians, he put it sheepishly back on again. "You don't know what he's up to—"

"We heard the call he placed to you last night," Van Wyck interrupted. "And we know about the things he's been sending you."

Good, Greg thought. *One less thing to worry about.* "Then the police are going to pick him up?"

"No."

Greg couldn't believe it. "If what Zeke said last night didn't qualify as a threat, what exactly do you guys *want?*"

Van Wyck's dark eyes were sober. "We want to keep you alive, Mr. Howland."

Greg felt the sudden need to sit down. *Where's a bus stop bench when you need one?*

"There's a café just up the street, sir," Van Wyck said. "Let's continue our conversation over a cup of coffee."

Apparently the FBI doesn't know everything about me, Greg thought, but he nodded. A strong cup of orange juice probably wouldn't stop his head from spinning, but a detailed explanation from this guy might. Greg had a dozen questions, maybe more, but admitted that he probably should wait until he was sitting down to hear the answers. "Lead on," he said, then added, "and what's your name again?"

"Van Wyck."

"I guess that means your first name's Agent."

The agent smiled amiably. "It's Steve."

Greg extended his hand. "Greg." He managed a thin grin. "And I hope you're on an expense account, Steve, because not only do I look like a penniless dumpster diver, at the moment I am one. There isn't a pocket in these pants that will hold fifty cents, let alone a wallet."

"The coffee's on Uncle Sam."

That's appropriate, Greg thought ruefully, *since we'll be discussing our common interest in "Uncle" Zeke.*

* * *

"Mom!" Clytie called from the living room. "Mom! Have you seen last night's paper?"

Margaret came in from the kitchen. "Clytie? I thought you'd gone to school already."

"Kimberly is waiting in the car," Clytie said breathlessly. "We came back because she remembered she has a civics project due, and she has to have the latest paper to finish it. I checked the recycling bin, but it wasn't there."

Margaret considered for a moment, then remembered. "I saw it in on the computer desk," she said, "under the scissors." She smiled. "I think your older sister might be saving it to shred at her leisure."

"Thanks, Mom!" Clytie called on her way out the door with the paper under her stubby arm. "And tell Andi I'll rip up any bad stuff about Greg myself!"

* * *

Greg accepted the tall glass of juice from the waitress, turned it with his fingers, and watched its water ring expand as he moved it across the checked plastic tablecloth, but he couldn't get around to drinking any of it.

Nor did Van Wyck touch his coffee. "I don't know how much you know about Zeke Martoni," he began.

"More than I want to," Greg said, "but apparently not enough."

"It was a bad day when you went to the police with that extortion rap."

Greg saw that the face he looked into was as certain as his must be amazed. "It seemed like a good idea at the time," he said, "what with Zeke out to wreck my life and all."

Van Wyck reached for his cup and lifted it. "Except that now there are certain people who think they may have to kill you."

Greg's lips formed a thin line. "I keep hearing that." He brought his hands up on the table. "Look, Martoni's a liar and a thief and an all-around scumbag but I don't think he's murdered anybody."

"We think he has," Van Wyck said as calmly as if they were discussing batting averages. "But he's not the one we're worried about. That's why we let him out of jail—to take the pressure off of you."

"Thanks," Greg said wryly. "It worked great."

"It's worked pretty well," Van Wyck agreed. "You're still alive." He sipped the hot liquid before returning the cup to the saucer. "It helps, of course, that you're a public figure."

"So you're saying nobody has to write my obituary until after the World Series?"

"You're relatively safe," Van Wyck said, "until it's time to take the witness stand against Zeke Martoni."

Greg leaned back against the upholstered booth. "This doesn't make any sense. If Zeke doesn't want to kill me, who does?"

"The Syndicate."

Greg waited two beats for Van Wyck to laugh. The agent didn't crack a smile. "You mean Syndicate with a capital S?" he asked incredulously.

Van Wyck lowered his chin in assent.

He only thought he woke up this morning, Greg realized suddenly. He must still be having nightmares. *FBI. Mob. Star athlete. Throw in a showgirl and you'd have a TV Movie of the Week, although a bad one.*

Greg waited patiently to wake up. And didn't. "May I ask *why* the Syndicate cares about me?"

"Martoni's not much more than a two-bit player," Van Wyck said, pushing his coffee cup to the side as he leaned forward earnestly, "but he has his fingers in it all." The agent began to tap the table with a spoon for each point enumerated: "Drugs. Illegal gambling. Weapons. Money laundering. Tax fraud."

"But I don't know anything about that stuff," Greg said, "outside of what happened with my brother." He wondered if Van Wyck knew about Jim and Zeke's gambling and decided that he must. He probably knew more about it, in fact, than Greg did himself. He propped an elbow on the table and raised his own fingers to his temple to massage a sore spot. "What do those people think I know?"

"It's not what they think you know, Mr. Howland. It's what they think you might do," Van Wyck said. "They think you might be able to put enough pressure on Martoni to convince him that he's finally going down."

"And taking some of them with him?"

Van Wyck nodded briefly. "Right now Martoni seems to believe that he's invulnerable. When you testify, and he finds out otherwise, he's going to want to deal."

"Won't it be too late to deal by then?"

"With who we're talking about and what Martoni probably knows, it'll never be too late."

Greg finally took a drink of juice but had a hard time swallowing it. He set the glass back on the table and pushed it away. "So you're telling me that the FBI is doing me a favor by letting Martoni play his stupid games and make my life miserable?"

"Yes, sir," Van Wyck said. "Consider it the lesser of two evils."

Greg nodded without conviction. Even if he believed all this, one aspect of this thing still puzzled him. "How come nobody told me any of this before now?"

"Our meeting today was an accident, Mr. Howland," Van Wyck said. "Actually, it was an error on my part. The Bureau elected to keep this covert for a number of important reasons. The one that most closely affects you is that any overt operation would likely result in a media debacle that would disrupt your career and further jeopardize your life."

"I guess there's no end to the favors you guys do me," Greg said. "Sorry I don't feel much like saying thanks." He gazed out the window at a city street that was slowly beginning to fill with cars and people. The FBI had followed him for months, and he never knew it. Was somebody else out there too, biding his time?

"Where do we go from here?" Greg asked.

"I don't make that decision," Van Wyck responded, "but it would be my guess that your agents will now pose as bodyguards."

"So except for my new little friends from the mob squad," Greg said, "life will go on as normal until I take the witness stand against Zeke Martoni. And you're telling me that that's when my *real* problems start."

"That, Mr. Howland," Van Wyck said, calmly lifting his coffee cup to his lips, "is an accurate assessment of your situation."

CHAPTER 35

Andi balanced the phone under her chin as she slipped out the front door, hoping to find a little privacy away from the madhouse the Reynolds' home had become. She had called Greg to tell him the good news about his double, and the front porch was the only quiet spot she could find to do it. For one thing, Zona was there to do her laundry. She had stopped matching knee socks only long enough to debate freedom of the press with Dawson, who had arrived with the latest, still unreported, news that Greg's double had finally been identified and arrested. Rufus was still there, too, of course, tearing around the house and generally terrorizing the inhabitants.

Andi leaned against the rail, looked out at the beautiful, blue afternoon sky, and even waved at the bodyguard in the car on the street. By this time tomorrow, thank goodness, Greg's name would be off every newspaper page but the sports page.

"See, Greg?" she said happily. "I told you things would get better." She smiled into the phone. "I'm glad you don't have so much to worry about now."

"Yeah," was all he said.

Andi frowned at the flat note in his voice. "You don't sound happy," she observed. "Dawson thought you'd be thrilled. He's so ecstatic that he's really putting his heart into arguing with Zona today."

"Good for him."

"Greg," Andi said, turning away from the blue sky, "what's wrong?" She could almost hear him pull himself together on the other end of the line. His "nothing" didn't surprise her. Nor did it reassure her in the least. "Please tell me what 'nothing' is bothering you this time," she pleaded. "And if you say, 'I'm fine,' I'm going to scream."

There was a long pause on the other end of the line.

"I wish you hadn't said that," Greg said quietly. After a few moments he added, "Andi, I dreamed last night that you screamed. I can't get it out of my mind today. I just can't . . . "

It was at least eighty degrees outdoors but Andi felt cold. Somehow she knew instinctively that the screaming she had done in Greg's nightmare hadn't been for herself, but for him. "You'll be home tonight," she said quickly. "You'll be home and you'll . . . sleep better." She shifted the phone into her other hand, restless, though with no true cause besides the awful, lost note in his voice. "Call me when you get to the castle," she said. "I need to know that you're home safe."

"It'll be after midnight—"

"I won't sleep until I hear from you," Andi said, knowing that it was true. "Promise you'll call me. And, Greg, promise me . . . "

It was almost a minute from the time Andi's words trailed off until Greg asked, "Promise you what?"

Andi couldn't understand the emotion she felt wringing her heart and welling in her throat. As she gripped the phone, she closed her eyes and imagined herself in Greg's arms—the only place in the world where she would ever feel safe and hopeful and whole. "Promise me that we'll live happily ever after."

"Andi, I can't—" he said, his voice deeper and more tender than she had ever heard it. But suddenly, before the first sob escaped her lips, his voice was strong again and resolute. "I promise."

* * *

"Men!" Zona May exclaimed, plopping herself down on the porch step next to Clytie as fascist, capitalism-loving Dawson Geitler got into his fossil-fuel consuming ozone polluter and drove away. And not a minute too soon. In two minutes Zona would have pulled out that old "secret admirer" note of his and given him explicit directions where to send it.

"Men!" Clytie sighed, hoping that her cousin—and her sisters—would go inside before Ian's beautiful beat-up beetle came up the street. Shy, sweet, poetic Ian. *Your eyes are as bright and intriguing as stars*, she repeated to herself. Every word, every syllable, every mauve-colored letter of that incredible note was now committed to memory. She'd have never believed it of him—a boy who stuttered and blushed when he gave oral book reports had not only written such beautiful prose but had been bold enough to slip it into her father's newspaper for her to find.

"Men?" Darlene asked eagerly, her bright eyes darting from Clytie to Zona and back, completely ignoring the fact that of the three other girls on the porch, Andi was the only one who met her eye. "What about men?"

The response was simultaneous:

"I hate them!" From Zona.

"I love them!" From Clytie.

And an abstention from Andi, who said instead, "Aren't you sick, Darlene? Shouldn't you be inside?"

"Men are the reason that God created cats," Zona told her cousins dolefully. "To make up to women for his next beastly creation: men."

"About cats—" Andi inserted hastily. "Greg admitted that he has a dozen kittens now and—"

"Don't thank me," Zona said. "Consider the kitties an early wedding gift. If you *must* marry a man, you deserve some compensation."

"But—"

"Men are wonderful!" Clytie exclaimed.

"Spoken," Zona intoned, "as a babe. You know nothing about men, Clytie."

"And you do?" Clytie retorted.

"What do you know about men, Zona?" Darlene asked. "Tell *me*."

"I'm telling you," Andi said, laying a hand on her little sister's shoulder and turning her toward the door, "that you are sick and you should be inside. Go 'chat' with one of your friends on the Internet."

What had she said now, Andi wondered, to make Darlene practically fly to the door with a promise—or perhaps a threat—that she'd be right back? With a sigh she watched her go, then turned back to

Zona and Clytie. They were both talking at once with the result that neither heard a word the other said. Andi looked on for a moment, trying to decide whether to retreat with dignity or try to referee the fray. She had just chosen the former when both young women stopped talking and turned to her.

"What do you think, Andi?" they asked in unison.

"I think," she said, "that I was just going inside."

"Answer the question first," Zona said. "The one that has been asked by every intelligent, interesting, independent woman since Eve—"

"The chicken," Andi said. "I think the chicken came first."

"Man cannot enter the celestial kingdom without woman," Clytie repeated stubbornly.

"Well that's obvious," Zona smirked, yanking the hems of her green shorts down over her knee and pulling up the edge of her argyle socks to meet them. "They'll have to have somebody smart enough to show them the way."

Clytie ignored the remark. "Andi wants to get married," she pointed out.

"Andi stumbled on a man with a hundred million dollars and fifteen cats," Zona countered.

"*How* many cats?" Andi asked.

"Fifteen . . ." Zona waved her chartreuse nails and shrugged. "Twenty. That's not the point."

"No," Clytie agreed indignantly, "it's not. Andi isn't marrying Greg for his money."

"Or for his cats," Andi added weakly.

"I'm never getting married!" Zona announced.

"I am!" Clytie proclaimed, knowing too well that her first priority ought to be a date to Homecoming next week.

They looked at Andi to break the tie. "Well, you both know that I'm going to marry Greg," she said. Then she thought of his twenty cats. "Maybe."

"Tell Zona how wonderful it is to be in love!" Clytie urged.

Andi thought of her most recent talk with Greg, how troubled he had sounded, and how his enigmatic pain tore at her heart. "Well—"

"Or, even better, Zona," Clytie added impetuously, "I wish you could find out for yourself. I wish you could get a letter like I did!"

"Letter?" Andi asked, fearing she would regret it.

"From a secret admirer," Clytie confessed with bright pink cheeks.

"I got a note from a secret admirer once," Zona said. "It was about as romantic as a dental chart." But with no makeup on her face, the sudden stain of color on her cheeks was hard to miss.

Even Andi blushed, but it was mostly from mortification.

"I know who wrote mine," Clytie said, leaning now toward her cousin conspiratorially. "Do you know who wrote yours?"

"Yes," Zona said. "Dawson Geitler."

Andi drew in a breath. But Clytie responded before she could.

"Dawson?" she cried. "Zona, that's awesome!"

Zona's response was halfway between a shrug and a nod. "Geitler's a chauvinistic, right-wing neat-freak," she said, but fondly.

"I think he's sweet," Clytie said. She scooted closer. "You're not going to break his heart, are you?"

Zona's color deepened. "Not before I break his neck, at least." She pulled a butterfly clip from her hair and fiddled with it. "So who's your Romeo?"

"Ian Lansky," Clytie sighed, her aqua eyes staring past Zona into space.

Zona glanced up at Andi. "I think it's safe to assume she isn't planning to break his heart."

His heart was not the one Andi worried about. Were Clytie and Zona talking about the same Darlene-induced and Dawson-generated note, she wondered, or not? It didn't sound like it could be the same letter from the way they described it. Then should she tell both of them about Darlene's scheme, or only Zona? Zona could easily embarrass herself if Andi let her go on thinking that Dawson had knowingly written her that letter. But if Clytie were disappointed so soon after Thaddeus' death, well, Andi honestly didn't think her little sister could cope.

She had yet to decide what to do when the front door swung open, and Darlene came back out with a paper in hand. She looked too pleased, Andi thought, to be up to anything but Disaster with a capital D.

Darlene gave her big sister a wide berth and handed her recently re-printed piece of computer-generated passion to Zona before Andi could intercept—though the attempt was valiant.

"Dawson asked me to give you this when he left," Darlene lied with perfectly innocent hazel eyes.

"He did?" Zona asked happily. "Thanks."

Andi watched Zona read the paper and grin. She knew all the way to the tips of her toes that this was bad.

"Not bad," Zona said, folding the note carefully. "You should see the way he spelled 'secret admirer' this time. I'd have never thought he'd be the type to go for cutesy."

"Do you like it?" Darlene asked eagerly.

Andi resisted, barely, the urge to strangle her little sister.

Suddenly, Clytie was on her feet. "Excuse me," she said. "Ian's coming!"

"Clytie!" Andi called. "Wait!"

Her sister turned at the bottom of the stairs. "I know, Andi," she said, her eyes shining. "I'm only seventeen years old. I'm too trusting. I need to think with my head instead of with my heart." The smile lit her pretty face. "Is there anything else you want to tell me *again*?"

Andi hesitated. She glanced at Darlene, who shook her head slowly. But could Andi trust her? Had Darlene sent Clytie the notes or hadn't she? Ian had stopped the car at the driveway and opened his door. Andi sighed. "Tell Ian I said hi."

"I like his car," Zona observed as she stood. "Well, tell Aunt Margaret I said thanks for letting me use the washer."

"Um, Zona," Andi said. "I have to tell you something about that, um, letter Darlene gave you." She watched Zona finger it with eyes as starry as Clytie's. "Um . . ." She pulled Darlene forward. "Darlene has to tell you something about that letter she gave you. Don't you, Darlene?"

"Yes," Darlene said. "Dawson said it was very important."

Andi pushed her back out of the way with a glower. "Listen, Zona—"

"I never thought I'd ever get anything like this," Zona said quietly. "You were always the pretty one, Andi. Ida June's the smart one, and Clytie's the nice one—"

"What am *I*?" Darlene interrupted anxiously.

In just a second, Andi thought, she was going to tell her.

"But me," Zona May continued as if Darlene hadn't spoken, "I've just been the odd one. It's rather nice all of a sudden to be told that

I'm unique and determined and have eyes as intriguing as stars." She giggled. It was the first giggle that Andi had heard from her cousin since the onset of their adolescence.

"But Zona . . ." she began helplessly. Looking into her cousin's face, Andi knew that she could no more tell Zona May that her love letter was a fake than she could drown Greg's passel of kittens. Maybe she could talk to Dawson Geitler instead. Dawson was a gentleman. Maybe he'd understand and be able to let Zona down gently and Zona would never have to know the letters hadn't come from him. "I'm glad you got the letter," she said, ignoring Darlene's triumphant look.

When her cousin climbed on her laundry-laden three-wheeler and pedaled away, Andi turned to her little sister.

"See?" Darlene said happily. "We did it!"

"We?" Andi put her hands firmly on Darlene's thin shoulders. "Darlene Reynolds," she said, looking into her sister's eyes and speaking very clearly so that not one syllable could be misunderstood, "if you *ever* tell Zona May—or anybody else—who really wrote those notes, I'm going to tell Mother and Dad who wrote them. Then you will never see another television show or enter another chat room as long as you live. Do you understand me?"

Darlene nodded reluctantly. "But can I still be the maid of honor when Zona marries Dawson?"

"Of course," Andi said sweetly. "And that will be when cats fly."

* * *

A few hours later, Dawson opened the front door of the castle and looked around curiously. A shadow moved in the trees. "Hello?" he called into the darkness.

The only answer was a tiny "mew" at his feet. He looked down at the scraggly little Siamese with a bright red ribbon around its neck.

"Gift wrapping them isn't going to help!" he called toward the citrus grove. "Greg isn't going to be happy about all these new cats." There was no answer and at last Dawson bent to pick up the kitten. A piece of paper fell from beneath the bow.

Dear "Secret Admiroror . . . ," it said. Dawson straightened. "Zona May?"

Apparently she was gone. Puzzled, he took the kitten into the house and closed the door. *I feel tumbling feelings in my heart as well* . . . Dawson dropped the cat, removed his glasses, polished them on his starched shirtsleeve, and returned them to the bridge of his nose. Then he read the rest of the note.

* * *

If the lights burning in the house were any indication, Dawson was still up when Greg got in from Houston that night. The Diamondbacks had won the last game on the Astros' home turf. That meant that tomorrow night—tonight, Greg amended, glancing at his watch as he pushed open the front door—he would be on the mound trying to win his team an all-expense-paid trip to the World Series. He knew he should feel ecstatic, but he mostly felt exhausted.

Geitler looked up when Greg entered. Seeing the big man behind his friend, he folded the note he'd been rereading and stuck it in the pocket of his robe. "Hi, Greg," he said, scrambling to his feet, "I didn't know you were bringing home a . . . teammate?"

"Try FBI agent," Greg said. "Dawson, this is Steve Van Wyck. Steve, this is . . . Never mind." He tossed his duffel behind the door and four kittens scurried over to investigate. "You probably know more about Dawson Geitler than I do."

"Most likely," Van Wyck agreed.

"The other agents spent their nights in the orange grove," Greg told Dawson, "but Steve here's a pretty good guy, and he's come all the way from Texas to watch my back. I figured it was stupid to make him stay outside when we have all these rooms." He looked around as if seeing his surroundings for the first time. "And all these *cats*."

His clear blue eyes registered his amazement. Or was it horror? "Dawson—?"

"Twenty-one," Dawson reported automatically, his eyes on Van Wyck.

"Andi is going to kill me," Greg said.

"About the FBI—" Dawson began.

"Andi is going to kill me unless the Syndicate beats her to it," Greg amended.

Dawson sat back down and fumbled in his pocket for antacids. Or aspirin. Or both. After a moment or two he said, "The Syndicate? That may require further explanation."

"Explanation's something Van Wyck here is great at." Greg shrugged out of his jacket, tossed it over a chair and bent to scratch Satchel between the ears. Then he scooped up Christy. He honestly couldn't remember when he had been so tired. Road trips and nightmares and shocking FBI revelations could do that to you. "I have got to sleep," he said flatly. "And I've got to call Andi first."

Dawson cleared his throat and his eyes darted again to the agent. "You haven't told her about . . . about . . . "

"No," Greg said. "The FBI and the mob haven't, uh, come up. And I'm not going to mention them—or the cats—unless she does." He tried to take a step, but Satchel was thoroughly wound around his ankles. "Does he do this to you?"

"I never see him unless you're here," Dawson said. "Apparently, he's a one-man cat."

"Apparently." Greg scratched the cat's head again, then pulled it gently out from between his feet. "I'm going to bed, Satch," he told it. "Go on, you know the way." The cat trotted obediently toward the hallway then turned to wait for Greg to follow. The ballplayer hesitated and motioned toward Van Wyck. "We've got an extra room now, right?"

"Two," Dawson said. He had not only had Greg's room restored, he'd set up a couple of spares just in case.

"And you'll find Steve anything he needs?"

"Of course."

"Thanks," Greg said. "Good night." In the hall, he turned. His friend looked like one of the great barn owls his father used to hunt back in Iowa. "Don't worry, Dawson," he said with a reassuring grin. "I had Van Wyck here checked out, too. He's a Yankees fan. We're safe until the World Series."

CHAPTER 30

Things could not have come together any faster, any tighter, or any more fortuitously if Zeke Martoni controlled the universe itself.

He took the final gift from the box to admire once again before he sent it. It was the crown piece of a truly masterful set. One brass bowl of the balance caught the glow of his thin cigar and reflected it back—a burning red-orange eye. He held the base in his hand and watched the equally weighted sides swing back and forth, at last reaching an equilibrium that Howland would never find.

His lips curved into a singularly satisfied smile.

It was good. It was almost too good. He set the weight carefully on the table and leaned languorously back into the supple leather chair to lift his feet up on the smooth, mahogany wood while he enjoyed a good cigar. Maybe later, he thought, he'd treat himself to some top of the line stuff, a well-deserved reward for a job well done.

True, the actor he had hired had been a disappointment, he admitted to himself as he eyed the balance through the hazy gauze of smoke. Zeke had designed the escapades to pull Howland's estimation down and set him up for the denouement yet to come. Instead, the ploy was up and Howland had emerged more popular than ever—which wasn't necessarily a bad thing, since it would only give him that much farther to fall.

Zeke blew a smoke ring and watched it rise. His perfect white teeth gleamed in the dim light. At least he had the satisfaction of knowing that the actor was in jail where dull-minded, weak-stomached men deserved to be. He'd talk, Zeke had no doubt of that, but it wasn't worth throwing *good money after bad to have him killed. Nothing he would say would amount to a hill of stinking turnips. By the time the Feds listened to the idiot and got around to coming after Zeke, he would be out of the country and Greg Howland would be living his worst nightmare—with a dead body in his house, the blood on his own spotless hands, and the love of his life lost.*

Or, Martoni thought, he would kill Howland himself and be done with it.

Both scenarios played themselves out in his mind with satisfying results. The first was compelling because the irony was so great and Howland's pain so exquisite. Martoni would like nothing better than to hold a grandstand seat for the event—to watch this self-righteous hero die day by day, inch by inch, of remorse and self-recrimination.

Only the drawback that he could not be there to watch that agony gave him pause. Experience was usually superior to imagination. Was it better then to shorten the interval if it meant he would then obtain the personal pleasure of being able to watch Howland suffer and then watch him die?

Zeke Martoni set the balance swaying with the slightest nudge from his elegantly slippered foot.

"Decisions, decisions," he said to himself. Then he laughed.

CHAPTER 37

Greg had firmly established rituals on the days he pitched and Andi knew it. He liked to wear the same clothes and eat the same foods and listen to the same music and think the same thought: baseball. It was all designed, she knew, to convert him from a man to a machine—a finely tuned, perfectly focused, almost infallible pitching machine—which was exactly what his team needed him to be tonight to win the National League Pennant. What Andi needed him to be was Greg, the man. But even more important to her than what she needed was to try to give Greg what he needed. Whatever that was.

She pulled her mane of curls off the back of her neck and secured it with a band. Men were so hard to figure out. If she were facing one of the greatest challenges of her life, she would want Greg by her side every moment, holding her hand. He, however, seemed to consider even her presence at arm's length about three blocks too close for comfort. Last night on the phone he had described her as a "distraction" and then seemed genuinely amazed when she took offense. The problem, as it turned out, had been one of semantics—and gender. If she had learned nothing else since falling in love, it was that men's thought processes were different from women's and that's all there was to it.

She slipped her arms into a Diamondbacks jersey but left it unbuttoned over the top of her purple tee. Andi wore Greg's number, of course—she and half the population of the state of Arizona. *Honestly, by the way some people talk, you would think this game is being played to determine the final outcome of Armageddon,* she thought.

A quick glance in the mirror caused Andi to frown. Purple and teal were not colors that flattered her titian hair and peaches-and-cream complexion, but she'd better get used to them just the same. The Diamondbacks weren't going to change over to ecru and forest green just because they suited her better. *On the other hand,* Andi thought with a smile, *if Greg asked them to they just might.*

The team had offered her and her family invitations to watch the game in any one of three skyboxes or four front-row blocks of seats on the field. Greg had nixed the latter offer (there mustn't be anyone within sight to remind him that he wasn't a pitching machine, after all) and was pleased when Andi chose to sit with Cleon and Laura Bisher in a suite on the second level behind first base. If tonight's game ended as everyone hoped, she would sit there for the National League portion of the World Series as well.

Hoping to give Greg the space that he needed to prepare for tonight's important game, Andi waited until she was sure he would have left for the ballpark before going over to the castle to speak to Dawson about Zona May. It had to be this morning since he and Zona would be in the skybox together tonight.

She left the bodyguard in the car and admired the grand old building again on her way up the stairs. How many more weeks until she could share it with Greg? *Too many,* she decided. Pressing the doorbell, she bent to pick up a small box that was in front of the door and was still rising when the door opened.

"Greg!" she exclaimed. He was so unexpected and so handsome and so close it set her head spinning and took her breath away. "I thought you'd be gone by now," she managed at last. "I, I came to see Dawson."

One eyebrow rose. "Dawson? Is this your way of saying I've been on the road too much lately?"

She smiled. "You have, you know."

"Yeah," he said gruffly. "I know."

He bent to kiss her then, a claiming kiss that left no doubt that if he would be a pitching machine later, he was a man now. Then he stepped back a good three feet.

"I didn't come to distract you," Andi said with a smile of immense satisfaction and pleasure that she *could* distract him. "I came to—"

"I know," he interrupted, "to see Dawson. I'm not gonna have to call him out to a duel or anything, am I?"

"No." She startled when a tall man came suddenly around the corner of the house.

"Okay, Mr. Howland," he said. "We're good to go."

Andi looked up at Greg, the question plain on her face.

He hesitated. "That's, uh, Steve," he said finally. "He, uh, needed a place to sleep last night."

He looked awfully well-dressed for a vagrant, Andi thought. But, knowing Greg, he had probably given the man some of his new clothes as well, they were roughly the same size.

"Hi, Steve," she said tentatively. When the man nodded, she wondered why Greg couldn't have stuck to collecting kittens. Wasn't the local homeless shelter he helped to fund enough without bringing the spares home? She'd see if Dawson could talk to him. Suddenly, she remembered the box in her hands and extended it to Greg. "This was in front of your door."

Greg took it but held it only a moment. At a motion from Steve, he tossed it to the other man.

This was definitely strange. "Who—?" Andi began.

"I've really got to go, Andi," Greg said sheepishly. "After the game I've arranged a pass for you to come down to the clubhouse with the wives and family." He looked unsure for a moment. "If you want to, I mean. Maybe you won't—especially if we win. It can be kinda, uh, boisterous. Maybe we'd better—"

"I want to be there," Andi assured him. She wanted to be anywhere Greg was. Forever.

"Yeah, but there'll be champagne and—"

"Twenty-six cases of champagne," Andi quoted from last night's newspaper "and twenty-seven cases of sparkling cider for you—one for every game you've won as a Diamondback—counting tonight, of course."

She watched his face soften and knew that he was thinking of kissing her again. Unfortunately, this time the pitching machine won.

"Then I'll see you tonight," he said. He pulled the door open wider and four kittens escaped onto the porch. "Dawson's in his office." He turned toward the triple halls. "It's down the center hall," he guessed. "Or maybe it's to the right. One of those."

Andi smiled. "I'll find it if I can get through all your watchcats."

"They're going, I promise," Greg said. He had just absentmind-edly picked up a kitten, and now he almost dropped it in his haste to prove the sincerity of his words.

"Yes," Andi replied, "I know they are." And while he was at it, Dawson Geitler and Steve Whoever-he-was had better be going as well. It might be a big old house, but she wasn't sharing it with anyone but Greg.

Andi found Dawson's office with little trouble. She had only to follow the sounds of Mozart and a ringing telephone. She tapped on the frame of the open door and smiled when Dawson looked up in surprise.

Every paper clip, every pencil, and every piece of paper was carefully arranged atop the immaculate, glass-topped desk but one. The errant paper was a plain sheet of notebook paper with rounded script written in purple pen. As she entered the room, Dawson snatched Zona's note and held it under his desk. "Andi."

"Hi, Dawson," she said. Now that she was here, the words she had planned so carefully scurried away as quickly as the kittens she'd met in the halls.

"You just missed Greg," Dawson began.

"I saw him," Andi said. "For a minute. He said you were in your office. I, um, came this morning to see you."

Dawson masked his surprise with a glance around the room. "I don't have a chair to offer, as you can see. Greg sits on the desk." Dawson stuck the note into his jacket pocket. "At least he does when I can get his attention at all. Business is never at the top of his agenda. Shall we go into the living room to sit down?"

"No," Andi said. "This will only take a minute."

"Then take my chair."

Always a gentleman, she thought. "Thank you," she said, "but I'm fine."

He stood since she did. "What can I do for you?"

Could you possibly love Zona May? she wanted to say. She cleared her throat. "I, um, don't know where to begin."

"Perhaps if you begin at the beginning."

He was so calm, so well organized, so precise Andi's heart sank. He could never love excitable, chaotic, careless Zona May. But he could still be kind. *Oh, please let him be kind.* She clasped her hands. *The beginning*, she reminded herself. "Do you remember Darlene asking you to write a secret admirer note?"

Dawson's eyes widened marginally behind his glasses. "Yes," he said slowly. "I wrote a note to Clytie at Darlene's request some weeks ago."

He was about to apologize, Andi saw, so she rushed ahead. "Well, Clytie never got that note."

"She didn't?"

"No," Andi said. "Darlene gave it to . . . to . . . to somebody else." She watched Dawson reach into his jacket pocket, but the hand didn't return. He was taking this as he took almost everything—calmly—and waiting for her to continue. No, she thought, he wasn't waiting exactly. He seemed to be lost in a thought process of his own. Hoping to call him back, she said, "Darlene gave it to . . . to . . . "

"She gave it to Zona May," Dawson said when Andi couldn't.

Andi sighed and nodded in assent—and relief. She didn't know how he knew, but she was glad that he did. Now for the next—and harder—part. "And somehow," she continued, "Zona figured out that the note was from you."

His hand was still thumbing something in his pocket and his eyes were on the rug. "She figured it out when we went to dinner," he said without hesitation. "Same notebook. Same pen. Same handwriting."

Andi was impressed. "Yes, that must be it." She bit her lower lip. "But she didn't know, of course, that Darlene had asked you to write the note or that you had written it to Clytie."

"No."

"And there's more," Andi said, relieved when at last his eyes rose and rather than the shock and possibly horror that she had expected to see, there was only bemusement and something else that she couldn't define. "Darlene gave her another letter, yesterday, that she'd made up on the computer. She said it was from you, too, and—"

Dawson interrupted by coming around his desk. "I'd appreciate it, Andi," he said, "if we could keep this between us. Zona need never know that I didn't write those letters."

Dawson Geitler wasn't a gentleman, Andi decided in a sudden burst of gratitude—he was a saint. Impulsively, she threw her arms around him.

"I guess you weren't kidding about me being on the road too much," Greg said from the office doorway. He held up the white ball cap. "I forgot my hat. And, Dawson, I also forgot to tell you that guy from *Newsweek* called again this morning when you were in the shower. Turns out he was looking for a reference. His number's on the caller ID."

The look Greg gave Dawson was decidedly pointed, and Andi watched the press agent lower his eyes uncomfortably. Surely he didn't think . . .

"Greg—" she began.

"Sorry, Andi, but I'll have to duel him later," Greg said from the hall. "I've gotta get to the ballpark before McKay shoots me."

"Take care of him, Andi," Dawson said quietly from behind her back. "Even when he doesn't want you to, take care of him."

She turned to respond but at the look of concern on his face, she couldn't think of a single word to say.

CHAPTER 38

How could Greg concentrate on winning a game of baseball when all he could think about was that stupid brass balance?

Balance of justice. Balance of power. Hanging in the balance.

But *what*, Greg wondered, slamming his glove on the dugout bench at the end of the first half-inning, was hanging in the balance? His game? His chance to testify against Zeke? His life?

The pitching coach handed him his jacket and Greg automatically pulled it halfway on, over his left arm, as the first of his teammates went up to bat.

"You okay?" the coach asked.

"Yeah," Greg lied. "Great."

The coach thumped his arm. The right one. The one that didn't count for anything. "Looking good out there."

Three batters up. Three batters down. Every Astro a victim of Greg's fastball. It didn't hurt that he'd imagined Zeke Martoni's face in the center of Jorge's mitt. He'd thrown the ball toward the imagined smirk with even a little more accuracy than usual. And much more force.

Jorge made an elaborate show of shaking out a sore catching paw for his teammates and the ESPN cameras. "We's hot tonight!" The catcher slid onto the bench next to Greg and began to remove his accoutrements so he could bat.

Greg couldn't help but shake his head at his friend's optimism that he'd make it up to the plate this inning. Jorge was the eighth batter. Greg was the ninth, and it was with mixed emotions that he considered the possibility of the Diamondbacks hitting well enough to reach either of their positions in the lineup this early in the game. On the one hand, reaching the bottom of the rotation would mean that they would have scored at least three runs. On the other hand, it would mean an at-bat for Greg. As if pitching wasn't enough under the circumstances, they might actually want him to hit the ball.

"You think we got 'em?" Andres asked, dropping a shin guard.

"I think it's a little early to break out the sparkling cider," Greg said.

"What's with you, man?"

Greg shot a sideways glance into the honest, anxious eyes and tried to shake it all off. Andi's family in the skybox and Dan Ferris in the front row and Martoni lurking who knew where. What good would it do him to blow the big game by dwelling on Zeke's latest "gift" anyway? He hadn't figured out the Jeep or the bug or the dream catcher until after the fact. Chances were good he wasn't going to figure out the balance a minute before Zeke wanted him to, either—and that might not be until a minute after it was too late. At the chill, Greg pulled the jacket across his back and stuck his right arm in it, too.

"You good?" Jorge asked in concern.

"Yeah," Greg said. "I'm good."

* * *

"Is he good or what?" Andi's brother, Brad, asked everybody in general and nobody in particular on the skybox balcony during the top half of the seventh inning. "He's pitching a—"

"Don't say it!" Enos shouted. He clutched his score book and adjusted his thick glasses authoritatively. "*Everybody* knows it's bad luck at a ballpark to mention a—one of those." He paused meaningfully. "It jinxes the pitcher."

"A what?" Zona asked. "You mean a no-hitter?"

"Argh!" Enos threw down his book. "If Greg loses a perfect game tonight, Zona, it's your fault."

"Argh!" Rufus echoed, though he clearly had no idea what was going on.

Andi waited for her cousin's sarcastic comeback or at least her unconcerned shrug. Her mouth opened in surprise when Zona turned to Dawson.

"I didn't mean to jinx Ace," she said meekly.

Andi's mouth opened wider when Dawson took her hand.

"You didn't, Zona," he said. "Enos, Rufus, it's all right. Just watch Greg."

Perfect advice, Andi thought, if ever she had heard it. And what a joy it was to be able to watch Greg with nothing else to worry her but him winning this game that meant so much to him. Her greatest fear—that Clytie would be heartbroken to be back in the box she had last shared with Thaddeus—had been resolved in a way that was nothing short of remarkable. Clytie had invited Ian to the game. When Andi heard her reciting to him many of the things about baseball that Thaddeus had once told her, and telling him all about Thaddeus as well, Andi knew at last that her little sister would be okay. She would always love Thaddeus, surely, but she could go on now and be better for the lost love, not broken by it.

The Jumbotron replayed Greg pumping a triumphant fist as the final Astro swung at air, ending the visitors' hopes of changing the 2-0 score before the seventh inning stretch.

Baseball. Andi sighed. If she wasn't very careful, she might begin to believe in the magic herself. All over the stadium, people leapt to their feet to cheer. In several places, excited kids had taped homemade "K"s along the rails in front of their seats to mark each of Greg's sixteen strikeouts. Signs waved and people danced with excitement. There was more to this game clearly than the commercialism that was all she had seen in it at first. There was also a sense of community and history and shared satisfaction she had seen no place else.

As the organ played "Take Me Out to the Ball Game," Andi looked down toward the Diamondbacks' dugout and wondered. How many of those supposedly grown men would still be here tonight playing their hearts out if they weren't paid a dime for it? She smiled and shook her head. The one in the middle—the tall, handsome blond one who had just pulled a purple sleeve over his surely aching arm—would be. She honestly didn't know if Greg Howland would ever grow up. Or if she would want him to.

She turned as Cleon Bisher came from the suite onto the balcony. He was with Trent Reynolds and a uniformed stadium attendant.

"Are you sure it's all right with the team?" she heard her father ask Cleon. "This game's for the pennant and all."

The team co-owner smiled. "I think it's safe to assume that whatever Greg Howland wants at this point, he gets."

Trent turned to the attendant. "And you'll take Enos down and bring him right back up after the inning?"

"Yes, sir," the attendant said, readjusting the plasticized credentials that hung around his neck as if to convince Trent of his reliability.

"Enos," Trent said, turning to his youngest son and unable to hide the smile on his face, "Greg wants to know if you'd like to spend the next half inning in the dugout."

Almost certainly, Andi thought, Greg had heard the whoop of delight from the field.

"Me, too!" Rufus cried anxiously. "Can I go, too?"

Trent shook his head. "Sorry, Rufus. You're a little too young to—"

Anything he might have said next was interrupted by a major tantrum. Brad reached for his little cousin and was rewarded with a new set of tooth marks in his thumb for his efforts.

Enos was already at the door when his father put a hand on his shoulder. "I'm sorry, son," he said, "but nobody in the stadium's going to get a moment's peace if you leave Rufus behind." At Enos' crestfallen look, he added, "Greg will invite you down for the World Series, I know he will."

Enos looked back at Andi, his thick lenses magnifying the tears in his eyes. She nodded reassuringly. "He will, Enos. I promise."

"I'll take them both," the attendant offered quickly.

He seemed a little too anxious to Andi, but trying to please Greg Howland often had that effect on people.

"I'll stay with them and make sure they're no trouble," the attendant added. "It's my job."

Trent was obviously leery.

"If we go now," the attendant said, "I can give them a chance to say hello to Mr. Howland and have them back up here before he goes out to pitch again."

By the looks on the two little boys' faces, you'd think they'd been invited to tour Disneyland after a quick stop by the North Pole. Andi knew what it would take to tell them no and knew her father didn't have it in him.

"Just let them say hello to Greg," he said, "and bring them right back."

Lucky kids, Andi thought as they left. She noted with a smile that the attendant took his assignment very seriously. He already had a firm grip on each boy's elbow.

She shifted her gaze to a picture on the skybox TV screen of the Diamondbacks' pitcher. He leaned forward on the bench with his elbows on his knees and his chin cupped in his palms, watching the game as avidly as any person in the stadium. Andi watched him blow a large pink bubble and smiled. If only she was the one on her way to the dugout, she thought. There was nothing in the world that she would like more right now than to distract Greg Howland from the game of the year for just a moment. Or two.

* * *

No distractions, Greg thought, forcing his eyes to remain on the field and his mind on the game. *You're almost through this thing.*

His teammates, as was the custom when a pitcher was on for a no-hitter, had stopped talking to him sometime during the fifth inning. Greg hadn't noticed. Nor did he know that he was six outs short of perfection. He only knew that the only way out of this thing was through. He had to keep walking out on that field, climbing that low hill, and throwing that little ball before they'd let him go home and worry about Zeke Martoni. And if he could throw enough strikes to whittle the number of those throws from fifty to twenty then better yet. That's what he'd do.

"Howland?" the bench coach said tentatively. "You're up."

So much for keeping his mind on the game. Sure enough, Jorge had just started his slow stroll to the batter's box. That put Greg on deck. He pulled off his jacket and took a helmet and a bat from his cubby as he looked over his shoulder at the scoreboard. One away; nobody on base. The possibilities flew through his mind. If Jorge got on first, he might be called on to bunt. If Jorge did anything else, Greg knew McKay would probably signal him to stay out of the way.

He was on the starting roster for a triple-digit fastball, not a barely triple-digit batting average.

He climbed the dugout stairs and took his place in the circle, careful not to raise his eyes enough to see a TV camera or a World Series scout or even the opposing relief pitcher. He focused on Jorge instead. Andres didn't make contact as often as the batting coach would like him to, but when he did—as he did just now—he had the raw power to make sure that that ball was gone. All Greg could think as he congratulated his friend at home plate was that now he wouldn't have to risk bunting into a double play.

As expected, he didn't have to worry about swinging the bat. With a three-zip no hitter, the manager confidently signaled Greg to stand as far back from the plate as he could while still remaining in the batter's box. *Why*, Greg thought ruefully, *take the risk of me accidentally hitting the ball and ending up on base? Only Casey struck out every time.*

It took five throws, he noted automatically, but the Astros' reliever sent him down. As he pulled off his helmet and walked back to the dugout with applause ringing in his ears, Greg wondered how the fans would react if he actually hit a long ball some day. He handed his helmet to a bat boy at the top of the stairs. Not that he honestly expected to find out.

"Here's the drink you asked for, Mr. Howland," the bat boy said eagerly. He extended a bottle of sports drink. "There wasn't any in the clubhouse, but somebody brought it in special."

"I didn't ask—" Greg began until something stopped him. "Thanks," he said, surrendering his bat and taking the bottle with him to the bench where his teammates had left him a wide spot for solitude.

He held the plastic bottle in his right hand while he slipped the jacket back onto his left arm. The Diamondbacks were at the top of the order again and, with a little luck and a line drive or two, it could be some time until Greg pitched. He dropped the bottle from his right hand to his left. It was sealed, but he still wasn't stupid enough to drink it.

Stupid? he asked himself. *Or paranoid?* Zeke wasn't behind every odd thing that happened. Maybe this was an honest mistake. Maybe one of his teammates had requested the drink. Maybe . . .

As Greg absentmindedly ran his thumb around the label he felt the tape. With a quick glance to each side, he peeled it down and off. The paper fell loose and into his lap. On the back was a simple pencil drawing of a balance. Beneath the scales in black block letters it said:

HOWLAND + BASEBALL = WORLD SERIES
CASTLE + KID - HOWLAND = DEAD KID

IF YOU'RE NOT ALONE HE'S NOT ALIVE

 CHAPTER 39

It was almost a minute before Greg had a thought or took a breath or felt his heart beat. When each of those things returned, however, it was in a rush. He glanced over at the nearest man on the bench. Surely Jorge could feel the pounding of his heart, or hear the ragged way he struggled to draw a breath, or at least see the tremor in his usually steady hands—the hands that held the note that meant that Zeke Martoni was finally through playing games.

Or that now he was playing them for keeps.

Jorge did notice but attributed it naturally to no-hitter nerves. He raised both thumbs, then, as superstitious as the rest of the team, he turned back away.

For the first time that night, Greg looked toward Cleon's skybox. Faces were impossible to make out at this distance but by squinting he could see Andi's red hair and Zona's yellow out on the balcony. Dawson was probably there, too, and maybe Brad. The small one must be Clytie and next to her . . . who? He was too big to be Enos, and the red-haired little boy was the one Greg was looking for. Could Enos be inside the suite?

He could be anywhere, Greg realized at once. *Including with Zeke.*

Or could he? Smuggling a sports bottle into a dugout wasn't even a challenge compared to many of the things Zeke had pulled off. But smuggling a child out of a crowded ballpark? The entire Reynolds family was here tonight, and surely they wouldn't let Enos out of their sight.

Unless they had a good reason.

Again the balance tipped toward terror. If there was a masterful liar in the world—a person who could charm birds out of trees and boys out of skyboxes—it was Zeke Martoni.

The same Zeke Martoni who was under constant surveillance by the FBI, Greg reminded himself, momentarily evening the scale. But he couldn't maintain the balance. He of all people knew how fast Zeke could disappear. Holding on to him was like holding on to slime: the tighter you squeezed, the more it slipped through your fingers.

Greg's hands clenched with his heart. Somehow, he knew, the FBI had lost Zeke. And if he didn't do something right now, he was going to lose Enos. He shoved the label into a pocket as he began to peel off the jacket. The Astros had executed a double play to end the inning, and a whole stadium full of people expected him to take the mound.

If you're not alone, the kid's not alive.

Greg knew his options were limited. He couldn't spare the time it would take to tell the truth to anyone in the dugout, nor take the risk of one of them failing to come up with a convincing lie to tell ESPN and, hence, the world. He could lie himself, perhaps, by pretending to be sick or hurt, but as Andi had pointed out, he was a lousy liar. He could think of only one other alternative, then, that might get him off this field and out of the ballpark fast enough to save Enos. He jogged out to the mound.

He'd given his teams, and the game of baseball as a whole, his best shot every time he put on a uniform, Greg told himself in an attempt to dispel any doubt over what he was about to do. But this was more important than playing in another World Series—more important than playing another game of baseball again ever. This was for Enos, and his life was more important than anything.

He shook off Jorge's first two signs. Puzzled, the catcher glanced at the manager and then flashed three fingers for the slider. Greg nodded tersely and adjusted the cap so low on his brow that he could see nothing but the glove. He didn't want this ball to get away from him and hit the batter.

He adjusted his stance carefully and pulled back. Then he threw as he had never thrown before, allowing his shoulder to turn too far too soon, forcing his torso out in front of his arm and leaving the arm to do too much of the work, unassisted by the position of his frame. The result was a ball that the batter never saw—clocked at 105 mph—and an awed silence from the crowd, followed by a roar of approval.

That and a sensation beyond pain that seared from Greg's shoulder down to the tips of his fingers and left him crouching on the mound, trying to catch his breath so that he could at last stand and leave the field.

Hundreds of thousands of people saw the look on Greg's face live or on TV. Most thought they knew what he was thinking: that he wouldn't pitch again that night, that he might not pitch again ever, and that the agony of that thought was simply too great for the young pitcher to bear. But they were wrong. Only one thing went through Greg's mind despite the pain and the noise and the terrifying mission that lay ahead, and it was a melody from a sacrament hymn. His mind raced to attach words to the familiar music and at last he was successful in part, ". . . *silently we pray for courage to accept thy will, to listen and obey . . .*"

Greg was willing to listen—knew he *had* to listen to save Enos. And he was willing to obey, too. He couldn't do it without the Lord and he didn't want to try. Then he remembered that there was a third thing that Bishop Ferris had counseled him to learn about obedience—to trust others and not try to do everything himself. As the manager and trainer ran across the field, Greg straightened and raised his eyes to the stands where Ferris had sat, but his friend was no longer there.

* * *

At least one person out of the tens of thousands of people who saw the agony as it crossed Greg's face perceived that it was something more than physical pain, and that person was Dan Ferris. He was out of his seat and on his way to the clubhouse before the trainer left the dugout. Since his seat was on the field level, he arrived several minutes ahead of Andi, who was through Cleon's suite almost before her family saw her go. Heedless of the bodyguard on her heels, she ran to the nearest elevator.

"Where's the clubhouse?" she asked breathlessly.

When the baffled operator didn't immediately respond, Andi fumbled in her purse for the pass Dawson had given her earlier. She thrust it forward anxiously. "Take me there now!" she said. "Right now."

* * *

Greg made it off the field and into the locker room.

Fifty thousand people down and two to go, he thought. But these two, the trainer and the team doctor, would be the toughest to get past. Not surprisingly, the men were more than a little reluctant to let Greg Howland take his multi-million dollar arm home with only the assurance that he would take two aspirin and call them in the morning.

"I'm fine, Doc," Greg said, pulling off his cleats with his right hand when the attempt to lift his left arm proved too much to bear. He stuck his feet hastily into his street shoes, considered tying them, and decided that the effort to involve his throbbing arm in the task far outweighed the benefit. "I'll check in tomorrow. First thing."

The doctor shook his head. "We'll need an MRI tonight, Greg."

"No can do." Greg tossed the purple ball cap he'd been wearing onto the bench and reached for the white one in his locker. "Van Wyck—now!" he said and was gratified when the tall FBI agent appeared within moments. Greg tossed him the warm-up jacket. "Check the pocket," he said as he stood. "But give me plenty of time. Martoni said 'alone' and I want to be sure he thinks that's what he's getting." He pushed past the doctor and winced at the pain when the trainer reached for his arm. "And, Steve, first give these two guys some of that 'explaining' you're so good at, will you?"

Greg jogged through the locker room and into the hall of the clubhouse, grateful that Van Wyck was there to keep the doctor from calling security. *When there's serious lying to be done, you're better off leaving it to somebody who does it for a living.*

He had just veered off toward the players' exit when he heard Dan Ferris enter the clubhouse and call out for him. "Over here!" Greg responded. "Hurry!"

He slowed his pace just enough to let the older man catch up if he ran. Even though he'd need to talk to him on the way into the parking garage, there was no one Greg would rather have at his side at that moment. It was not only a sure bet that he'd need Bishop Ferris' professional help, it was an absolute certainty that he'd need his prayers as well.

* * *

Andi skidded to a stop in front of the clubhouse door and waved her pass in front of the beaked nose of a well-starched security guard.

"I want to see Greg Howland," she said breathlessly.

The man took her pass and examined it carefully. And slowly.

Who was this man, Andi wondered, some kind of foreign exchange guard from Buckingham Palace? "May I go in now?" she asked anxiously.

"You're Andi Reynolds?"

"Yes!" she said. "Do you need to see ID?" She was reaching for her wallet when the guard handed back her pass with a small, white envelope. She stuck them both in her purse and waited for him to open the door.

He didn't budge. "I was to give you that message before you went into the clubhouse after the game, Miss Reynolds," he said. "The stadium attendant who gave it to me said that it's urgent."

"Who?" Andi asked in bafflement. "What message?" Had he given her something when he handed back her pass? When the guard nodded toward her purse, she hastily opened it again and saw the envelope. With a quick glance of annoyance over this petty waste of precious time when Greg was hurt, Andi snatched it out and tore it open along the flap

"Miss Reynolds?" the guard asked in concern a moment later.

The bodyguard had taken her elbow, Andi realized at last, and was practically holding her upright. Had she fainted, or was she only about to? Blood pounded in her ears and a cold nausea gripped her stomach. She was going to faint, she thought, or she was going to be sick. She pressed her free hand to her lips to stifle the scream that must surely escape in another moment. If she lost control now, she would scream and scream and perhaps never stop.

The security guard finally opened the door. "You can take her in to the wives' lounge to sit down," he told the bodyguard.

"No!" Andi cried as she stepped back and crumpled the note in her hand before either of them could see the horrifying words written on it. Words from Zeke Martoni that were terse and perfectly clear, telling her precisely what she must do—and do alone—if she ever wanted to see Greg again.

"I . . . I've changed my mind," she said. "I need to . . . to . . ." She cast a quick look up at her bodyguard and felt panic tighten her throat. "To go to the restroom," she managed at last. She turned and fled down the hall back toward the very public part of the ballpark, knowing that her only chance to protect the man she loved was to lose the man he had hired to protect her.

Somehow, she would. Andi Reynolds had stood with Greg under the stars at her family reunion and vowed to herself that she would do *anything* for him. Now she was going to have to prove it.

CHAPTER 40

The castle was dark and perfectly still.

Greg knew that there must be FBI agents somewhere among the shadowy trees in the orchard, and a police SWAT team monitoring his movements from a mile or so up the road, waiting for him to enter the building before they moved in. But there was no indication of anyone anywhere. Nothing stirred except the waxy leaves of the citrus trees, fitful in an early autumn breeze.

He pushed open the front door, hoping that Zeke Martoni believed him to be as much alone as he felt, and entered the foyer without reaching for the light switch. Enough moonlight filtered in through the open windows for him to see that the hall and front living areas were empty of everything but shadows. The kittens had apparently scattered—or taken shelter en masse under Dawson's bed. From force of habit, Greg looked down at his feet for Satchel then glanced up at the high balustrade, but the big cat was also in hiding. Or so Greg wanted to believe.

All around him the old house was quiet. Dark.

Empty?

Greg felt the sweat on his face and chest turn cold. He'd broken every speed limit and run more than one stoplight on the race here from the ballpark. There was no possible way he could have made it any sooner. Surely Martoni knew that. He tried to force down a fear that perhaps it had been too late even before he had left BOB, but the bile lodged in his throat.

"Martoni?" The word carried into the empty halls and echoed back. *Three floors. Twenty-seven rooms. No time.*

And an awful dread of what he might find when at last he guessed correctly. Greg's nails dug into the palms of his hands yet he scarcely felt the pain shoot up his injured arm because of the all-consuming agony in his heart. Why hadn't he trusted his instincts and stayed away from Andi's family despite her pleas? Or why hadn't he at least told her the whole truth so that she would have understood the danger and decided to keep him at arm's length herself? Greg couldn't believe what he had done to her. To Enos. To them all. He closed his eyes to halt the sudden swaying of the room. Why was wickedness allowed to exist? And why, when he had come so far and tried so hard, would God suddenly forget—

I will not fail thee nor forsake thee.

There had been two voices in his head all along, Greg realized at once. One was shrill and terrified and damning. The other was quiet and calm and encouraging—and almost impossible to hear over the first. Unless he made a real effort to listen.

Be strong and of good courage.

Greg opened his eyes and the room was still again.

"Martoni!" he hollered. "I'm here!"

His words were flung back by the stone walls, but Greg didn't hear them. He was listening to another voice.

The Lord thy God is with thee whithersoever thou goest.

Upstairs, he thought suddenly. *He'll be in the room with the balcony.* Zeke would be able to see for himself if Greg had come alone.

But with that sweeping view of the valley, had he seen the police come as well?

Greg dismissed the appalling thought almost as quickly as it had come and bounded up the grand staircase, two steps at a time, before he could lose his nerve. Faith cannot coexist with fear, and Greg knew that he would need all he could muster of the former to save Enos. Unarmed and unprepared, faith was all he had to get him through the next few minutes—the most challenging and difficult minutes of his life—minutes in which he would face Zeke Martoni and win at last.

Or else lose everything.

* * *

It was here someplace and she would find it.

Andi ran her hand desperately along the smooth river rocks of the cistern searching for the right one. She didn't wonder how Zeke Martoni had learned that she knew of a secret entrance into the castle, or why he would want her to use it tonight. Nor did she think it ironic that the one reckless thing she had done as a child now made it possible for her to do the most reckless thing she would ever do as an adult. She hadn't thought of anything at all, in fact—except for Greg—since reading the terrifying note that said if she didn't come here at once, he would die.

Fortunately, ditching her bodyguard hadn't required much thought. Tonight's man, besides being retained for brawn rather than brain, was a regular. Since she'd docilely accepted his presence for the last several weeks, he had no inkling that tonight she was anything but what she claimed and certainly appeared to be: suddenly and deathly ill. It had been simple then to leave him waiting patiently outside one entrance to the ladies' room while she slipped out another.

And after that she'd run to her car, repeating Greg's name to herself and to the Lord all the way to Mesa. It was not a chant so much as it was a prayer, and it got her safely here, though she hadn't noticed a single landmark along the way.

Just as she felt the sting of frustrated tears behind her lids, one cool, round rock gave beneath her hand, and Andi knew that she had at last found the latch. She pulled straight up and a metal bar came with it, releasing the door. She knelt and pushed against the stones with all her might. They moved inward a few inches and then a few more, but it wasn't enough. She sat on the ground then and braced her back against a nearby tree to use the greater strength of her legs to force a door that hadn't been in regular use for almost a century. Even then, she managed to move it only a few feet before her legs were fully extended and her leverage lost, but this time it was enough. She could just manage to squeeze through.

The stairs were as steep as she remembered them, but the tunnel seemed narrower and much lower. Crouching at the entrance, she shuddered as she brushed away a cobweb and tried to peer into the inky darkness. There were no words for what she felt and one way only to keep her from wondering—imagining—fearing—what might lay ahead.

Andi said Greg's name again, softly and aloud. Then she turned on her tiny flashlight and stepped into the blackness.

* * *

There was a light at the top of the stairs, Greg saw finally. It came from one of the inner rooms, one without windows, the one across from the room with the view. The door was ajar and yellow light slanted through it, cutting the darkness in half.

Satchel had come out of hiding and Greg was sorry. He pushed the cat aside with his ankle. "Go," he whispered. "Scat." But he knew it was still at his heels when he reached the doorway and cautiously opened the door a little further.

Although Greg thought he had imagined every possible scenario in the last interminably long hour, he hadn't imagined this.

"Greg!" Enos said happily. He jumped up from the floor where he'd been carefully arranging new baseball cards into parallel columns. "Zeke said you were coming! Didja pitch a no-hitter? Didja win the game? Didja bring me the ball?"

Greg was too numb to respond. Too numb, in fact, to do more than lay his hand on the excited child's shoulder. A hand, he noted with some dismay, that shook despite his best efforts to still it. His thoughts raced. He had faith, of course, and he'd hoped for the best, but this was too easy. Way too easy. His eyes fell on Rufus crumpled on the floor near the door then sought Enos' questioningly.

Enos looked over his shoulder at his cousin. "He fell asleep in the car," he offered brightly, "so Zeke had to carry him inside. Nothing wakes up Rufus."

"Where—" Greg cleared his throat. "Where is Zeke?"

"Looking for me, kid?" An angular form took shape from the shadows in the hall and stepped forward.

In contrast to Greg's rumpled uniform, Zeke Martoni was immaculate. As always, Greg thought, he was dressed to kill. But this time he had the snub-nosed revolver in his hand to prove it. The young ballplayer pushed Enos into the room and stood in the doorway between Martoni and the children. "Enos, stay back," he commanded.

But the child had been given baseball cards and promised a party by the man he thought was Greg's friend. He reached up to pull on his hero's belt loop. "When's the party?"

The corners of Zeke's mouth curled upwards. "Any minute kid," he said. "We're just waiting for our last guest to arrive."

"Then we'll have cake?"

"Enos!" Greg said tersely. "Get away from the door. Right now."

Confused and hurt at the tone in his hero's voice, Enos stepped sulkily back—and into Rufus. The other little boy sat up and rubbed his eyes. From his position on the floor, Rufus could see what Enos had not. "Is that a real gun?" he asked sleepily.

"Zeke," Greg said, trying to speak calmly and think clearly and pray fervently all at the same time, "you've got what you want now. Let the boys go."

"You're wrong, Grego," Martoni said, raising the gun and using it to motion the younger man further back into the room. "But I'm gonna get it soon." He smiled when Greg took an obedient step backward, herding Enos as he went and wondering how he could gather up Rufus, too. "I'm gonna get it *real* soon."

Enos' eyes were wide behind his glasses now and terrified. His lower lip quivered as he looked up at Greg. "He said we were gonna have a surprise party after your game, Greg. He said—"

"Ssh, Enos," Greg interrupted. "It's okay. Just hold on to the cat for me." He nudged Satchel out from between his feet and toward Enos as the child's words finally registered with his brain. *Party?* "Last guest?" he said, mostly to himself.

"I've been waiting a long time to finally meet that little redhead of yours." Martoni paused to enjoy the shock and dread that registered so quickly on Greg's candid face, then he ran his free hand up to preen an immaculate sideburn in satisfaction. "I might as well break it to you now, kid," he added with a great show of mock sympathy. "The lady thinks she's coming here to you, but she'll be leaving with me. Us getting acquainted will be just one more thing you'll have to think about."

Greg could no longer feel his heart hammering in his chest. Most likely it didn't beat at all. Surely Andi wouldn't have—couldn't have—

"Martoni—" he began, but the word was spoken so low he barely heard it himself.

"Don't thank me for the party, Grego, until you've heard what else I've got planned," Martoni said with a slow smile. "Since you're the guest of honor at this little bash, and since I got two boys for the price of one tonight, I'm gonna let you choose which kid you want me to kill." He moved the gun back and forth in a slow arc. "Eenie, meenie—" As Greg struggled to draw a breath, Zeke's smile widened to reveal a row of gleaming, white teeth. "If you can't choose fast enough to suit me, Grego, I can always kill them both."

To Greg, Martoni looked like the jackal he was—all teeth and menacing intent and glowing black eyes. Meeting those eyes, he knew at once that Zeke was high, not on liquor that might have dulled his reactions, but on chemicals that would make him faster, more alert, and even more deadly. Greg ran a hand over his face and into his hair. How had he brought the people he loved to this? And, more important, how was he going to get them out of it?

"You'll have to kill me first," Greg said, thinking that he'd only said aloud what Martoni had planned all along.

But he was wrong.

"Not a chance, kid," Zeke said. "If I'd wanted you dead, I'd have taken care of that little detail weeks ago. I want you sorry you were ever born." His eyes burned into Greg's as he considered his options. "I probably *will* have to shoot you, Grego," he admitted, "to keep you out of the way. But I promise you, you'll only wish I'd done a better job of it. You'll wish you were dead, all right—every time you close your eyes and see the dead kid or imagine your girl—"

Greg took a reckless step forward and Zeke swung the gun from the center of his broad chest toward Enos cowering now atop his baseball cards with only the cat for cover. "So you're telling me you're ready to choose now, kid?" Martoni hissed, cocking the revolver. "Move one more inch and it's just like saying the word."

Greg froze. *Where*, he thought in desperation, *are the police?* If they showed up on the stairs right now and he charged Zeke, the man would have to use the only shot he'd get on him rather than Enos or Rufus. Yes, he'd insisted on coming alone and yes, he'd insisted they give him time, but this was ridiculous.

Why don't they come? Before Andi— Greg stopped himself before he could finish the sentence in his own mind, since the only scenario he could possibly bear was the one of her being safely intercepted by the police before she reached the front door. *Maybe,* he thought, *I can hurry the police along a little.*

He moved incrementally back in front of Enos and noted with gratitude that Rufus was not only too still to draw much of Zeke's attention, but seemingly unconcerned with what was going on around him as well. Greg said, "You'll never get away from here, Zeke."

"I'm touched that you're worried about me, kid," Zeke sneered as he brought his left hand up and laid it delicately on his chest. But his right hand—the one with the gun—never wavered. "Especially when you've got so much on your own mind." He shifted the gun back to Greg's heart. "Let's cut to the chase, Grego. I don't have all night to—"

"Greg?" Andi called from somewhere just outside the room.

That it was impossible and unthinkable were both moot points, Greg knew now, because it was true. She was here in the castle and ascending the back stairs at that moment. He felt the blood drain from his face and probably from his heart, as he realized in a swift flash of horror that he was living the nightmare he'd had in Houston. No matter how hard he prayed—or how hard he willed Andi away—she came closer still.

"Andi, no!" he cried out desperately, and then for the police microphone he said, "Bishop, now!" But he knew it was probably too late on both counts. He had only himself to rely on, and if he so much as moved, Zeke would shoot Rufus or Enos; but if he remained still, Martoni would have Andi for a shield. Why had he been stupid enough to think that he could handle this by himself? Andi and Bishop Ferris had been right about his pride and stubbornness all along.

I'll take help now, Greg told God and the universe at large, *from anyone, anywhere. Please send me help.*

And just like that he got it.

"I don't like you," Rufus said matter-of-factly from his place at Zeke's feet. Then he bit the man's ankle.

Greg saw the gun come down as the pain and surprise registered on Martoni's face and knew that this was the only chance he was going to get. But just as he lunged forward, the gun came back up. There was a flash of orange, a crash of thunder, and as he fell, Greg heard Andi scream.

HAPTER 41

Everything happened at once and largely without Andi's notice.

For the rest of her life, all she would remember of the next few moments of pounding boots and big guns and loud voices was Greg lying face down on the floor.

Stifling another scream and heedless of the arms that reached out for her, Andi flew down the hall and threw herself down beside Greg. He wasn't dead, she saw at once with a thousand psalms of thanksgiving. His chest heaved and he made a low, strangled sound somewhere deep in his throat.

"Don't try to move," she said anxiously when she saw him press his palms to the floor and heard him moan with the pain of trying to push himself up. "Lie still, Greg."

"Andi—"

"Hush." She lay herself over him protectively to keep him warm and still, and to will her life into him. When she felt another sickening lurch, she looked up frantically for help and was stunned to see Enos and Rufus in one corner of the room, obviously unhurt but being restrained by—of all people—the man she had seen with Greg at the castle this morning. Her eyes widened, but she lowered them almost immediately. It was all simply too much for her to think about right now when she wanted only to think about Greg.

"Andi," he said again. "I—" but the rest of the words were lost in another fit of strangled coughs.

"I love you, Greg," she whispered fervently into his ear. "I can't live without you." She was relieved and immeasurably grateful when, as if sent directly from heaven itself, Bishop Ferris knelt at her side.

"We've got an ambulance, Greg," he said. "Hold on just a few more minutes, son."

Finally, despite Andi's efforts to keep him still, Greg rolled to his right side. She squeezed her eyes closed, knowing that she couldn't bear what she might see.

"Greg?" she heard Bishop Ferris say incredulously. "You're okay?"

The strangled sound was more distinct as he sat up, and more easily understood. Andi's eyes flew open as she searched Greg's muscular chest. It was shaking still, but obviously unharmed. She raised her eyes in wonder to look into his face and saw that he was—laughing.

The sound that came from her own throat then was something between a sigh and a sob. Holding out both hands to him, she saw helplessly that they trembled beyond all reason.

Immediately remorseful, Greg gathered her up with his strong right arm and pulled her close. "I'm sorry, Andi," he whispered into her hair, his voice rich and low and full of raw emotion. "So, so sorry."

After a minute or more of holding her so securely that Andi believed—hoped—he might never let her go, he raised his face to Dan Ferris. She felt a last chuckle escape him in spite of his best efforts to contain it.

"I was gonna play the hero," he told the bishop ruefully, "but I tripped over that stupid cat."

"That 'stupid' cat saved your life, Greg," Ferris said, clasping him affectionately on the shoulder and looking, Andi thought, as relieved as she felt.

"Yeah," Greg agreed, "him and God and Rufus."

At the sound of his name, the little boy broke away from Van Wyck and did a fairly good imitation of a human cannonball on his way across the room to Greg. Enos was only a few paces behind, and Andi moved marginally away to make room for the little boys. She could only imagine what these three had been through together these last few minutes. Her eyes filled with tears of love and gratitude as she watched Greg pull them into his lap, but she also winced when he did as Rufus tugged on his painful arm.

"I'm sorry I bited," Rufus said, lowering his chin to his chest.

Andi watched Greg ruffle the child's hair and thought for a moment that he might cry. But he smiled instead. "Hey, Rufus," he said thickly, lifting the little chin with one finger, "you can bite that guy anytime you want to. Tell your mother I said so, okay?"

"Is he a bad man?" Rufus asked with wide, hazel eyes.

Andi's heart clenched as Greg held the two little boys very close and then reached for her hand. "The worst," he said finally.

Sitting safely now on Greg's lap, Enos had forgotten his previous terror. "You should have seen those SWAT guys slam Zeke up against the wall, Greg," he said excitedly. "It was way cool."

Andi watched Greg try to suppress a grin and fail. "Sorry I missed that."

As she had known all along, the man of her dreams still had a lot of little boy left in him, too. It shouldn't have surprised her then that—with what he most treasured now safe—Greg would recover as quickly as Enos and let his thoughts turn to his second love. Still, her jaw dropped slightly when he asked Dan Ferris hopefully, "Did you catch the final score of the ball game?"

Ferris glanced at Andi and rubbed the smile from his face with a hand. "Sorry, Greg," he said. "I must have been listening to the wrong channel on the police scanner. Nobody mentioned it."

Greg turned. "Steve?"

Van Wyck shrugged, but a paramedic who had just arrived in the hallway overheard the question.

"The D-Backs won it three-zip, Mr. Howland," he reported eagerly. "When you came out, they put Westen in and he held 'em. Between the two of you, it was a perfect game!"

"We're going to the World Series!" Greg and Enos whooped in unison.

You could have been killed tonight, Andi thought as she watched Greg jump to his feet with the boys and twirl Rufus around in a celebratory circle, sore arm or not. *We could all have been killed.*

If Greg had not, at that exact moment, set Rufus down and knelt to gather her up into his arms instead—and if he had not euphorically kissed away everything that was left of her fear and confusion, Andi might well have killed him then and there herself.

* * *

If asked to define "celestial" a few days later, Andi would have responded: "This very moment." She sat on the balcony of the castle with Greg and a half dozen kittens, and sighed at the splendor of the copper and gold sky above the White Tank Mountains to the west.

The wrought-iron glider swayed gently when he removed a kitten from his lap then used the same arm to pull her closer. The glider was the only piece of "furniture" Greg had ever purchased himself and was a replica of one from Andi's back porch.

Andi nestled her head in the hollow of his neck, then remembered and pulled away in concern. "Does it hurt?" she asked. "Should I move to your other side?"

Greg made a fist and flexed the not inconsiderable biceps. "Man of Steel," he grinned. "I'm pitching the last game of the World Series, you know."

Andi leaned back in resignation. So he'd said. So everyone in the nation—with the possible exception of the New York Yankees—hoped. His team would be back from the East Coast segment of the series tomorrow, and Greg would be back on the bench the next night after only one priesthood blessing, several shots of steroids, and five days of physical therapy. Then, for better or worse, he'd be on the mound the night after that. Every sports pundit with a microphone said it would be a miracle if he ever pitched again as he once had. But Greg Howland didn't hope for miracles anymore, Andi knew. He counted on them.

And why not? Zeke Martoni was locked away in maximum security—for his own protection—and wouldn't be out anytime in their lifetimes. And with all the FBI had on him, they no longer needed Greg's testimony to convict. That meant that, thankfully, the threat to his life was gone, along with the federal agents, wired ball caps, bodyguards, and long months of trepidation. All that faced them now, Andi thought blissfully, was to write "and they lived happily ever after" on their wedding cake.

After Greg unloaded all these cats.

The six kittens, all of various colors and sizes, had followed him out to the balcony, and two were now in his lap. Satchel was under his feet, of course, but Andi hoped the big tabby would stay there forever. He had saved Greg's life, and she would cook him salmon every week for the rest of his life to show her gratitude.

But the kittens had to go.

"Greg," she began, raising her face toward his and willing herself not to become distracted when he kissed the bridge of her nose, "Zona's going to take all these cats, right?"

"I wouldn't count on it," he said slowly. One side of his mouth turned up. "Don't tell me I know something that you don't."

"As I recall, you've known quite a lot that I haven't over the past few weeks," she said. But she was unable sustain a frown in the face of that eternally endearing lopsided grin. She reached up and tugged playfully on his ear. "But that's one thing that better change, Howland." She tugged a little harder. "Starting right now."

"I give," Greg said with a chuckle. "I'll squeal—Dawson's quitting pretty soon. He got a job working for *Newsweek*."

Andi recalled the morning in his office and knew at last what he had meant. "But why?" she asked curiously.

Greg sobered. "I think he's realized that there are more important things he can do with all that talent than help me sell shoes." His eyes, Andi noted, were filled with admiration for his friend. "But he is going to have to write one more press release first." Greg reached for her hand and ran his thumb across the diamond-and-emerald ring on her finger. "He's going to have to break the news that we're getting married."

Andi drew in a breath. "You don't want to keep our engagement a secret anymore?"

"No," Greg said, "not unless you want to." His eyes were searching and a little worried. "But you've got to remember, the publicity might be pretty intense for a while—"

"I'm not afraid."

Greg raised her fingers to his lips. "No," he agreed, "you're not afraid of anything."

Andi felt a tingle where his mouth brushed her knuckles, and it spread all the way down to her toes. At last the world would know that she and Greg had made earthly promises to one another, and soon they would make eternal ones. She was thrilled with the prospect of belonging to him forever. She was thrilled with everything in life, in fact . . . except for the kittens. And he was avoiding the issue.

"About Zona—" she began again.

"Did I leave that part out?" he asked innocently. "It seems that Dawson's first assignment will be on Kiribati. Somebody's building a school there." At Andi's pointed look, he shrugged. "Yeah, but more than they need money they need doctors and teachers. Dawson's just the guy to get the message out, don't you think?"

"Yes," Andi said. "But about Zona—"

"You know what they say," Greg continued, "about a picture being worth a thousand words—?"

"*Zona?*" Andi exclaimed suddenly. "And *Dawson?*" She was sitting upright now and her emerald eyes were huge. "Zona and Dawson are going to Kiribati *together?*"

"Yeah," Greg grinned. "I was worried about Dawson, too, at first. Then I figured that if he can cope with the dirt and the germs and having no place to plug in his computer modem, he can probably deal with Zona May."

Andi was quiet for several seconds as she considered the end result of the Darlene-Maybe-Not-Such-A-Disaster. "My goodness," she said at last. "That's amazing."

She finally settled back into the swing and absentmindedly stroked the silky puff of kitten that had curled into her lap. The other cats, for the moment, were forgotten. "Well," she told Greg, "*I* happen to know a couple of things in the romance department that *you* don't." She waited for curiosity to get the best of him but received only the slightest raise of a sandy eyebrow. "Sterling Channing and Justine Fletcher are engaged," she announced happily. "They'll be married in the spring."

"No double wedding," he said quickly.

"No," Andi said. "I'm not sharing an altar with anyone but you." She snuggled closer. "And you'll be more interested in the next news," she promised. "Clytie has a date to Homecoming."

Greg had been playing with one of Andi's curls, but dropped it at the mention of Clytie's name. "That's great!" he said. "With who?"

"The paperboy," Andi answered. "His name is Ian."

"Ian," Greg repeated. "That beats Prince Iggy by a long shot, doesn't it?" When Andi looked puzzled, he grinned. Then he asked cautiously, "Will I like this guy?"

"You ought to," Andi said. But she knew that realistically Clytie was going to have a difficult time finding any boy Greg thought was good enough for her. "I think the reason Clytie likes Ian is because he's so much like you."

"So, you're saying that he's handsome and brave and—"

"Big headed?" Andi teased. "No, but he's sweet and shy and kind of clumsy."

"And I thought you were marrying me because I'm so dashing." His hand had moved back into her curls. "You must really want those free baseball tickets, then." The kittens on their laps scattered as he deftly turned her face toward his. Cy got its claws snagged in Andi's skirt on the way down, but Greg didn't notice. "Not that I care why you marry me," he continued, his voice deepening, "as long as you do. I promised you happily ever after, Ariadne Reynolds, and I intend to keep that promise."

His face was so close now it was almost impossible for Andi to think of anything but kissing him. Still she managed to disentangle the kitten from her skirt and say, "Then there's one thing you could do for me, Greg—"

"Win the World Series?"

His fingers stroked the back of her neck, and she knew that only moments separated her from oblivion. She murmured, "No, you could find homes for all these cats."

He leaned a little closer. "Except for Satchel?"

His voice was deep and tender, and his lips were much too close to hers for reason. "Of course we should keep Satchel," she said.

"Can we keep Christy?" he asked, kissing her temple and causing her to nod despite herself. His lips moved to her earlobe. "And Cy?"

"All right," she whispered. Whichever kitten Cy was, it was her new favorite.

His lips were inches away from hers. "And Tinker?"

"Uh, huh—"

"Chance?"

In desperation, Andi raised her palms to each side of Greg's face, pulled him forward, and covered his lips firmly with her own before he could name even one more kitten. As her eyes closed, she could feel the warmth of the sun on her face and the warmth of Greg's lips on hers. In fifty years, six months, and perhaps a day or two, she and Greg would sit on this very glider on this very balcony as the sun set behind the Arizona mountains—molten of gold in honor of their golden wedding anniversary. Their children would be grown by then, and perhaps one or two of their grandchildren would have children of their own. And, Andi thought, if Greg had his way, those great-grandchildren would be romping with kittens as far as the eye could see. Despite herself, she smiled.

Then Greg deepened the kiss, and the kittens and kids and even the sunset were lost amidst the falling of the stars. No matter how many days or years or eons passed, Greg would always kiss her this way, and her knees would always weaken and her heart would always throb and she would know throughout all time the true definition of celestial: eternity with the one you love.

ABOUT THE AUTHOR

A native of Arizona, Kerry Lynn Blair lives in West Jordan, Utah, with her husband, Gary, and two of their four children. One is a full-time missionary.

Besides baseball games, Kerry likes to while away hours at libraries, thrift shops, and on Temple Square. She also enjoys reading, speaking to women's and youth groups, and watching movies filmed before 1950. She is the author of two best-selling LDS books, also published by Covenant, *The Heart Has Its Reasons* and *The Heart Has Forever*.

Kerry loves to correspond with readers, who can write to her in care of Covenant Communications, Box 416, American Fork, Utah 84003-0416 or e-mail her at **KerryLynnBlair@aol.com**. Her website is **kerrylynnblair.com**.

ON A WHIM

CHAPTER 1

To: Jillybean@azhot.com
From: Whims1@byu.edu
Dear Jill: Get me out of here! I've only
been at Wymount two days, and already I've had
at least a dozen people ask me if I babysit.
Like I really want to spend my senior year
changing diapers and wiping noses. They
couldn't pay me enough to do it, if any of
them had money, that is. No joke. Everyone
here is dirt poor. Their cars look like they
were rescued from the dump, and just yesterday
I heard someone talking about the "cute" kids'
clothes Deseret Industries has right now. Too
weird.

I'm still not speaking to my mom, which
sorta makes breakfast difficult. I mean, it'd
be nice to just say, "Pass the milk," rather
than going after it myself, but I'm determined
to punish her. After all, she deserves to be
punished for feeling "prompted" to move up

```
"prompted" to move up here right before my
last year of high school. I tried to tell
her I felt prompted to stay in Tempe and
live with you guys for the year, but she
didn't buy it. Maybe I'll forgive her one
day for all of this, but I doubt it. Gotta
go. Write soon. Your best friend with no
life—Whimsy.
     P.S. Haven't seen Josh yet. I'm sure I'll
run into him one day, not that it's a big
deal. I'll tell him hi for you when I do.
```

The Cougareat was practically empty. I sat near the front and tried hard not to glance up from my book to see if Josh Iverson was walking past. As if that was likely. Fall semester was still a week away. Anyone with half a life wasn't going to be at the Wilkinson Center at nine in the morning. Besides, Josh was probably at football practice or autograph-signing practice or even brunching with BYU's elite. I, on the other hand, was sitting alone in the Cougareat, reading *Pride and Prejudice* for the hundredth time, and wishing that Josh would walk in, buy me a Coke (decaffeinated, of course), and confess his undying love for me. Was that too much to ask?

The words on the page blurred in front of me, and I began to daydream of Josh leading BYU to a solid victory, and then, over the roar of the crowd, I would hear the announcer ask if a Whimsy Waterman would please come down to the field. And there in front of everyone in the stadium, including his old girlfriend Holly, Josh would spit out his slimy mouthpiece and say, "I love you, Whimsy. Will you marry me?" To which, of course, I would say, "Yes."

I closed my eyes and just as Josh was about to seal our engagement with a kiss, I heard someone from behind me say, "You're an English major. Am I right?"

I turned around and saw this table washer guy standing right behind me. A blue apron hung off his lanky frame, and his thick, dark hair was cut short enough for boot camp. For some reason he made me feel uncomfortably transparent, almost as if my daydream had just been broadcast on the Jumbotron at Cougar Stadium, and he had been there

to see it. My neck went as red as my hair, and I stammered, "Uh, wh—
what did you say?"

The Table Washer smiled then glanced at the floor. "This is going
to sound stupid," he said, "but from clear over by the Chinese food, I
thought you looked like an English major. So, uh . . . I'm just
wondering if I'm right."

I'm sure you can understand why I didn't want to say something
like, "College student? No, no. You've got it all wrong. In a few weeks
I'm starting my senior year of high school. And as for majors—I
haven't a clue what I want to be when I grow up." The truth was definitely too embarrassing to admit. Besides, I didn't want to hurt his
feelings. So, with a look of amazement, I held up my copy of *Pride
and Prejudice* and said to the guy in the apron, "Good guess."

He seemed relieved. He put down his squirt bottle and rag on the
table and said, "I liked *Pride and Prejudice,* not that I'm an English major.
I had to read it in high school. Austen's a good writer, but I think it's weird
she wrote about all that romance stuff, but in real life she never married."

Trying to sound like an English major, I said, "Yes, I thought that
was peculiar, too."

The Table Washer shrugged. "Who knows? Maybe she was better
off just imagining that kinda stuff in stories. I mean, it's possible no
one she liked ever asked her out."

"It's definitely possible," I said and felt the weight of my own
dismal dating reality press down on my shoulders. The truth was that,
since turning sixteen, I'd only been asked out once and that was by
Tim Darby. A nice guy, but he picks his nose in public. I mean, if he
had tried to hold my hand, I would have gagged.

The Table Washer put his hand to his heart and said, "I'm Matt
Hollingsworth."

"I'm Whimsy Waterman," I said, "and no, Whimsy is not my
real name."

"Wait. Let me see if I can guess. It's gotta be a little unusual. I'm
gonna have to say . . . Gertrude."

"Just as bad. It's Wilhelmina."

"Really? I think Wilhelmina's kinda cool. It's sorta old-fashioned,
but it's still pretty. So no one ever calls you Wilhelmina?"

"Not unless they want to die." Oops. That was probably too

"I'll be sure to make a note of that," he said and smiled.

"Obviously, I've never liked my name, and the funny thing is, I was named after my grandmother, who didn't like the name either. She went by Willie."

"So how did you get Whimsy?"

"Growing up, my best friend, Jill, had a lisp. My parents used to call me Whimmy, and she turned it into Whimsy. Somehow it stuck. But I spell it without the *e.*"

"Oh, um . . . so are you from Provo?"

"No. I'm from Tempe, Arizona."

"Never been there, but I hear it's a great place. Some friends of mine went to the Fiesta Bowl last year. They couldn't believe people have gravel lawns."

"I know. So far the one thing I like about Provo is the green grass." My neck ached a little from looking up at Matt, but it wasn't like I wanted him to leave. I mean, since arriving in Provo a few days earlier, life had been dull, boring, blah! Having a guy showing interest in me was a definite improvement, and the fact that he mistook me for a college student didn't hurt my ego any. I mean, sure, he needed braces and a protein shake, but still, he was cute, especially when he smiled and his blue eyes squinted into crescent moons.

I was about to ask him if he wanted to sit down when he said, "So where do you live?"

"Wymount Terrace." For some reason the look on his face made me want to say, "Houston, we have a problem."

Nervously looking at the ground and fidgeting with his apron, he said, "Really? I hear Wymount's a great place. Oh, uh, well, it's been good talking to you, but, uh, I'd better get back to work." And then, grabbing his squirt bottle and rag, he left.

I slumped in my chair and mumbled, "For your information, Mr. Table Washer, not everyone at Wymount is married. I'm not, my mom's not, and neither are the two-year-olds."

* * *

When I got back to Wymount Terrace, the first thing I did was call Jill. "Jill, he thought I was married. I'm so stupid. I never should have told him where I live."

"Look on the bright side. You'll probably never see him again, and if you do, just tell him you got your marriage annulled."

"That ought to win him over."

"Whims, forget the busboy. What I want to know is if you've called Josh yet?"

"Well, uh . . . not exactly."

"I knew it! Girl, when it comes to guys you're like a decade behind the times. Just call him. You know he wants you to. Why else would he have written his dorm number on your hand before he left?"

"He wanted to save a tree?"

"Whims, don't you get it? The only bright side to your mom starting law school is that you get to date Josh Iverson."

"I *get* to date Josh Iverson? Jill, there are thousands of pretty girls up here for him to date."

"But you're the one he wrote his number on."

Somehow that sounded offensive, like I was a piece of property to be claimed. Crossing my fingers, I said, "Just to get off the subject, I promise I'll call him."

"Today?"

"Okay, I'll do it today. But I'm telling you right now, he's not interested. I mean, not that it wouldn't be nice if he were. But Jill— he's the next great BYU quarterback, and I'm just some skinny redhead who knew him in high school."

Jill loves dramatic pauses, so she paused long and hard. Then she said, "You know that infomercial on positive thinking? You know, the one with the guy who has around ten extra teeth?"

"Yeah?"

"Buy his book."

"I know I'm a pessimist. But look at my life—there's nothing to be positive about it, no silver lining. Just one awful thing after another. My mom gets accepted to BYU law school, I have to say good-bye to you and spend my senior year of high school up here with a bunch of strangers, and then live in married-student housing where I'm surrounded by loud, runny-nosed kids. I don't need to set promptly at five every morning. And to top it all off, I meet a guy that I'm slightly interested in, and I make him think I'm married."

"Uh, like I said. Whims, buy the book."